THRICE THE BRINDED CAT HATH MEW'D

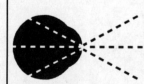

This Large Print Book carries the
Seal of Approval of N.A.V.H.

A FLAVIA DE LUCE NOVEL

THRICE THE BRINDED CAT HATH MEW'D

ALAN BRADLEY

THORNDIKE PRESS
A part of Gale, Cengage Learning

Farmington Hills, Mich • San Francisco • New York • Waterville, Maine
Meriden, Conn • Mason, Ohio • Chicago

GALE
CENGAGE Learning®

LIBRARY OF CONGRESS CATALOGING-IN-PUBLICATION DATA

Names: Bradley, C. Alan, 1938- author.
Title: Thrice the brinded cat hath mew'd : a Flavia de Luce novel / Alan Bradley.
Description: Large print edition. | Waterville, Maine : Thorndike Press Large Print, 2016. | Series: A Flavia de Luce mystery | Series: Thorndike Press large print core
Identifiers: LCCN 2016035017 | ISBN 9781410492265 (hardback) | ISBN 1410492265 (hardcover)
Subjects: LCSH: De Luce, Flavia (Fictitious character)—Fiction. | Large type books. | BISAC: FICTION / Mystery & Detective / General. | GSAFD: Mystery fiction.
Classification: LCC PR9199.4.B7324 T48 2016b | DDC 813/.6—dc23
LC record available at https://lccn.loc.gov/2016035017

Published in 2016 by arrangement with Delacorte Press, an imprint of Random House, a division of Penguin Random House LLC

For Shirley — then, now, and always

Thrice the brinded cat hath mew'd.
Thrice, and once the hedge-pig whin'd.
Harpier cries: — 'Tis time, 'tis time.
Round about the cauldron go;
In the poison'd entrails throw.
Toad, that under cold stone
Days and nights hast thirty-one
Swelter'd venom sleeping got,
Boil thou first i' th' charmed pot.
Double, double toil and trouble;
Fire, burn; and cauldron, bubble.

Fillet of a fenny snake,
In the cauldron boil and bake;
Eye of newt, and toe of frog,
Wool of bat, and tongue of dog,
Adder's fork, and blind-worm's sting,
Lizard's leg, and howlet's wing,
For a charm of powerful trouble,
Like a hell-broth boil and bubble.
Double, double toil and trouble;
Fire, burn; and cauldron, bubble.
— William Shakespeare, *Macbeth* (IV.i)

ONE

The winter rain slashes at my face like icy razor blades, but I don't care. I dig my chin deep into the collar of my mackintosh, put my head down, and push on against the buffeting of the furious wind.

I am cycling madly towards the village of Bishop's Lacey, fleeing hordes of Hell's hobgoblins.

The past twenty-four hours have been a nightmare. All I can think about is getting away from Buckshaw.

Gladys's wheels groan horribly beneath us. The biting cold has penetrated her steel bones and seized the tendons of her brake cables. She judders wickedly on the slick tarmac, threatening to skid off the road entirely and pitch me into the icy ditch.

I want to scream into the wind, but I don't. One of us, at least, must keep her wits about her.

I try to put my thoughts in order.

In spite of having been banished to Canada and then re-banished back home from Miss Bodycote's Female Academy — in what may or may not have been double disgrace — I have to admit that I had been looking forward to being reunited with my family: Father; my two elder sisters, Feely and Daffy; our cook and housekeeper, Mrs. Mullet; and most of all, Dogger, Father's general factotum and all-round right-hand man.

As every traveler does on an Atlantic crossing, I had daydreamed about my return to England. Father, Feely, and Daffy would be at the docks to greet me, of course, and perhaps even Aunt Felicity would put in an appearance. WELCOME HOME FLAVIA banners would be waved, a few discreet balloons, and all that sort of thing. Discreet of course, because, like myself, none of us de Luces wear our hearts on our sleeves.

But when the ship berthed finally at Southampton, there had been only Dogger standing motionless in the rain beneath a dark umbrella.

With the strangeness that comes of separation, I had offered him my hand, rather than giving him the crushing bear hug that was in my heart. I regretted this at once, but it was too late: The moment had passed and the opportunity was wasted.

"I'm afraid I must be the bearer of rather bad news, Miss Flavia," Dogger had said. "Colonel de Luce has been taken ill. He is in hospital with pneumonia."

"Father? In hospital? In Hinley?"

"I'm afraid so."

"We must go to him at once," I said. "What time will we be there?"

We still had a long journey ahead of us, Dogger explained. The five-twenty boat train from Southampton would take us up to London and to Waterloo Station, where, just after seven in the evening, we would have to change to a taxicab for a dash across the city to another train at another station.

We would not reach Doddingsley until late in the evening, and would not arrive at Bishop's Lacey, Hinley, and the hospital until even later. By then, visiting hours would be long over.

"Surely Dr. Darby —" I said.

But Dogger gave his head a sad shake, and it was not until that moment that I realized how grave Father's situation must be.

Dogger was not the kind of person who would tell you that everything would be all right when he knew perfectly well that it would not. His silence said everything.

Although there had been so much to say,

we had spoken little in the train. Each of us had stared out blank-faced through the rain-streaked glass at a rushing landscape that seemed in the gathering twilight to be the color of old bruises.

From time to time I glanced at Dogger, but found that I could no longer decipher his face.

Dogger had suffered horribly with Father in a Japanese prison camp during the war, and still, from time to time, experienced flashbacks of such terrifying intensity that they left him little more than a weak, whimpering child.

Once, I had asked him how he and Father had survived.

"One tries to keep a stiff upper lip, mentally," he had said.

I had worried about Dogger almost constantly during my absence, but in writing — although missing me — he had seemed to be otherwise well enough. Dogger's had been the only letter I'd received from home during my incarceration in Canada, which tells you pretty much all you need to know about the warmth of the de Luce family.

Oh, of course, there had been that sarcastic footnote by my newly discovered cousin, Undine, who had been dumped by Fate and her mother's horrible death on the doorstep at Buckshaw. Undine's place in the family remained to be seen, but I didn't hold out much hope for her. Because she was still a child — whereas I was twelve, and much more knowledgeable about the ways of the world — I wasn't particularly looking forward to renewing our brief acquaintance. But if I found, when I got home, that she'd been pawing my belongings while I was away in Canada, there would be mayhem at the manor house.

It had been well past dark when the train crawled at last into Doddingsley station, where Clarence Mundy's taxicab stood waiting in the rain to take us to Buckshaw. The cold air was damp and penetrating. A yellow fog hung round the dim lights on the platform, giving them a ghastly, ghostly glow, and making me feel as if my eyes were brimming.

"Nice to see you again, miss," Clarence whispered, tugging at the peak of his cap as I got into the car, although he otherwise remained silent, as if I were an actress — in costume and makeup — about to make my entrance at stage left, and he the stage manager, bound to respect my role by keeping a respectable professional distance.

We rode to Bishop's Lacey and Buckshaw in silence, Dogger staring fixedly ahead and me gazing desperately out through the glass as if trying to penetrate the darkness.

Hardly the homecoming I had expected.

Mrs. Mullet met us at the door and folded me into her arms and bosom.

"I've made you up some sangridges," she said in a curiously rough voice. "Beef and lettuce — your favorites. Left 'em on the dresser by your bed. You'll be tired, I 'spect."

"Thank you, Mrs. M," I heard myself saying. "It's very thoughtful of you."

Could this be Flavia de Luce speaking? Surely not!

In my present state of mind, slices of dead cow garnished with sprigs of the local vegetation were a particular horror and abomination, but something made me hold my tongue.

"They've all gone up to bed," Mrs. Mullet added, meaning Feely, Daffy, and presumably Undine. "It's been an uncommon 'ard day."

I nodded, reminded suddenly of my late-night arrival at Miss Bodycote's Female Academy. Dark entrances, I thought, seemed to have become a regular part of my life.

Wasn't it odd that my own flesh and blood had not waited up for me, or was I expecting too much? I had only been gone since

September, but surely, one of them . . .

I stifled the thought.

Surely there was someone to welcome me home. Even a stuck-out tongue from Undine would have been welcome. But no — it was far past her bedtime. Undine would be off in the world of whatever vile dreams fueled her waking life.

And then I thought of Esmeralda: *Esmeralda!*

Dear, sweet, precious Esmeralda, my pride and my joy. The fact that she was a Buff-Orpington hen made no difference whatsoever. Love is love, wherever you may find it — even when it's covered in feathers.

"I'll be back in a jiffy," I said to Mrs. M. "I just want to say hello and good night to Esmeralda."

"It's late, dear," Mrs. Mullet said, putting her hand on my elbow. "You'll need to be fresh to go visit your father in the morning."

"No," I said, "I want to see Esmeralda," and I turned away before she could stop me.

"Miss Flavia —" she called as I strode across the foyer. A quick glance back showed Dogger shaking his head, as if to discourage her.

The garden was in wet darkness, but I still

knew my way to the greenhouse well enough.

"Esmeralda!" I called out, not wanting to startle her in her sleep. "Guess who's home! It's me — Flavia!"

I opened the glass door and reached inside for the electric light switch. For a moment my eyes were dazzled by the glare of the naked bulb.

In the corner, Esmeralda's cage was empty.

At moments of great surprise, the human mind is easily derailed, sometimes causing us to act quite irrationally. Which is why I picked up the cage and looked underneath it — as if Esmeralda had somehow managed to reduce herself to the thickness of a piece of newspaper and had slid, chuckling, under the cage, as a practical joke to welcome me home.

A wisp of dust raised itself up into the air and disintegrated in the draft from the open door. It was obvious that the cage had not been touched in quite some time.

"Esmeralda?"

The hair stood up on the back of my neck and there was panic in my voice.

"Esmeralda!"

"We're sorry, dear. We meant to tell you —"

16

I spun round to find Mrs. Mullet and Dogger standing in the doorway.

"What have you done with her?" I demanded, but I think I knew the answer even before the words were out of my mouth.

"You've eaten her, haven't you?" I said, my words suddenly cold with fury. I looked from one of them to the other, hoping desperately for a no: for some simple, obvious, harmless explanation.

But none came. And it was just as well: I wouldn't have believed them anyway.

Mrs. Mullet wrapped her arms around herself, partly against the cold and partly for protection.

"We meant to tell you, dear," Mrs. M repeated.

But they didn't need to tell me. It was all too clear. I could already picture it in my imagination: the sudden throwing open of the cage, the seizing of that warm, fat feathered body, the frenzied, terrified clucks, the ax, the chopping block, the blood, the plucking, the gutting, the stuffing, the stitching, the roasting, the carving, the serving . . . the eating —

Cannibals.

Cannibals!

I elbowed my way roughly past them and fled back into the house.

■ ■ ■ ■

By choice, my bedroom was at the far corner of the unheated east wing, next door to the chemical laboratory that had been set up by his family in the days of Queen Victoria for my late great-uncle, Tarquin de Luce. Although Uncle Tar had now been dead for more than twenty years, his laboratory was still the wonder of the chemical world — at least, it would have been if they'd known about it.

Fortunately for me, the room, with all its chemical marvels, had been abandoned until I had seized it as my own and set about teaching myself the craft.

I climbed onto my bed and retrieved the key from where I'd hidden it in a baggy bulge of wallpaper that drooped from the ceiling. Plucking an ancient india rubber hot-water bottle from a drawer of an equally ancient dresser, I unlocked the laboratory and stepped inside.

I put a match to a Bunsen burner, filled a flask with water, and sat down on a stool to watch it boil.

Only then did I allow myself to burst into hot, bitter tears.

It was here, on this very spot, that Esmeralda had so often perched on a test-tube rack, watching me boil one of her eggs in a beaker for tiffin.

There are those persons, I suppose, who would criticize me for loving a chicken to distraction, but to them I can only say "Boo and sucks!" The love between animal and human is one that never fails, as it does so often among our own sorry tribe.

My mind went over again and again what Esmeralda must have felt at the end. It tore at my heart so fiercely that I had to quit thinking about her, and think about another chicken instead: a chicken I had once seen fleeing the hatchet in a farmyard, while I was cycling near Bishop's Lacey.

I was doing this when there was a light knock at the door. I hastily dried my eyes on my skirt, blew my nose, and called out, "Who is it?"

"It's Dogger, miss."

"Come in," I said, hoping there was not too much coldness in my voice.

Dogger stepped silently into the room. He spoke before it was necessary for me to do so.

"Regarding Esmeralda," he said, waiting to judge my reaction.

I swallowed, but somehow managed to keep my lips from quivering.

"Colonel de Luce was obliged to go up to London to deal with the Inland Revenue. In the train, he came into contact with the influenza virus — there's been a great deal of it about this year: even more, in certain locations, than in the great epidemic of 1918. The onset was remarkably rapid. The influenza progressed into bacterial pneumonia. Your father was in urgent need of a hot, nourishing broth. He was very ill and unable to keep down anything else. I take full responsibility, Miss Flavia. I made sure that Esmeralda did not suffer. She was in that blissful trance which one induced by scratching her under the chin. I'm sorry, Miss Flavia."

I deflated like a leaking balloon as the anger went slowly out of me. How could I hate someone who had probably saved my father's life?

I could find no words to fit the situation, and so I remained silent.

"I fear our world is changing, Miss Flavia," Dogger said at last, "and not necessarily for the better."

I tried to read between the words, and to reply with understanding.

"Father," I said finally. "How is he? The truth, Dogger."

A shadow flickered across Dogger's brow:

the ghost of an unpleasant thought. From what I had been able to tease out of him in the past, I deduced that Dogger had once been a highly qualified medical man, but the war had beaten him to a pulp. In spite of all that, and for all that it cost him, he was still unable to dodge an honest question, and I loved him all the more for it.

"He is gravely ill," Dogger said. "By the time he returned home from the city, he already had a feverish cough with a temperature of 102. The influenza virus does that. It also kills the natural bacteria of the nose and throat, which then allows the lungs to be invaded. The result is bacterial pneumonia."

"Thank you, Dogger," I said. "I appreciate your honesty. Is he going to die?"

"I don't know, Miss Flavia. Nobody knows. Dr. Darby is a good man. He's doing everything he can."

"Such as?" I could be remorseless when necessary.

"There is a new drug from America: aureomycin."

"Chlortetracycline!" I said. "It's an antibiotic!"

Its discovery and extraction from a soil sample in a field in Missouri had been mentioned in an issue of *Chemical Abstracts*

& Transactions which — because of Uncle Tar's lifetime subscription, and the failure of my family to notify the editors of his demise — was still being delivered to Buckshaw like chemical clockwork more than two decades after his death.

"Bless you!" I blurted, certain that Dogger had somehow taken a hand in Father's treatment.

"It is Dr. Darby who should be the recipient of our gratitude. Not forgetting, of course, the drug's discoverer."

"Of course not!"

I made a mental note to send up a bedtime prayer to — Dr. Duggar, was it? — the American botanist who had extracted the stuff from a mold sample in the soil of a garden plot in Missouri.

"Why did he call it aureomycin, Dogger?"

"Because of its golden color. *Aureus* means 'gold' in Greek, and *mykes* means 'fungus.'"

How simple it all was, when you got right down to it! Why couldn't life itself be as straightforward as a man bending over a microscope in Missouri?

My eyes were heavy. *Iron eyelids,* I remember thinking. I stifled a yawn.

I hadn't slept properly for ages. And who knew when I would have another chance?

"Good night, Dogger," I said, filling the hot water bottle. "And thank you."

"Good night, Miss Flavia," he said.

When at last my red eyes came open in the morning, they fixed upon the shrouded beef and lettuce sandwich, which still crouched accusingly on my dresser.

Perhaps I should eat the thing, I thought, *in spite of my revulsion.* I'd been given so many lectures all my life about wasting food during a time of rationing that guilt had become automatic: It came on by itself, like a burglar alarm.

Trying to keep my gorge from rising, I reached for the plate and lifted the tea towel.

Beneath it lay two toasted crumpets — still warm — with a slathering of honey on both sides, just as I liked them.

"Dogger," I said aloud as I propped myself up in bed, "your price is above rubies. You are the crème de la crème — you're the cat's pajamas."

I chewed, in something close to contentment, letting my eyes wander round the room. It was good to be home again, propped up against my own pillows, listening to the familiar *tick-tock* of my own clunker of an alarm clock, searching for the spots in the ghastly yellow Victorian wall-

23

paper where — if you squinted slightly — the wormy red squiggles in the pattern seemed to form a devil's head peering out of a mustard pot.

This was all mine now — or soon would be — I remembered, to do with as I pleased. Hard to believe, but it was true. When my mother Harriet's will had come to light after ten years, it was a shock to everyone — especially myself — to discover that she had left Buckshaw to me.

Everything.

All of it.

The whole kit and caboodle.

Not that everything was settled yet. There were still tons of paperwork to be sifted, I supposed, but in the long run, Buckshaw was in the bag.

I suppose that might sound callous, but it was true. I had tried during much of the past year to keep from thinking of the weight of responsibility that would eventually fall upon my shoulders: on that future day when all the paperwork had been dealt with and I was at last the chatelaine . . . mistress of Buckshaw.

My relationship with my sisters had not exactly been a day at the fair — not even at the best of times. The very thought of how they would react when I owned the very beds they slept in — even the spoons they ate with — was enough to give me the judders.

Feely was engaged to Dieter Schrantz, of course, and would soon be gone: perhaps as early as next summer. But Daffy — and it was Daffy whom I really feared — would be a force to be reckoned with.

She had the same devious mind that I had. And mercy, simply because we were sisters, was out of the question.

Both of them had been in bed when I arrived last night, so that my reception still remained to be seen. Breakfast would be a battlefield.

I needed to keep a sharp eye out and antennae tuned.

I got up, dressed, washed my face, and plaited my pigtails as neatly as I could. Appearance was important. I needed to show them that I had learned *something* at Miss Bodycote's Female Academy — that I was not the same simple little sister they had sent packing in September.

Sophistication was what was called for.

Should I put a flower behind my ear? I dismissed the idea as soon as it popped into my head. Flowers would never do, what with Father in hospital: It might seem to be a celebration. Besides, it was December, and flowers were thin on the ground. I had spotted a potted poinsettia in the foyer, but its blood-red color was hardly in keeping with the gravity of the situation.

Perhaps I would just stroll in, sit down at the breakfast table, and light a cigarette. That would certainly signal a new maturity.

But the problem was this: I didn't smoke. It was a filthy habit. And furthermore, I had no cigarettes.

Slowly I came down the east staircase, shoulders back and chin up, as if I were balancing an invisible Bible on my head.

The old P&D: poise and decorum. Feely was always yattering on about it, and I had picked up a few extra tips from a dog-eared back issue of *The Lady's Friend* in the waiting room of the dentist's office before setting out on my voyage to Canada.

Poise was keeping your knees and your lips together, your eyebrows and your nostrils apart.

Decorum was keeping your mouth shut.

I needn't have bothered: There was no one in sight.

For a few moments I stood alone in the middle of the foyer, which seemed somehow larger and more empty than usual. *Barren* was the word. *Desolate.* There was an unaccustomed coldness about the place.

Ordinarily at this time of year, there would have been a Christmas tree: not as grand, of course, as the one in the drawing room, but a seasonal welcome to visitors nevertheless. There would have been paper garlands, with holly wreaths and dangling mistletoe, and the warm dusty air resuscitated by the smell of rosemary, and of oranges and cloves.

But as far as I could see, there was not a trace of Christmas at Buckshaw this year. It was as if some curse — some ancient and ancestral chill — had fallen upon the house, as it does in the tales of Edgar Allan Poe.

A shiver shook my shoulders.

Get a grip on yourself, Flavia, I thought. This was no time for sentimentality. I was about to face my family. Where was I? What had I been thinking?

Oh, yes: poise and decorum. I needed to be as crisp and cool as a colonial cucumber.

I walked casually, but briskly, into the dining room, pulled out my chair without allowing it to grate on the floor, and unfolded the linen napkin fussily into my lap.

Perfection. I was proud of myself.

Daffy's nose was in a book — *The Parasites,* by Daphne du Maurier, I couldn't help noticing — while Feely appeared to be examining her own reflection in one of her highly polished thumbnails.

I helped myself to a lukewarm kipper.

"Good morning, sisters dear," I said, with just the slightest touch of sarcasm.

Like a pair of sick suns rising, Daffy's eyes came slowly up above the binding of her book. I could tell she hadn't slept.

"Well, well," she said. "Look what the cat dragged in."

"How's Father?" I asked. "Has there been any news?"

"He's in hospital!" Daffy snapped. "As you very well know. Put there by being made to drag himself up to London."

"That's hardly my fault," I snapped. "I understand he contracted pneumonia on the train."

Less than a minute in the room and already the knives were out.

"Hardly!" Daffy spat. She was seething. "*Hardly!* Your father is at death's door and yet you sit here quibbling about —"

"Daphne —" Feely said, in that voice of hers which would stop an army tank dead in its armored tracks.

Mrs. Mullet had come into the room and was busily bustling about, trying to pretend that everything was tickety-boo when it wasn't.

"Bacon'll be along directly," she said.

"The Aga's a chore to light when it's been let go out overnight. My fault, though, what with Colonel de Luce an' all."

I glanced at an imaginary wristwatch. "What time is Clarence coming with the taxicab?" I asked. "I'm anxious to see Father."

"Bless you, not till half one," Mrs. Mullet said. "Visitin' hours aren't till two. Don't make a face, dear. It might freeze, and then where would you be?"

And so my hopes of rushing to Father's bedside were dashed, just like that. I tried to swallow my disappointment.

"How's Dieter?" I asked, turning to Feely and attempting to start a civil conversation.

"How would I know?" she spat as she threw down her napkin, jumped up from the table, and stormed from the room.

She and Undine passed in the doorway. Undine stopped and cupped a hand behind her ear, as if listening to Feely's rapidly retreating footsteps.

"Cousin Ophelia is overwrought," she said in her overloud, froggish voice. "She and Dieter have had a big bust-up. It's about having babies, I expect. Hello, Flavia. Welcome home. How did they treat you in Canada?"

She came striding awkwardly across the

room and stuck out her hand. Besides stabbing her to death with a crumpet fork, I had no choice but to give it a quick, limp shake.

Undine stood there staring out at me from her great white moon face, as if expecting me to make a speech. Her watery blue eyes, framed and magnified by the large black rims of her spectacles, gave her an odd and ageless look: She might have been eight or a hundred and eight. She looked like some child's crayon drawing of a de Luce.

When I didn't answer, she leaned over and helped herself to the remains of my kipper.

"We saw Uncle Haviland yesterday," she said, meaning Father. "He looks dreadful."

Even before my brain could work, I was on my feet.

That Undine — a distant cousin of the nth degree — could see Father and I could not was not just unbearable, it was the last straw.

I got up from the table and, as if in a trance, left the room.

It was the first time in my life I had ever walked out of anything, and if the truth were told, it felt damnably good.

Which explains why I am bicycling to Bishop's Lacey in the freezing rain.

I need desperately to get away from Buck-shaw: to get away from my family. My destination is the vicarage, and the person I intend to call upon is Cynthia Richardson.

Who would ever have believed it?

Cynthia and I have had an animal aversion to each other that began years ago when she spanked me for scraping chemical samples from the stained-glass windows of St. Tancred's.

It was, I think, only when I discovered that she and her husband, Denwyn, the vicar, had tragically lost their only child, a daughter, beneath the wheels of a railway train on the platform at Doddingsley, that the tide began to turn, and Cynthia and I had now, in the past year or so, become firm friends.

There are times when even family can be of no use: when talking to your own blood fails to have meaning.

I suppose when you stop and think about it, in the great scheme of things, that's what vicars' wives are for.

I dismounted and leaned Gladys against the churchyard wall. She would be quite safe here until I was ready to go home. As Gladys was rather fond of churchyards, the wait would be something of a treat for her, in spite of the rain.

"It's nice to be home," I whispered, giving

her a pat on the seat, but not in a sentimental way. "Enjoy yourself."

I walked through the wet grass, wiped my feet on the steel scraper at the door, and tugged on the bellpull. From the depths of the vicarage came a distant, muted jangling.

I waited. There was no answer.

I counted slowly to forty — which seemed to be a reasonable interval: not short enough to seem a nuisance and yet not long enough for anyone inside to think the caller had gone away.

Another yank on the pull resulted in the same far-off clattering.

The house sounded empty.

Perhaps Cynthia was in the church. I hadn't thought of that. So much of her time was taken up with flowers, leaflets, surplices, hymnals, Brasso, and beeswax, to say nothing of parish visits, meetings of the WI, the Mothers' Union, the Altar Guild, Brownies, Girl Guides (in which she served as Brown Owl), Boy Scouts, Wolf Cubs (in which she was sometimes acting Akela), the Restoration Fund (of which she was chairwoman), and the Parish Council (of which she was secretary).

I waded back across the wet grass, but the church was empty. It was now raining harder than ever and my feet were cold and wet.

As I walked back towards Gladys, there came a call from the direction of the vicarage.

"Flavia! Yoo-hoo! Flavia!"

I didn't recognize the voice as Cynthia's, but it turned out to be her all the same.

She was huddled behind the front door, holding it open no more than a crack. As I stepped onto the veranda I could see that she was clutching closed a shabby pink dressing gown.

She looked awful.

"Welcome home," she croaked. "I've got a beastly cold, so I won't give you a hug. Denwyn and I were sorry to hear about your father. How is he?"

"I don't know," I said. "We're going to see him this afternoon."

"Come in . . . come in," Cynthia said, opening the door just wide enough to squeeze through. "I'll put the kettle on and we'll have a nice cup of tea."

That was Cynthia all over. She had her priorities straight: welcome, hug (whether delivered or not), explanation, sympathy, and tea, in that order.

She had tactfully left the sympathy until

33

near the end in order to make it seem less serious.

It was a tactic I had used myself on occasion — burying the bad bits among the good — and I appreciated her thoughtfulness.

"Milk and two sugars, if I remember rightly," she said, when the kettle had boiled and the tea was steeping. "Your shoes and socks are soaked. Give them to me and I'll put them on the hearth."

I handed them over and picked a few blades of wet grass from between my toes.

"And how was Canada?" Cynthia asked, stifling a sneeze. "All lakes, moose, and lumberjacks, as expected?"

This was something of a private joke between us. She had confided, as I was leaving for Canada, that her father had once been a log driver on the Ottawa River, and that she sometimes thought of following in his spiked boot steps.

"Pretty much," I said, and left it at that.

"But how are *you*?" I added. "You look a fright."

Cynthia and I were great enough pals that I could get away with it.

"I *feel* a fright," she said. "I must look like something the cat dragged in."

Daffy's very words to me, I thought.

"I hope you're not contagious."

"Good heavens, no! Dr. Darby was good enough to look in. He tells me I'm past that stage. Just as well. I have Wolf Cubs at half five and Scouts at seven. Pray for me, Flavia!"

"You ought to be in bed," I said. "Bundled in flannels and sipping hot toddy with milk."

Hot toddy and milk was a prescription I'd once heard Mrs. Mullet's husband, Alf, recommend to Father. "It's a sovereign remedy," Alf had said. "Good for what ails you, man, beast, or angel."

Father had remarked later that Alf's advice was ambiguous but well-meaning.

"Do you have any rum or brandy in the house?"

"I'm afraid not. Sacramental wine is my limit." She giggled nervously, as if giving away a great secret.

"I could run over to the Thirteen Drakes and beg a bottle. I'm sure Mr. Stoker would be happy to put it on tick. It's not as if —"

"Thank you, Flavia, but no. It's very sweet of you. I've so much to do, I hardly know where to begin."

And then suddenly, shockingly, she was in tears. I handed over a clean handkerchief and waited for her to subside. Some things simply can't be rushed.

35

After a while, the sobs became wet snickers, and the snickers became a weak grin.

"Oh, dear! Whatever must you think of me?"

"I think you work too hard," I said. "What can I do to help?"

"Nothing," she answered. "I shall simply have to let some of my chores slide. I shall ring up and tell people the truth: that the vicar is away and that I'm ill."

"Is the vicar away? I didn't realize that. How awful for you."

"The bishop called one of his snap inspections of clergy. 'The Brains Trust,' he calls it, in order to make it sound jolly. At the diocesan office, of course. Denwyn won't likely be home until late."

"You're sure there's nothing I can do?"

"I wish there were," she said. "But the tasks of a country vicar and his churchmouse wife can only be — hold on — wait a minute — yes, there *is* one thing."

"I'll do it!" I said, not caring what it was.

"I hate to send you out in the rain, but our car's cracked a piston or a connecting rod or some such impossible part, and Bert Archer says he can't get it back to us before next Wednesday."

"Don't worry," I told her. "I feel better in the rain."

It was true. The human brain performs more efficiently when taking in humid air than it does in hot or cold dry weather. My theory is that this is some kind of throwback to our fishy ancestors, who lived in the sea and breathed water, and some day when I have sufficient time, I intend to write a paper upon the subject.

"Do you know where Stowe Pontefract is?"

Cynthia's voice broke in upon my thoughts.

Of course I did. It was only a mile or so as the crow flies from Bishop's Lacey; two miles, perhaps, if the crow has to ride a bicycle and keep to the roads and lanes. In spite of its spelling, the name of the place was pronounced "Stowe Pumfret," and it was something of a joke in Bishop's Lacey.

"It's a hamlet," Daffy had once told me. "Too small to be a village — too big to be an omelette."

It was done Stowe Pontefract style, people in Bishop's Lacey would sometimes say, meaning seldom, poorly, or not at all.

"Yes, I know the place. It's between here and East Finching," I said. "First road to the right at the top of Denham Rise. Just past Pauper's Well."

"That's it!" Cynthia said. "Thornfield

Chase is no more than a quarter mile in."

"Thornfield Chase?"

"Mr. Sambridge's place. Although I'm afraid it's not nearly so grand as it sounds."

"I'll find it," I said.

I could be there and back in an hour. It was not yet mid-morning. Plenty of time to get home and scrubbed for my first visit to Father.

"What would you like me to do?" I asked.

"Just deliver an envelope to Mr. Sambridge, dear. He's a very clever wood-carver. More of an artist, I suppose. Denwyn's been trying to entice him into replacing — or at least restoring — some of the carved medieval angels on the hammer-beam ends. The poor man suffers dreadfully from arthritis — to be quite frank, he's as stiff as a board — so that we hate to ask him to come in again. Still, Dr. Darby says keeping active is the best thing for it. Shocking what the deathwatch beetle can do once it gets into old oak. You're sure you don't mind?"

Whether Cynthia was talking about Mr. Sambridge's joints or the carved angels, I couldn't work out, and I didn't want to ask.

"Not at all," I said. "I'd be happy to help."

And it was true, although what I was happy about was not so much being help-ful, but being able to get away from Buckshaw, Undine, and my blasted sisters, even for a couple of hours. A ride in the rain would do me good. It would blow out the cobwebs that had been forming in my cranium for quite some time.

To the north of Bishop's Lacey, the road rises steeply in a series of folds. I stood on Gladys's pedals and pumped for all I was worth. There was no traffic, but if there had been, the drivers would have seen a red-faced girl in a yellow mackintosh swerving slightly and wobbling from side to side as she fought the hill and the furious gusting of the north wind.

Like an aeroplane, a bicycle is capable of stalling at too low a speed, and one has to be prepared to step off and push at any moment. Even with the lowest gear engaged, it was a rough go.

"Sorry, Gladys." I puffed. "I can only promise you that it's downhill all the way home."

Gladys gave a little squeak of delight. She loved coasting as much as I did, and if there was no one in sight, I might even put my feet up on her handlebars: a bit of bicycle artistry that she loved even more than ordinary free-wheeling.

The turnoff came sooner than I expected.

A weathered fingerpost pointed east in the direction of Stowe Pontefract. The road was no more than a narrow, rutted lane, but at least it was level. Dense, wild holly hedges grew on either side, their scarlet berries sparkling in spite of the gray, watery light. These pretty but poisonous berries, I recalled with pleasure, contained, among other things: caffeic acid, quinic acid, chlorogenic acid, kaempferol, caffeine, quercetin, rutin, and theobromine. "Theobromine" means, literally, "the food of the gods," and is the bitter alkaloid found also in tea, coffee, and chocolate. An overdose could be fatal.

Death by means of a lavishly large box of chocolates delivered to a rich and elderly aunt was not just something that happened in mystery novels. No, indeed! It was probably no coincidence that holly and chocolates were always somewhere about at Christmas: the time of year when mortality rates peaked among the aged.

This pleasant train of thought was interrupted by the appearance of a pair of crumbling brick pillars on my left. A cracked wooden signboard, its painted letters peeling as if it suffered from eczema, read: THORNFIELD CHASE. I braked, turned carefully into the drive, and dismounted.

All that remained of the estate was a Gothic hunting lodge, and what was left of that was in sad disrepair. A carpet of green and black moss covered the sagging roof, the doorframes were rotten, and the windows were as dull as dead eyes. A dismal *drip-drip-drip* came from the plugged gutters, the remains of which hung in metallic tatters.

What an odd place for a so-called master carpenter to live, I thought. There must be more than a little truth in that old proverb: The cobbler's children and the blacksmith's horse are always without shoes.

What were Colonel Haviland de Luce's children without?

That part of my mind switched itself off.

A derelict Austin sedan stood under the trees, a liberal spattering of bird droppings suggesting that it had not been recently moved. I glanced quickly in through its spotted windows. A pair of soft leather driving gloves was visible — one on the seat, the other on the floor. Nothing else.

I turned and slogged through dead wet leaves to the door.

A tug on an old-fashioned bellpull — an ivory knob in a brass plate — produced a surprisingly bright and crisp ringing from somewhere inside the lodge.

41

In case someone should be watching me through a peephole, I brought the envelope out from beneath my mackintosh and arranged my features into what I thought might pass for eager efficiency: one elbow crooked and slightly raised, brows slightly beetled, lips lightly pursed — a cross between a Post Office telegram boy and Alice's white rabbit.

The gutters dripped.

I rang again.

"Mr. Sambridge," I called out. "Mr. Sambridge . . . are you here?"

No answer.

"Mr. Sambridge, it's Flavia de Luce. I have something for you from the vicarage."

"Something" sounded more tantalizing than "a letter." "Something" might be money, but then, I imagine, so could "a letter."

But my choice of words made no difference anyway: Mr. Sambridge was not responding.

I suppose I could have dropped the envelope through the mail slot, but that is not the way of Flavia de Luce. Cynthia had given me an errand to run, and I would carry it out come hell or hobnails. It was a question of honor and — yes, let's face it — curiosity.

I lifted the flap, applied my eyes, and peered through the slot at a painted brick wall with a single coat-hook, upon which hung a Norfolk jacket of the style worn by gamekeepers.

"Hello?" I said, speaking into the opening. "Mr. Sambridge?"

I tried the door, knowing even as I did so that it was pointless, but to my amazement, it swung open easily and I stepped inside.

Aside from the boxy little entranceway — constructed to keep the weather from blowing directly in — the ground floor of the lodge was a single large room, and it was clear that this was Sambridge's woodworking shop. The smell of fresh shavings filled the air: The room was fragrant with the sappy scent of the forest.

A workbench stood in the light of a window, littered with knives, planes, saws, and files, and an assortment of sharp cutting tools: some with flat, some with curved, and some with V-shaped blades. There was a vise, and wooden and rubber mallets of different sizes.

On a stand stood a magnificently carved oak eagle, not quite finished, its vast wooden wings raised and spread, its beak open in a silent shriek, its feathers slightly ruffled, as if rising up like a puff adder to defend its nest from mountain climbers. It was a lectern, of course, and I knew that the eagle represented Saint John the Evangelist.

Once installed in whatever church it was destined for, this bird would strike secret terror into the hearts of all the little children lining up for their first communion — as perhaps it was supposed to do. Even *my* neck was bristling slightly.

As a wood-carver and an artist, Mr. Sambridge was a genius, no doubt about it.

A small cooker, a sink full of soiled dishes, its slow *drip-drip* matching the sound of the ruined gutters outside, and slipping in and out of time with the Black Forest cuckoo clock on the wall.

Tick . . . tock . . . tick . . . tock . . . DRIP . . . tick . . . tock . . . tick . . . DRIP . . . tock . . .

And so forth.

The hands of the clock were at 10:03.

A few books and a cold fireplace completed the ground floor. A narrow staircase led to the upstairs.

"Hello?" I called again, as I set foot upon the first step.

The man might be an unusually sound sleeper.

Or perhaps he drank. Anything was possible. Even if he *did* carve evangelical eagles.

"Mr. Sambridge?"

44

A stair tread creaked and I froze — but realized almost at once that I was frightening myself. "Getting in a state," as Mrs. Mullet called it.

I gave a carefree little snort to relieve the tension. The man had gone out and left his front door unlocked. There was no more to it than that.

Technically, I suppose, I was trespassing — perhaps even housebreaking. I'd have just a quick peek into the upper room and then make my exit. I'd leave the envelope on Mr. Sambridge's workbench, where he couldn't miss it. I might even scribble a little note giving my name and the time of day — so that he would know who'd been in his cottage, and when.

Everything on the up-and-up . . . all shipshape and Bristol fashion . . . all according to Hoyle.

But that was not the way things turned out.

At the top of the stairs was a door.

A closed door.

There is a certain type of person to whom a closed door is a challenge — a dare, a taunt, a glove thrown down — and I am one of them. A closed door is more than a mystery to be solved: It's an insult. A slap in the face.

As anybody with two older sisters can tell you, a closed door is like a red rag to a bull. It cannot go unchallenged.

I stepped forward, put my ear to the panel, and listened.

Dead silence. Not even the usual amplified roar of an empty room that you expect when you use a wooden door as a sounding board.

I put my hand on the knob, gave it a twist, shoved open the door just wide enough to let my eyes rove over the room.

What a disappointment.

In alphabetical order: bed (neatly made), bookshelf, chair, chamber pot, clothes press, table, and a thin Turkey carpet: all very orderly. All surprisingly neat and clean.

No monsters, no madmen: none of the things you always expect to come leaping out at you when you're snooping round a stranger's house.

I pushed the door a little wider, but with a sudden thump, it seemed to meet with some obstruction. It jammed just past the halfway mark.

I stepped into the room, and as I did so, the door swung slowly closed of its own accord.

It must have been off balance, I decided later, because of the weight of Mr. Sambridge's body.

I spun round.

He was hanging upside down, lashed to the back of the door — his arms and shackled legs spread in the shape of a human "X."

Two

The expression on his darkened face was ghastly: a look of sheer horror. The eyes bulged out in a stare that might have been amusing if their owner had not been dead. The nostrils were flared and cavernous, like those of a horse about to bolt: as if they had flung themselves open in one last desperate attempt to draw in oxygen. The corners of the open mouth, inverted as they were — turned up instead of down, in mockery of a smile — made it clear that the man had, at the instant of death, been terrified.

How had he come to be strung up in that helpless position, hanging like a hawk from a tree in its tangled jesses, left to struggle helplessly until death freed him?

Saint Andrew had been crucified in just such a spread-eagled way. I remembered that from an exchange visit we had paid several years ago to the Girl Guide troop at Hinley Presbyterian Church. Although the meeting itself had been pretty much of a washout — on account of snobbery — the great stained-glass window behind the pulpit and the "common table," as the Presbyterians called their altar, had been most instructive.

The center panel depicted Saint Andrew, who was, as I had expected he would be, fastened to his cross like a giant asterisk, arms and legs flung wide, as if he were a paratrooper whose parachute has not yet opened.

But Mr. Sambridge was, as I have said, hanging upside down — unlike Saint Andrew, who had at least been put to death in an upright position.

It was Saint Peter, I remembered, who, at his own request, had been crucified head downwards.

This fact in itself was incredibly interesting. Surely such a bizarre death — and in such an interesting position — coming to a wood-carver who specialized in ecclesiastical subjects could be no coincidence. Was there a hidden message here, having to do with his past?

My first thought, of course, had been to go for help. But it was clear — and it would have been even to someone less accustomed to death than myself — that Mr. Sambridge was beyond assistance.

I was fairly certain, anyway, that there was no telephone at Thornfield Chase. I had not noticed one in my quick survey of the downstairs room. And surely, if there had been a telephone installed, Cynthia or the vicar would have rung up Mr. Sambridge, rather than sending me on this errand.

Too late for doctors or ambulances. Too late for Mr. Sambridge.

For the time being, at least, I had him all to myself.

And I might as well say here and now that, at that very moment, a sudden sense of vast relief swept over me, as if a long-hidden and unexpected sun had risen. I felt as Atlas must have felt when some good Samaritan finally took pity upon him, and lifted the weight of the globe from his poor aching shoulders.

For quite some time now, I had not been myself. Much as I hated to admit it, the events of the past several months had shaken me rather badly. I was not at all the Flavia de Luce I had once been. Whether that was a bad thing or a good one remained to be seen, but until I managed to work it out, the feeling was one of bearing an enormous invisible burden: the weight of the world.

I want to know who I am before it is too late — before I am no longer the same person — before I become someone different. Although there are days when this seems a furious race against time, there are others when it seems to matter not a tinker's curse.

But now — suddenly — in a flash — an instant — a twinkling of the eye — everything changed.

Somewhere in the universe, a cinder had fallen through the grate and bounced out onto the open hearth.

And yet none of those tired old phrases — in spite of their suggestion of speed — manage to convey how quickly that change came over me.

Before you could say "Jack Robinson!" or "Snap!" (I was ashamed of myself for using these tired old phrases, but for some reason I couldn't seem to help myself), I felt as if I had been suddenly possessed by my former self — as if from some molten furnace, a new Flavia de Luce had been poured into my old shoes.

No . . . not a *new* Flavia de Luce, but the old one, yet tempered now, and hard as steel.

It's amazing what the discovery of a corpse can do for one's spirits.

I licked the tip of my mental pencil and began to make notes.

Age, I thought: *about seventy, at a guess.* We had been taught to estimate ages in Girl Guides, not only by physical characteristics but also by comparison. The latter method told me that the man was much older than Father, who was fifty, and younger than old Canon Eastlake, who, at ninety, had crept quavering back to St. Tancred's last summer to be presented with a purse of money for his half-century of services to the Building Fund.

I ticked off the main indicators: gray hair and bushy gray beard tending to white, wrinkled facial skin (dark as it now was and dragged down by gravity), faded gray eyes (yes, they were open, and staring at me), scandalously bushy eyebrows, and a profuse undergrowth of hair in the ears.

I stuck a curious finger into the surprisingly warm mouth, remembering as I did so that fingerprints cannot be taken from dead lips. Mr. Sambridge possessed a remarkably good mouthful of natural teeth for someone his age, whether ritually maintained or expensively corrected I could not tell.

As someone who has spent hours of agony strapped down in Dr. Frankenstein's chamber of dental horrors in Farrington Street, I could only respect — and hate — anyone who still possessed such a spotless set of choppers.

That would do for basics, but I knew that I could be much more thorough.

My task was complicated, though, by the position of the body, and by the fact that much of its blood had settled in the head.

Cutting him down was out of the question. If I had learned one thing from Inspector Hewitt in the past, it was not to meddle with dead bodies.

At the very thought of my old friend, I felt my face flushing. How exciting it would be to call in the inspector: to be the one to break the news of Mr. Sambridge's death. But before I could do so — and before I could receive the inspector's generous and wholehearted praise with an entirely innocent heart — I needed to remove any traces of my own investigation.

But before turning things over to the police, there was much to do, and I'd better get on with it. My time here was limited. I needed to get back to Buckshaw in time for the taxi to visit Father in Hinley; that was one thing that couldn't be delayed.

I also had to consider the possibility that someone — the postman, perhaps — would come to Thornfield Chase and find me there alone with Mr. Sambridge.

Gladys, parked outside, would be a dead giveaway. There wasn't time to go downstairs and move her to a hiding place, and to be caught doing so would be even more difficult to explain.

No, the best thing was to get on with it, and hope for the best.

Father had once lectured us: *In even the most desperate of situations, you must always put efficiency first. Efficiency is paramount.*

And he was right. How wise my father was!

Efficiency was everything.

The problem at hand was in making a careful study of Mr. Sambridge's features, hampered as I was by the fact that he was hanging upside down and cutting him loose, as I have said, was out of the question.

The solution came to me at once. I stepped to one side, threw my hands above my head, bent sideways at the waist, planted my right hand down firmly upon the carpet, flung myself into a half cartwheel, and ended up in a handstand, face-to-face — nose to nose, almost — with the corpse.

Much better!

At once — and in spite of the grimace — it looked much more human. Everything seemed to snap into place.

There must be a part of our brain, I thought, *that is designed to recognize human features: a part of the brain that switches off when the face is upside down. I must remember to research this theory at a more convenient time.*

But for now — and with a sharp shock of recognition — I realized I had seen this face before.

The ocean wave of gray hair, that large, bulbous forehead, the long ears, and the sad eyes had triggered some overgrown memory circuit. The only trouble was, I could not remember the *where,* the *when,* or the *who* of it.

No time for that now, I thought.

At this short range, my view of the dead man's face was almost microscopic: I could see the pores on his nose (large, but clean) and the myriad of minute red blood vessels in his nose, broken and spreading in all directions like a map of the Amazon and its tributaries.

Aha! I thought. *He drinks.*

But wait! Although I had not yet searched the house thoroughly, I had come across no liquor bottles.

Used *to drink,* I decided.

Was it my imagination, or did the corpse's

face show a little relief at my change of mind?

Around the clearly defined outline of his beard, the cheeks, chin, and neck were clean-shaven without the slightest sign of stubble, which seemed to suggest that he had died early in the day, soon after shaving, rather than later.

I turned my attention to the hair again, which now, hanging down towards the floor, appeared to me, in my inverted position, to be standing on end in fright, but was otherwise a healthy bush, as if its owner had faithfully used a patent hair tonic from birth.

"The hair of a much younger man," said the voice of the Whisperer in my ear. *"Is it possibly a wig?"*

Lowering myself to balance on my head and one elbow, I reached out carefully for a handful of strands and gave them a sharp tug, thinking as I did so that (a) you can't hurt the dead and (b) as with lips, you can't leave fingerprints on hair.

But this was no wig. The hair was natural. And — I should have thought of this before — it matched perfectly the color of the hair in the man's ears and nose.

People who dye their hair, beards, mustaches, and eyebrows for nefarious purposes seldom think to include their earlobes and nostrils.

I studied the skin. The cheeks and forehead were liver-spotted, as were the backs of the hands, which hung helplessly to the floor, the fingers turned in and clawlike — as if their owner had died clutching, like a drowning man, at the proverbial straw.

I examined the fingernails. As I had suspected they would be, several of them — notably the first three on each hand — were broken. And under each of these, partly dried blood was caked. The fingertips themselves were raw and covered with abrasions, a word I had learned from Dickens's *Martin Chuzzlewit,* in which the eldest Miss Pecksniff found abrasions on the knobby parts of her father's anatomy after he had been knocked down the front steps. I had heard it again from Dogger as he dressed my wounds the first time Gladys shied and dumped me onto the gravel drive.

The abrasions made it likely that the blood under the nails was the corpse's own.

If his wounds had been inflicted *after* Mr. Sambridge was hung up by his heels, the source of the damage could not have been more than an arm's length away. It — or they — would have been within reach.

I lowered my feet and sprang out of my

headstand.

I didn't have far to look. The contraption by which Mr. Sambridge was suspended was a sort of windlass: an ingenious system of ropes and pulleys attached to the back of the door — not so very different from the rack upon which medieval torturers stretched their victims in the Tower. At the heart of all this was a hand-carved wooden gear assembly, which looked for all the world like a waterwheel in the millstream of some quaint Victorian village. In miniature, of course.

A wooden pawl, or tongue, fell into the teeth of a ratchet gear, assuring that it could turn in only one direction, unless released. The device was a simple one: a mechanism I had learned to recognize when Dogger taught me the art of lock-picking.

The pulleys had been beautifully hand-carved, apparently from single blocks of oak, and polished by someone who was proud of his work. They must have taken weeks of patient work. I could still smell the beeswax with which they had been lubricated.

I could smell something else, too: a whiff of sulfur, or something very like it.

Had the Devil been here in his horns and hooves, leaving behind the smell of brimstone? Had Mr. Sambridge met his end in some bizarre ritual, at the hands of a group of village Satanists?

I shook off a growing shiver before it overcame me.

If Mr. Sambridge *had* been murdered, it had been no spur-of-the-moment killing. Someone had gone to a great deal of trouble to rig up such an infernal device.

A pair of hemp ropes ran up and through the wooden pulleys, ending in leather-padded loops which encircled his ankles.

For a distance of a foot or more, both above and below the dead man's knees, the fibers of the rope were stained with moist blood. It was obvious that, before dying, he had clawed at his bonds in a frantic attempt to free himself.

But his struggles had been in vain. He was caught up like a fly in a spider's web.

His face, as I have said, was livid, as might be expected of someone who had died while hanging upside down. Whether or not the congestion was postmortem was something that would only be determined at the inevitable autopsy.

I tried to put myself in his position: to imagine how he must have felt as he waited upside down for death to come.

While I myself have never died, I *have*

mastered the art of standing on my head for lengthy periods of time, in order to stimulate my thinking processes. Dogger had assured me that doing so should not be fatal: Only people with dicky hearts would be at risk during an extended headstand.

Had Mr. Sambridge suffered heart troubles?

If he had, his medicine cabinet might well hold the answer. A prescription for anything containing thiocyanate, nitroglycerine, or any of the veratrum alkaloids derived from the corn lily or false hellebore, for instance, would be highly suggestive.

I'm sorry if I seem to digress, but that is precisely what I was thinking at the moment. It's the way my mind works. Things are not the same in real life as they are in, for instance, the fictional world of Sherlock Holmes. Brains, in reality, do not go *clickety-clickety-clickety-click* from *A* to *B* to *C* to *D* and so forth, rushing like a train along the rails, until at the end, with a happy *"Toot-toot!"* they arrive at their destination, *Z,* and the case is suddenly solved.

Quite the contrary. In reality, analytical minds such as my own are forever shooting wildly off in all directions simultaneously. It's like joyously hitting jelly with a sledge-hammer; like exploding galaxies; like a display of fireworks in which the pyrotechnic engineer has had a bit too much to drink and set off the whole conglobulation all at once, by accident.

It was not until this point that the room itself began to attract my notice. I had been so occupied with the remains of the late Mr. Sambridge that I had not really — other than a quick glance — registered the contents of his bedroom.

My first impression, now, was that I had been miraculously transported through time and space and dumped into the bedroom of Geppetto, the wood-carver in *Pinocchio.*

I looked round in astonishment at the furniture, which was remarkable, to say the least.

The four-poster bed, for instance, was made up of what seemed to be an entire squadron of carved angels: plump wooden cherubs that simpered and leered at one another as they swarmed to their mischievous task.

What came to mind was that line from *Hamlet:*

And flights of angels sing thee to thy rest.

But these cherubs were not singing the terrified night-shirted figure to his rest, but rather, so far as I could make out, dragging him down relentlessly by his knobbly carved wooden knees towards the pit of carved flames which formed the foot of the bed. The victim's mouth was open, his tiny teeth like bat's teeth as he fell, in a silent scream of agony.

Much like — I couldn't help thinking — the real Mr. Sambridge.

Two falling figures, tumbling headfirst into eternity: one of wood and one of flesh and blood.

What was I to make of that?

On the wall beside the bed was what seemed at first to be an eighteenth-century lady's fan: a large, lacy, delicate semicircle which proved to be, upon closer inspection — or so I guessed — a large specimen of coral, which looked for all the world like a silhouette of an ancient tree in winter.

A bedside table was decorated with carved serpent legs supporting a marble slab top, upon which had been placed two shillings and sixpence, a key, a silver pocket watch with chain and fob, a fist-sized gargoyle carved from some dark wood such as ebony, the stub of a pencil, a bit of gray fluff indicating that these objects had previously been in someone's pocket, and a £1 ticket on the Irish Hospitals' Sweepstake.

I remembered with a pang how Daffy and I had clubbed together last June to buy Father, as a birthday present, a ticket on this same race.

"It's the most valuable prize ever offered," I'd told him, brimming over with excitement as I handed him what I prayed would be a winner. "More than £22,000."

Twenty-some thousand quid would go a long way, I thought, *to easing Father's money worries.*

Father's brow had clouded and furrowed, and I was left standing awkwardly with the ticket in my outstretched hand.

"I appreciate your thoughtfulness, Flavia," Father had said. "It is very kind of you, but I cannot accept."

He seemed as embarrassed as I was.

"You must never indulge in gambling," he said. "Nor must you stand to profit from the frailties of others. Lotteries, as you very well know, are against the law."

"But —"

"No, Flavia. That's enough. I have spoken. You may go."

And with that, he had turned back to his stamp collection.

I was too crushed to tell Daffy what had happened.

Can you revoke a prayer? I wondered.

In the following weeks I had then counter-prayed each night in bed that the ticket would be a loser. To win would be a calamity. While I was perfectly capable of keeping my own trap shut, I knew that the seller of a winning ticket was also awarded a sum of money. In my case, the seller was Tippy Hogben, who, under cover of her market stall at Malden Fenwick, did a brisk business in such black-market goods as tea, butter, and sugar.

And if Tippy won so much as a shilling, I was as good as dead. Gossip would cook my goose.

It wasn't the giving of the ticket to Father that was a crime, but the buying of it, which was my responsibility alone. At the last minute Daffy had begged off our jaunt to Tippy's stall on the grounds of having a ferocious headache, so that, in the end, I was left to do the dirty deed alone.

Now, six months later, the very thought of an Irish Hospitals' Sweepstake ticket still made me queasy, which was one of the reasons I didn't touch this ticket of Mr. Sambridge's.

The other reason was fingerprints.

I couldn't help wondering if the deceased had checked his ticket. It seemed unlikely. If he had, and if it were a loser, he'd have thrown it away; if it were a winner, he'd have handed it in and claimed his prize.

I needed to examine the back of the ticket to see if it had been endorsed, and it didn't take long to think of a solution. Leaning over the table, I touched the tip of my tongue to the thing and flipped it over.

"Necessity is the mother of invention," Daffy had once told me, and as far as I knew, no one had yet come up with a system of tongue-print identification. I would put it on the list of clever innovations I intended to suggest some day to Inspector Hewitt.

But not during this case, of course.

To my disappointment, the reverse of the ticket had not been written on: no seller's name, no endorsement by the buyer.

I repeated the tongue trick and flipped the ticket back into its original position. A little damp, perhaps, but it would soon dry off.

But wait! Had I done myself in?

Would they test for saliva? Would Sergeant Woolmer think to do a spit test on this flimsy piece of evidence?

A German researcher named Mueller had, more than twenty years ago, suggested such a test: one in which the presence of an enzyme called alpha-amylase could indicate the presence of saliva. But to the best of my knowledge, Mueller's test could not distinguish the alpha-amylase found in human saliva from that found in certain bacteria and fungi, or, for that matter, in the saliva of certain apes.

A possible defense, if I were accused, might be that the ticket had come into contact with fungus, or some kind of earthy bacteria: that it might, for instance, have fallen out of Mr. Sambridge's pocket during a walk in the woods and landed in a mushroom ring.

Or been licked by a playful chimp at the zoo.

I smiled at the thought — smiled for the first time in many months.

It was the chemistry that caused this lifting of the spirits. Chemistry lifted you up out of the mud and flung you up among the stars.

Except, of course, when it didn't.

Things could so easily go wrong. Even the alchemists of the Middle Ages, deluded as they were, recognized that the Devil often inserted himself into chemical operations.

One had to be careful.

It would never do to second-guess the members of the detective police force.

Nevertheless, one didn't often hear of murder victims — if indeed Mr. Sambridge were one — being spread-eagled in a vertical position.

Could I have stumbled upon some bizarre act of human sacrifice?

A quick sniff of the air told me there was no lingering odor of smoke or candles; no stink of burning baby fat or anything like that, which was just as well. I don't think I could have dealt with it. While I'm blessed with an extraordinarily strong stomach, there are some things that are beyond bearing.

No, there was just that little whiff of sulfur, which might have just as well come from a lighted match.

I gave a sigh of relief as I confirmed that there were no traces in the room of soot or ash, no chalked pentagrams on the floor, or any of the other beastly things that Daffy delighted in reading aloud to me after dark from the spine-curdling novels of Dennis Wheatley.

But just as I was congratulating myself on my level-headedness, there came a scratching sound from the direction of the corpse. I whipped quickly round and saw that it was moving.

THREE

I practically shed my skin.

The corpse's hands were moving slowly towards me. In fact, the whole dead body was in motion.

It swung slowly into the room as the door came open with a groan.

There was a breathless pause and then something began to ooze through the crack and into the room.

It was a cat. Not, as you would expect, a black cat, but rather a tortoiseshell. Still, you never knew, and I was taking no chances.

"Hello," I said. "What's *your* name? Grimalkin? Grissel? Greedigut?"

The cat replied with a noncommittal "Meow."

It makes no sense, I know, to be chatting to a cat while its probable former owner is dangling dead on the door, but that's the way things are in real life. We have a tendency to prattle away in the face of fear, as if pretending that things are normal will make them so.

Some people have gone to the chopping block saying, "I hope we're not too late?"

In any case, it didn't really matter. The cat wrote me off with a single glance, sniffed hopefully at the hair of its late master, then stalked across the room, jumped up onto the bed, and began to wash itself.

"Nice kitty," I said, as one does.

Without the cat, I might not have thought to examine the bed. I dropped down onto all fours and had a look underneath.

Nothing. Not even dust balls. For a man, and an apparent bachelor, Mr. Sambridge was a remarkably good housekeeper.

Back on my feet, I ran my hands beneath the pillows. Nothing there. Not even pajamas.

At the head of the bed, and off to one side, was a hand-carved bookcase.

Life with my sister Daffy had taught me that you could tell as much about people by their books as you could by snooping through their diaries — a practice of which I am exceedingly fond and, I must confess, especially adept.

Mr. Sambridge did not have many books — perhaps a dozen in all. Several of these, such as the King James Bible and Robert Burton's *Anatomy of Melancholy,* were well thumbed, but the remaining volumes seemed unread: as fresh and crisp as if they had just arrived from Foyles in the morning post.

And, oddly, there were several copies of the same books, each in mint condition in a fresh dust wrapper.

I recognized them at once by their brightly illustrated covers: *Rainy Day Rhymes, Hobbyhorse House, The History of Crispian Crumpet,* and *Pirates in the Garden:* those immortal childhood classics by Oliver Inchbald.

Who, in England, or for that matter, anywhere else in the Empire or beyond, hadn't had these books read aloud to them even before they could manage bread and milk? I myself still had distinct memories of:

Splash! Sploik! Splonk! Splink!
Jumping in the rain
What a jolly mess, I think
Here I go again!

Or worse:

Captain Congleton's kangaroo
Is coming tonight for the Irish stew.

I still have several disjointed recollections of the unfortunate Miss Gurdy reciting this nonsense mechanically and without expression as she forced a spoon of gruel upon me in a high chair.

To someone like myself who had already been exposed to *real* poetry, these childish rhymes were an enormous letdown. I thought in particular of one rainy afternoon when I was very young that Daffy, in a far corner of one of the attics, had rehearsed "Westron Wind":

"Westron wynde, when wyll thow blow
The smalle rayne downe can rayne.
Cryst yf my love were in my armes
And I yn my bed a-gayne."

Outside, the small rain had raced down the leaded windowpanes, adding blurred but vivid images to her words.

Reminded of another song, Daffy went on:

"Marti'mas wind, when wilt thou blaw,
And shake the green leaves from the tree?
O gentle death, when wilt thou come?
For of life I am wearie."

71

The words had touched something so deep inside me that I shivered at their sound. Although I did not know it at the time, the feeling was one of loneliness: a feeling I would later come to know — and later yet, to treasure.

Captain Congleton's kangaroo, my aunt Fanny!

Using my handkerchief to avoid leaving fingerprints, I picked up one of the copies of *Rainy Day Rhymes* and opened it to a random page:

Splash! Sploik! Splonk! Splink!
Jumping in the rain
What a jolly mess, I think
Here I go again!

There was no getting away from this stuff, even at the scene of a murder.

But then I thought, *Hold on!*

Could it be that there was a message here for me? Had the book fallen open at that particular page for a reason? Was it like those cases I had heard about where people would seek solutions to their problems by sticking a finger at random into the Bible?

Prognostication, Daffy called it, and said it was a load of old horse hockey.

What a jolly mess, I think. Here I go again.

Were the words not meant to point up my present predicament? They could hardly have been better chosen. And besides, it was raining outside: *Splash! Sploik! Splonk! Splink! Jumping in the rain.*

Gladys would certainly appreciate this weird reflection of our actual lives. The sounds perfectly described her progress along a puddle-filled lane.

"Stick to the facts," Uncle Tarquin said inside my head.

I leafed slowly through the pages: Here was Crispian Crumpet building sand castles by the sea, and here he was feeding a pony an apple over a wicket gate. Here he was gluing feathers to his forearms for a poem called *The Child Icarus,* and here, roasting a chestnut on a stick over an open bonfire.

I wondered if Oliver Inchbald's real-life son, upon whom the books were based, had actually done these things, or whether they were make-believe, the result of the author's overheated imagination?

I had never noticed it before, but in spite of his many messy doings, the boy was always pictured as crisp and clean, as spotless as any saint. No filth in the world of Crispian Crumpet. Sickness and sadness were unknown quantities, like x and y.

Why was this obnoxious child's life so

filled with honey and sunshine when my own was rain and ruin?

With a sigh, I closed the book and returned Crispian to his shelf.

His life and mine were as unalike as noonday and darkness.

"Stop it!" Uncle Tarquin snapped, and this time I obeyed.

Only then did the strangeness of my discovery strike me. Why on earth would a grown man — a grown *older* man at that — have a set of children's books at his bedside?

And multiple copies, at that?

Could it be a case of second childhood, like old Mr. Terry, the former verger at St. Tancred's? Mr. Terry, according to Mrs. Mullet, baked mud pies in the oven if he were not watched carefully, and chased robins round the vicarage garden with a salt cellar.

I had another look at Mr. Sambridge. Even dead, he didn't look like someone who had lost his marbles. Surely the vicar and his wife would have noticed: Cynthia Richardson would hardly have sent me alone, and without any warning or explanation, to the house of a man who was known to be utterly gaga.

Someone like that would hardly be able to make a living by ecclesiastical wood-carving.

Perhaps he was a book collector.

I know that there were people who are as barmy about books as Father is about postage stamps. My sister Daffy, for instance, can prattle on about flyleaves, colophons, and first editions not only until the cows come home, but until they have put on their nightcaps, gone to bed, switched off the lights, and begun snoring in their cowsheds.

Again using my handkerchief, I lifted the Oliver Inchbald books one at a time from the shelf and turned to the title pages: first editions, every single one of them. No inscriptions.

As I have said, as pristine as if they had just come fresh from the booksellers.

Below the title and the name of the author, each book bore the imprint of its publishers — Lancelot Gath, London — and the address in Bedford Square.

Nothing else: no bookmarks, underlinings, or tipped-in clippings.

Except for one: a rather grubby copy of *Hobbyhorse House,* lacking its dust wrapper, which, unlike its mates, was lying flat across the Bible and Shakespeare.

I opened it. This one, too, was a first edition. The owner's name was printed in crude and spidery block letters of green ink, which had bled horribly into the absorbent paper of the page:

Carla Sherrinford-Cameron.

My heart leaped with joy — and something else.

I *knew* Carla!

What in the name of all that is holy was Carla's copy of *Hobbyhorse House* doing in the bedroom of an elderly wood-carver who lived miles from her home in Hinley?

There was only one way to find out, and that was to question Carla. Even if she didn't have the answer, it would satisfy my need to ask.

Meanwhile, there was the question of Mr. Sambridge. Who had killed him and why?

Time was running out and I needed to get back to Buckshaw. There would be no second chance to view the scene of the crime. This would be my only opportunity, and I meant to make the most of it.

Before continuing with the corpse, I made what I thought was a professional examination of the room: swift, yet rich in detail.

I ran through a mental list even as I was inventing it: nothing overturned, nothing spilled, no dust marks to indicate that some object — a blunt instrument, for instance — had been moved, or taken away from the room. There was, in fact, no dust at all: further indication that Mr. Sambridge was an uncommonly good housekeeper.

Back to my list: nothing on the floor, no fresh scuff marks or abrasions, nothing under the carpet, nothing behind the pictures on the wall (a view of the sands at Margate, labeled as such, and a rather decent watercolor of a wooded glade: one of those works that captures the place so perfectly that you think you've seen it before).

A ewer, a pitcher, a water tumbler, and a toothbrush and tooth powder on a bedside table completed my survey. I had already satisfied myself that Mr. Sambridge still possessed almost all of his own teeth: an event so rare as to be remarkable in its own right, as I knew from my visits to Farringdon Street, with its framed warnings, and alerts inspired by the Blitz:

Gum disease is the silent enemy. It strikes while you're asleep!

Home defense. Lights out on tooth decay!

Avoid the blackout. Brush after every meal!

These placards had taught me that our precious English teeth were in short supply, relatively speaking, and that we ought to guard them like the Crown Jewels.

The cat, still grooming itself on the bed, seemed to sense that I was finished. It jumped down and, with its tail in the air like a flag, stalked to the door to be let out without so much as a glance at the inverted Mr. Sambridge.

I followed it out and shut the bedroom door behind me (handkerchief in hand, of course) making sure that the latch engaged. The thought of a cat being locked in too long with someone in Mr. Sambridge's condition was too much even for someone with *my* strong stomach. There were certain details that even Edgar Allan Poe hadn't dared write about.

Next on the agenda was to notify the police: a matter which required a great deal of thought. I mustn't be rash and yet, at the same time, must not seem ever to be anything less than cooperative. Inspector Hewitt would judge me on my professionalism, and I didn't intend to let him down.

Or myself, for that matter.

Outside, in the slackening rain and accompanied by the cat, I strolled casually over to where Gladys was waiting. There was a cottage directly across the lane from Thornfield Chase, and it was more than likely that whoever lived in it had seen me go into Mr. Sambridge's house. In the villages of England, there's precious little that escapes the neighbor's eye.

As if to illustrate my thoughts, a bit of lace

fluttered at a window.

I had been seen.

Obviously, the cottager didn't know that Mr. Sambridge was dead. If he or she did, he or she should have been out to challenge me, or should, at least, have called the police.

It seemed to me that the best choice was to amble off with a casual air, as if I were just another girl with a bicycle, taking the country air. To reinforce that impression, I wheeled Gladys over for a closer examination of the holly hedge growing by the gate, remembering, as I did so, that the stuff was often planted in such a position to ward off lightning and witchcraft.

Which of the two had Mr. Sambridge feared?

With a quick and obvious glance over my shoulder, to give the impression that I was checking to see if anyone was watching, I snapped off a sprig of holly with a few colorful berries, and, with a spirited toss of my head, poked the holly jauntily — but carefully — into my hair behind the ear.

Flavia Sabina Dolores de Luce.

So I had once identified myself to a nosy librarian.

Although I refrained from kicking up my heels, you could almost hear the castanets.

Job done. The lace curtain settled too casually back into place.

The cat got up from where it had been sitting beside the gatepost and walked towards me, its tail in the air, as if it wanted to tell me something.

"Meow," it said.

"Sorry, kitty," I said. "I can't take you with me. Go catch a mouse. Be a good cat until someone comes for you."

Gladys and I pushed off on the road home. There was still plenty of time to think.

From Pauper's Well, the road down Denham Rise is long, steep, straight, and tempting. With my chin down on the handlebars, I pedaled us up to speed, and then sat back to enjoy the mad downhill rush.

I fancied I was Donald Campbell, that Gladys was his speedboat *Bluebird,* and that we were tearing across Coniston Water at 170 miles an hour. With the world rushing by in a blur, it was easy to see how one could become addicted to racing, and it was only halfway down that a close encounter with a cow made me back off on the old sauce for our final descent into Bishop's Lacey.

By the time I rode into the high street, I had retransformed myself into a slow and precise-pedaling Miss Prim: a shoulders-back, straight-spined model of deportment, all right angles, like a carpenter's square or a middle-aged spinster: a person who couldn't possibly be involved in murder.

Without even thinking about it I found myself pursing my lips into a "prunes and prisms" shape as I gave a crisp nod to Tully Stoker, the landlord of the Thirteen Drakes. Tully was standing on a stool, putty knife in hand, putting the last touches to a new pane of glass in the window of the saloon bar.

Steadying Tully's stool was a thin, slightly frail gentleman I'd not seen before, and I couldn't help wondering what had become of Tully's potboy, Ned Cropper.

Ned was another of Feely's innumerable suitors. Although he was not gifted with many of the so-called social graces, Ned had taught me how to produce a two-fingered whistle that could be heard as far away as Culverhouse Farm.

Had something happened to him in my absence? Had Ned been sacked — or met with some mishap? I surely hoped not. Perhaps he had given up on Feely, married someone else, and emigrated to Australia, say — to take up farming, or perhaps even to open a pub of his own. If he had, Tully's daughter, Mary, would be furious in a heartbroken kind of way. She had adored Ned since they were both of them in nappies.

I made a note to quiz her later.

But for the moment I needed to concentrate on how I was going to report Mr. Sambridge's demise.

I managed to contain my excitement until I reached the vicarage.

"He's dead!" I shouted as I burst through the door, not even bothering to knock. "Mr. Sambridge is dead!"

Cynthia was all wide-eyed as I flew into her arms in the kitchen and buried my face in her shoulder. I resisted the urge to beg her to summon the police. There are times when you have to let nature take its course.

I allowed myself to be made a nice cup of tea, and to refuse — in spite of my secret drooling — a plate of Peek Frean Bourbon biscuits.

"You poor thing!" Cynthia said, and I let her comfort me. She needed it more than I did.

"Was it awful?"

I clamped my teeth down on my lower lip and nodded dolefully.

"I understand," she said. "You don't want to talk about it. I'll ring up Constable

Linnet. He'll know what to do."

He would indeed, I thought. He'd know enough to call in Inspector Hewitt and his men, Detective Sergeants Woolmer and Graves.

I was already feeling a warm glow of anticipation at matching wits with them once again.

"Here, blow —" Cynthia said, producing a handkerchief from thin air, and I blew.

FOUR

"Flavia, Flavia, Flavia," Inspector Hewitt said.

He had sent Graves and Woolmer off to secure Thornfield Chase, but decided to interview me personally before going there himself.

A wise choice, I thought, *and a flattering one.*

In the December rain, the vicarage was especially damp and soggy, with an aura of boiled eggs and old books — a perfect setting for our encounter: dark, brooding, and simply reeking of secrets and tales told in an earlier time.

Cynthia, discreet as always, had taken herself off to the farthest corner of the house, leaving the inspector and me to speak frankly to each other.

"Did you touch anything?"

His first question did not please me.

"Of course not, Inspector. I know better

than that."

"Mmmm," he said, not confirming or denying my words.

Since Cynthia had already explained to him about sending me on her errand, there wasn't much left to talk about except the scene of the crime itself.

"Did you see anyone, going to or returning from Thornfield Chase?"

I told him about the twitching lace curtain. Best to be up front about it, just in case the resident busybody had reported my presence.

"Nobody else?"

He was quizzing me closely, testing my powers of observation.

"No. Nobody, Inspector. Not until I was back in Bishop's Lacey. Mr. Stoker was replacing a windowpane at the Thirteen Drakes."

"Hmmm," he said, rubbing his chin. "Seems odd in this day and age, doesn't it? Cycling all the way to Thornfield Chase and back without spotting or being spotted by a single living soul?"

I could play this game, too.

I shrugged. He could hardly hold me responsible for the geographical distribution of the entire population of Great Britain at one particular hour on one particular rainy day.

"I was merely thinking aloud," he said, but only after an unnerving pause. "How long do you suppose he had been dead?"

"Not long," I said instantly.

"Judging by?"

It was too late. I had already fallen into his trap.

"The slight discoloration of his face. Posterior hypostasis, I believe it's called."

Actually, I knew jolly well what it was called, but I didn't want to damage my chances by being too superior too soon.

"Excellent!" Inspector Hewitt said, and I couldn't help swelling a little. "And the time?"

"The kitchen clock was at 10:03," I told him.

"Thank you, Flavia," he said. "That's extremely helpful. I thought you might have noticed."

Was it getting warm in here, or was it just me? My face was flushing and there was nothing I could do about it.

I faked a cough but it was too late.

"It was because he was hanging upside down," I added, trying to be helpful. "The posterior hypostasis, I mean. It might have been more advanced —"

"Thank you," the inspector said. "But please say no more. I haven't yet visited the scene, and I prefer to form my own first impressions."

I took this to be a lie — or at the very least an outright evasion. A corpse was either upside down or it wasn't. It had nothing to do with who saw it first. But if it *was* a lie, it was one that I appreciated: the kind of lie I might tell — and often have told — myself.

The inspector closed his notebook with an audible *snap!* and got to his feet. He had written down no more than the time of day I had given him.

I must admit that I didn't want him to go. Until that moment I hadn't realized how much I had missed having his undivided attention — having him all to myself — from time to time.

Was it love? I didn't know, but it wasn't pleasant. I'd do anything to keep him with me for even a few moments more.

"How's Mrs. Hewitt? Antigone."

"She's very well, thank you. I shall tell her you were asking."

He turned to go.

"Actually," he said, stopping with his hand on the doorknob, "she wrote you in Canada, but her letter came back stamped 'RTS.'

Return to sender. Address unknown."

I gasped. "That's impossible," I said. "Did she mail it to Miss Bodycote's Female Academy, in Toronto?"

"I believe so," he said. "But that's neither here nor there now, is it? Now that you're here."

I could only nod dumbly.

What cretinous clod would have sent back Antigone's letter? Could other mail have been returned? Could this be why a single letter from Dogger was the only communication I had received from Buckshaw during my entire incarceration in Canada?

My face must have mirrored my thought.

"Oh, well," Inspector Hewitt said. "Welcome home, regardless."

And that, for what it was worth, was the sum total of my encounter with Inspector Hewitt. Although pleasurable, it hardly lived up to my expectations.

In another moment he was gone, and I was on my own again.

As usual.

I shouted up to Cynthia who, judging by her voice, was somewhere in the distant attics.

"Thanks, Cynthia. I'm leaving now."

"I'll be right down," her muffled voice came back.

"Don't bother," I called. "I have to get to the hospital."

And before she could say another word I was out the door, had seized Gladys's handlebars, and was pedaling homewards.

Even as I turned in at the Mulford Gates and rode along the avenue of bare chestnut trees, Buckshaw seemed strangely quiet — as if it had been abandoned.

Although it was not the busiest place in Bishop's Lacey, there was often someone coming or going, whether it be Mrs. Mullet or the postman, a delivery van or the occasional taxi.

Now it stood strangely bare and silent. No taxi was parked on the gravel sweep, as it ought to have been if we were going to Hinley and the hospital.

I parked Gladys and opened the front door.

Silence. I cocked my head and made use of my near-supernaturally acute hearing — a sometimes troublesome trait I had inherited from my late mother, Harriet.

Not a sound. The house was perfectly quiet.

I walked — tiptoed, actually — to the center of the foyer and listened again.

"AGGHH — ahh — AGGHH — ahh —

AGGHH — ahh — AGGHH!"

The bloodcurdling two-toned yodel seemed to be coming from all directions.

Something heavy struck me between the shoulders, and down I went, tumbling ace over teakettle, onto the floor in a heap.

"Caught you!" Undine shrieked. "I'm Tarzan of the Apes and you're a marauding warthog."

Winded, I rolled over and lay on my back, staring up dazedly at a long, heavy rope, which was now swinging lazily to and fro in the foyer. It seemed to be attached high above, to one of the upper staircases.

"What are you doing?" I demanded furiously. "I might have been badly injured. You might have broken my spine. What are you doing rigging up a rope in the house? I'm going to tell on you."

This was rather a weak threat, and I think Undine sensed it. With Father in hospital, there was really no one in authority to report her *to*.

"To Dogger," I added.

"Ha!" she said. "Dogger already knows. He helped me rig up the rope."

I reeled back as if slapped in the face.

Dogger? Rigging a rope for Undine to play her childish games?

My mind refused to process the thought.

It was as useless as if some comic farmer had tried to get a tractor started by stuffing hay into the petrol tank.

"I don't believe you," I said.

"It's true, Miss Flavia," Dogger said quietly. He had suddenly appeared behind me in the way he sometimes does.

"Miss Undine was very much missing her homeland and her mother. I thought that if we could re-create something of the former, if not the —"

"Thank you, Dogger," I interrupted. "I understand."

Even though I did not. There were probably good enough reasons for his betrayal, but I was not yet ready to be pacified.

Undine's mother, the late Lena — of the Cornwall de Luces — had brought her to Buckshaw from Singapore before coming to a grisly end here in the parish church.

What a vine-swinging ape-man could possibly have in common with Singapore was beyond me; perhaps the recently rigged rope served only to remind the child of Johnny Weismuller films she had attended with her mother in happier days.

Meanwhile, the rope swung slowly and accusingly back and forth between us, like an awkward stage prop in one of those tiresome mystery plays in London's West End.

For just an instant it reminded me of another rope: the one — or ones — by which the late Mr. Sambridge was suspended in his bedroom at Thornfield Chase, but before I could focus upon it more sharply, the thought was gone.

"Miss Undine has been looking forward for quite some time to surprising you," Dogger said.

"And I *did*, didn't I?" Undine crowed. "Come on, Flavia, admit it. I scared the stuffing out of you, didn't I?"

"Yes," I admitted. "You certainly did."

I was seized by the sudden and inexplicable urge to sweep this lonely little girl up into my arms and hug her until the jelly came out, but luckily, I was able to suppress it. The de Luce blood is stronger, after all, than sentiment.

What was coming over me? I wondered. Was my brain going soft?

Would I soon be reduced to one of those gibbering idiots said to be locked away in a walled-up tower room by so many of our titled English families?

Although homesickness can take many forms, one's eventual homecoming can be even more terrifying than being away. Could it be one of those illnesses Dogger had once told me about, in which the cure is far worse than the disease?

I was thinking not so much of Undine as myself.

"I suppose I'd better go powder my nose and get ready for the hospital," I said, trying desperately to make light of an otherwise awkward situation.

"I'm afraid we'll not be going today," Dogger said quietly. "Matron feels that Colonel de Luce needs his rest, and Dr. Darby agrees."

The taste of disappointment in the mouth is more bitter than gall: more bitter even than brucine or strychnine, which are two of the most sour substances known to humankind.

My fury was incandescent. I felt as if I were going to burst into flames: as if I were about to spontaneously combust. I hardly dared draw another breath for fear of fanning the fire.

Where, then, did the power come from — the power that made me nod wisely as if I were in full agreement? The power that made me float as gracefully up the staircase as if I were Vivien Leigh in powdered wig and silk brocade?

Don't tell me there are no such things as miracles.

I know better.

■ ■ ■ ■

I was lying on my bed with my hands clasped behind my head. As sometimes happens when you're frustrated, snippets of verse kept popping, one after another, into my head:

O Timballoo! How happy we are
When we live in a sieve and a crockery-jar!

Edward Lear had written that, and Mr. Lear was a very wise man. Living in a sieve and a crockery jar was a near-perfect description of my present situation. Shakespeare himself couldn't have phrased it better.

When I was down beside the sea
A wooden spade they gave to me
To dig the sandy shore.

This one was Robert Louis Stevenson.

As a child, I had thought it was a nursery rhyme about burying someone on the beach, but was disappointed to be told that it was merely about puttering in the stupid sand.

Crispian Crumpet had built sand castles, too, hadn't he, in those books by Oliver Inchbald? Like a grave digger, Crispian was always doing something with shovels.

For instance:

Crispian Crumpet is digging a hole
Down by the garden wall.
"Where will it take you?" I ask him politely.
"To China," he says, "Or Bengal."

"What will you do when you get there?" I
   ask him
Down by the garden wall.
"I shall buy tigers or tea," he says brightly
"Or a red rubber rug for the hall."

Why had Mr. Sambridge kept immaculate first editions of this nauseous drivel on his bedside table? And why was Carla Sherrinford-Cameron's name inked into one of them?

Had Carla killed the old wood-carver? It seemed unlikely, but stranger things had happened, as I knew all too well, not only from listening to the detective adventures of Philip Odell on the wireless, but also from my own life.

Was there some hidden link between the girl and the owner of Thornfield Chase? Could he possibly be her grandfather?

My thoughts were interrupted by the sound of the doorknob being rattled. Since

Dogger didn't rattle doorknobs, I had already worked out who it was most likely to be.

"Go away!" I said.

"Open the door," came Undine's voice.

I just knew it!

"Go away. I'm sleeping."

"Let me in, Flavia. It's vitally urgent."

I couldn't help smiling.

"Just a minute," I said. I took my time about letting her in.

"I'm sorry if I discommoded you," she said. "Abu used to say that 'discommoded' was when you shoved someone off the loo. She was being facetious, of course."

"Abu" was the name she had called her mother back home in Singapore. "Possibly," I said. "What do you want?"

"Feely promised to take me to the Advent concert at St. Tancred's, but now she's begged off with a headache. She ought to marry Dieter and sort it out for once and for all."

"Hmmm," I said. I didn't want to become involved in Feely's love strategy — not, at least, through Undine.

"The concert begins at half two," Undine said. "They're having gingerbread for the children and oolong tea for the grown-ups.

I adore oolong tea. You can pilfer some for me."

Although I was flattered to be classed as a grown-up, I was not all that fond of oolong tea, which I found to leave a fishy taste in your mouth and a faint craving for rice.

"No, thanks," I said. "I've got better things to do."

"Such as . . . ?"

"Don't be a pest. Go swing on your rope and eat a banana. Oh, and by the way, give my regards to Jane."

Undine regarded me with sad eyes. "You don't love me, do you?"

"Of course I love you! I could simply smother you with HP Sauce and eat you up. Gobble! Gobble! Gobble!"

Talking to Undine brought out a part of me that I didn't particularly like, but giving in to it was easier than trying to reason with her.

"Ugh!" Undine said. "You're repulsive. Come on, Flavia. Carla Sherrinford-Cameron is singing, and you wouldn't want to miss *that*, would you?"

She opened her mouth wide and jabbed her forefinger rapidly in and out, as if inducing a vomit.

Ten minutes later, under a leaden sky, we

were galloping across the rain-soaked fields towards the village.

FIVE

Carla Sherrinford-Cameron, her hands clasped together at her waist like lobster's claws, was singing "The Lass with the Delicate Air," and I found myself wishing I had thought to bring a firearm with me — although whether to put Carla out of her misery or to do away with myself, I had not quite yet decided.

With her huge eyes, lank red hair, and pale buttermilk skin, she looked like a sea creature by Botticelli: a googly-eyed mermaid dredged up in a fisherman's net, caught between two worlds with nowhere to hide.

It could only have been Fate, operating flat out and in top gear, that had plunked Carla almost literally on my doorstep at the very instant she was required. It saved me a most tiresome trip to Hinley and although I could easily have looked up her address in the telephone directory, the fact that a fond Fate had snatched Carla up by the scruff of the neck and dumped her at my feet as a dog brings a bone was oddly satisfying.

Carla was a student of the Misses Lavinia and Aurelia Puddock, those musical spinster sisters whose musty talents made a misery of every public event in Bishop's Lacey.

Although she lived in Hinley, several miles away, Carla came by bus to sing in our village at frequent intervals, on the principle that it was better to be a big frog in a small pond than a tadpole in a large one.

"With the deh-heh-heh-heh-heh-heh,
heh-heh-heh-heh-ell-hick-cut air
Men call her the lass with the del-hick-cut air."

Her voice hung shrill in the air like a shot partridge.

I have nothing against singing provided it's done properly — I do it myself occasionally — but there are times when enough is too much, and this was one of them.

Perhaps in unconscious imitation of Carla's pose, I wrung my hands.

"Men call her the lass with the-uh . . ."

In the brief and dramatic silence that followed her hovering high E — which is called

100

a fermata, my sister Feely had told me, and can be held for as long as the performer wishes — my knuckles gave off a sickening *crunch!* All ten of them.

Simultaneously.

All of us in the parish hall, including Carla and me, whipped our necks round to locate the source of the ghastly disturbance.

Undine gave out a horrible, wet snicker, followed by a thumbs-up, and a grin of outright admiration.

To give her credit, Carla was game. She went on to the end:

"del . . . lick . . . hut air."

And then she fled.

I found her sobbing in the churchyard.

I remembered that the poet Walter de la Mare had once written:

It's a very odd thing —
As odd can be —
That whatever Miss T eats
Turns into Miss T.

If Mr. de la Mare was correct, Carla must be in the habit of feasting on fireflies. Her red face fairly glowed with the heat of her body, and her forehead was glossy with a greasy dampness.

"I *hate* you, Flavia de Luce!" she spat. "You've ruined everything. I hate you! I loathe you! I despise you!"

"I'm sorry," I said. "It was involuntary."

Involuntary was perhaps too grand a word — too pretentious for the occasion — but it slipped out of me before I could stop my mouth.

It launched Carla into a cold, full-fledged fury.

"You de Luces are so . . . so . . . blooming *superior,*" she said, her voice dripping with the venom of a sack of vipers.

"Look, Carla," I said, trying to calm her, "it's a question of mechanics, not malice. When you put pressure on your metatarsals —"

"Oh, *bugger* your metatarsals!" Carla snarled, and I sucked in my breath noisily and widened my eyes, as if I were scandalized.

"Carla!"

The first step in gaining the upper hand is always to seize the moral high ground, and to be able to do this with no more than a single word is nothing short of genius.

I also let my jaw fall open in astonishment — which was gilding the lily, perhaps, but if a dab of gold paint here and there — as in the Sistine Chapel, for instance — hadn't ruined Michelangelo's reputation, why should it ruin mine?

The thought of gilding reminded me: Here was a golden opportunity.

"I know how you feel, though," I said, putting a hand on her shoulder. "We're two of a kind, you and I."

We were no such thing, but the second step was: Create a kinship with your subject.

Carla looked up at me with something approaching hope. I came close to feeling sorry for her.

"We are?" she asked, and I knew she was mine.

"Of course we are!" I said with a laugh. "Everyone knows how dreadfully your family treats you."

It was a shot in the dark, but I knew at once that it had struck blood, bone, and gristle.

"They do?" she said, something dawning on her face.

According to my sister Daffy, Tolstoy had written something about happy families being all alike and unhappy ones each unhappy in its own way. "Like us," she had added with a horrible grimace. Well, Tolstoy was wrong. It's the other way round — at least in my limited experience.

I knew nothing whatsoever about Carla, but it seemed a safe enough bet that she must have a family.

"You're quite right," she said suddenly. "They *do* treat me dreadfully. They think I'm going to be a failure."

"Whatever makes them think such a thing?" I asked.

"Because they're such failures themselves. Mother is a failed sculptor and Father a failed advertising man. I wonder what I shall fail at when I'm old enough?"

"How old are you? Right now, I mean. Today."

"Sixteen," she mumbled, casting her eyes down as if being sixteen were an indictable criminal offense.

"But let's talk about happier things," I said, putting the other hand on her other shoulder.

She looked up at me doubtfully.

" 'The Lass with the Delicate Air,' " I said. "You were actually singing about yourself, weren't you?"

I paused to let the oblique compliment sink in. Carla was not the brightest star in the firmament.

"And you sing it so beautifully," I said, shoring up the dam, just in case.

"Do you really, really think so?" Her great wet eyes swam up towards me.

It says somewhere — in the Book of Proverbs, I think — that lying lips are abomination to the Lord, but they that deal truly are his delight.

I considered my words carefully before I spoke them. "I don't just *think* so — I *know* so," I told her, giving her shoulder a tender squeeze.

I would probably burn in the fires of Hell for an eternity of eternities for such a flaming fib, but I didn't care. Paradise would just have to get along without me.

"It always reminds me of that other wonderful song, 'Who Knoweth Where Fate Will Fetch Her' — based on the poem by Shelley. I'm sure you know the one."

I was equally sure she didn't, since I had invented it on the spot.

Carla nodded knowingly.

I had her! A counter-fib cancels out any number of prior fibs by the party of the first part. Somewhere up above, Saint Peter would be blotting his big book and cussing at the two of us like billy-ho!

". . . or," I went on blithely, " 'King of the Sands.' "

I proceeded to quote:

"I shall make you a house of mud
With a one and a two and a three-a-ringo,
With mud-made walls and a mud-made
    floor
Just for you and me, by jingo!

"Oliver Inchbald," I said. "Everybody knows that one. It's from *Hobbyhorse House*. I've always thought that the poem is about loneliness, actually. The speaker is expressing the wish to return to the mother's womb: to build a sanctuary and share it with a friend. Don't you agree?"

The concept of returning to the mother's womb had been explained to me at great length and in great detail by one of the more advanced girls at Miss Bodycote's Female Academy, but I still wasn't sure if she had been pulling my leg.

Carla nodded weakly. This was not going to be as easy as I thought.

"Perhaps you could set it to music," I said. "With your great gift, you ought to —"

But before I could say another word, Carla's voice, quavering at first, began to rise up in song. Even though she was inventing the eerily thrilling melody on the spot, the hair on the back of my neck began to arise like a snake charmer's cobra.

"I shall make you a house of mud
With a one and a two and a
   three-a-ringo . . ."

And so forth.

At the words "Just for you and me," Carla scrambled to her feet, flung her arms around me and gave me a bone-breaking hug.

I had overplayed my hand.

"You poor kid," I said, and I almost meant it.

"Everyone has read *Hobbyhorse House,*" I added, waiting for her snuffles to subside. "Or had it read *to* them, at least. I expect you did, too."

This seemed to brighten her a bit. She wiped her eyes on her ruffled sleeves.

"My auntie Louisa actually *knew* Oliver Inchbald. Can you believe it? He had a mad purple pash for her — or so she said."

"Oliver Inchbald? They must have been very young."

Inchbald, I recalled from the dusty back issues of *The Bookman* and *The Illustrated London News* that formed a rising tide in all the cupboards and crannies of Buckshaw, had been happily married for donkey's years to a honey-haired dough lady who spent her days knitting ditty bags for sailors and mittens for the homeless poor.

"It wasn't all that long ago," Carla said. "Not long before he died. Auntie Louisa worked for his publishers, and —"

"Lancelot Gath, Bedford Square, London!" I blurted out.

"That's right," Carla said. "How ever did you know that?"

I tapped my temple knowingly with my forefinger. "I keep my eyes open," I said. Even though it didn't quite make sense, I could see that she was impressed.

Already a plan was beginning to take shape in my mind. It would be risky, but that's what life's about, after all, isn't it?

"Tell me about your auntie Louisa. She must have been awfully bright, to work for a publisher, and all that."

"She was. She died a couple of years ago in an Aqua-Lung accident in the Mediterranean."

"A *what*?"

"An Aqua-Lung. It's a kind of underwater breathing apparatus. She was diving on a Roman shipwreck with Jacques Cousteau."

"Holy cow!" I said, and I meant it. "I'm sorry to hear that."

"It's all right," Carla said. "She always said she'd prefer to die on her way to the moon than under a runaway bus. And I suppose in a way, she did. Auntie Louisa was always something of an adventurer — or *adventuress,* as Mama always says."

I knew from Daffy's small talk that the word could be taken in more ways than one.

"I'll show you a photograph of her some time, if you like. She's smoking Albert Einstein's pipe, and he's wearing her slippers."

"Sassafras!" I said.

"She was like that, you know. Madcap, Mama always says. She taught Winston Churchill to rhumba and beat the author of Jeeves at croquet."

"P. G. Wodehouse," I said. Daffy was always going on about the man and cackling to herself in the middle of the night when she ought to be sleeping.

"Yes, that's it. Auntie Loo — everyone called her Loo, even her own mother — knew everyone who was anyone. She was unbelievably popular in certain circles."

"I see," I said. I would need to consult with Daffy, who had the uncanny, almost supernatural ability to read between the lines. Even though it would mean negotiating a truce with my sister, it would likely be well worth my while.

"Do you know what I envy about you?" I asked.

This is one of those trick questions to which no one on earth has ever answered

"Yes." If you need a "No" to keep things going — to keep the barn door open — this is the way to get one.

"No," Carla said. "Tell me."

"I'll bet she used to read aloud to you, your auntie Loo. Oliver Inchbald, and so forth. Isn't it wonderful to think that her ears heard him reading from his own works, and your ears heard her. What a treat for you that must have been, getting it second-hand, almost straight from the horse's mouth, so to speak."

This was stretching things a bit, but it seemed to prime Carla's pump.

"Oh, yes," she gushed. "I begged her to tell me again and again about the punting and tea cakes in the Backs at Cambridge, and the Dixieland Jazz Band at the Hippodrome — and again, after hours at the Kublai Khan Club in Soho."

"And Crispian Crumpet?" I suggested.

Carla closed her eyes, threw her head back, and chanted:

"Crispian Crumpet is christening his tricycle.
'I name thee Icicle,' says he . . .
'Icicle, nicycle, pearl-without-price-icle
Icicle Thricicle, thou shalt be!'

"Silly, isn't it?" Carla said, interrupting herself.

I didn't say so, but it wasn't silly in the least. In fact it was, in my opinion, probably the best poem Oliver Inchbald had ever written. As someone who had herself administered the rite of Holy Baptism to a bicycle, it touched a very deep chord.

"Some people have little need for human companionship," I said, as if to no one, and Carla squeezed my hand. "Obviously, your auntie Loo was not one of them."

"No," Carla said. "Everyone adored her. They were always comparing her to a warm summer's breeze. When she died, the postman had to bring the mail in a sack. It was very tragic."

"But Oliver Inchbald was already dead by then?" I asked.

"Oh, yes. For some years. As a matter of fact, it was Auntie Loo who was called upon to identify his body."

"Really?" I couldn't hide my interest. "How do you know that?"

"Because she told me so. *It was I who was called upon to identify the body.'* Those were her very words. I remember them quite distinctly."

My mind was running away with itself.

"Why would she be called upon to identify

his body? Why not his family?"

"Well, Auntie Loo said it was because his wife had become deranged, and his son point-blank refused."

"Good lord," I said. "I wonder why? Was there something unusual about the way he died?"

"I suppose you could say so. He was pecked to death by seagulls while he was bird-nesting. On the island of Steep Holm. It's in the Bristol Channel."

"Nesting season?" I asked.

You didn't need to be a radio panelist on *Puzzle Corner* or *What Do You Know?* to deduce that fascinating fact.

"I think so," Carla said. "Auntie Loo said there wasn't much left of him but a few ribbons, his wallet, and his pipe."

"Crispian Crumpet — Crispian Inchbald, I mean — must have been devastated. What a way to lose your father!"

"I suppose," Carla said. "Although by then he was no longer a boy. He was at Oxford, I think, and was already doing something in cinema films, lighting or sound or something. I don't remember. He was very artistic — like his father."

"Was?" I asked. "Isn't he still alive? Crispian, I mean?"

"As far as I know. Auntie Loo used to

send him a Christmas card every year, but he never wrote her back. *'He's a bit of a rum 'un,'* she used to say."

Crispian Crumpet? A rum 'un? I could hardly believe it. Whatever could have become of the famous little boy who baptized his bicycle — the little boy who was digging a hole to China (or Bengal) — the dear little boy who wanted to build his father a house of mud, for just the two of them?

I realized with a pang that I had often wished to do just that myself.

I had a brief vision of kidnapping Father from the hospital in Hinley and whisking him off to some distant island in the tropics — just the two of us — where I would build him a hut of mud and grass: a new Buckshaw, free of all the cares and worries that had brought him so low. There would be an annex, of course, for his stamp collection, and another for my chemistry lab.

And there we would live upon turtle's eggs and coconut milk, tuning in on a short-wave wireless set to the BBC whenever we felt like a bit of Bach or Philip Odell.

It would be heaven on earth, and we would hang in our hammocks, Father and I, as we talked quietly to each other and watched the setting sun.

113

"He got himself into some kind of trouble with the law," Carla said. "Auntie Loo wasn't sure what it was, but it had something to do with the racetrack."

"A betting man, was he?" I asked.

Carla shrugged.

Undine chose that very moment to interrupt. She came charging out of the parish hall like a deranged bowling ball, arms flailing and veering alarmingly from side to side.

"Flavia! Gravia! Quavia, Slavia!" she shouted at the top of her lungs, as if the whole world had just gone deaf. She climbed up onto a teetering tombstone, where she stood wigwagging her arms for balance. "I'm the king of the castle, and you're the dirty rascal!" she bellowed.

"Pipe down!" I said. "There's a concert going on inside."

"It's finished," Undine said. "The gingerbread was better than the music. I'm already hungry again. Let's go home."

"I must apologize for my cousin, Undine," I said. "She can be quite uncouth."

"Not at all," Carla said. "I admire her frankness."

"See?" Undine crossed her eyes and stuck out her tongue.

"I've enjoyed our little talk," Carla said. "Perhaps we can continue it another time."

"I'd like that," I told her. "Oh, by the way: I couldn't help wondering if you still have all your Oliver Inchbald books? I'd like to borrow them one of these days," I added, ". . . just for old times' sake, and because of their association with the author. I promise I'd look after them."

"Of course I have," Carla replied, with just a trace of a glare. "I wouldn't part with them for all the tea in China."

"Oolong!" Undine shouted. As I seized her by the arm and dragged her away, she made a remarkably coarse sound with her mouth.

Outside, the temperature had plummeted and, as we made our way across the hardening fields in the growing darkness, a light snow began to fall. Here and there, distant electric lights came on in other people's homes, mere pinpricks in the gloom. *Mirages of happiness,* I thought. *If you walk towards them, they will never grow any closer. Eventually they will vanish into thin air, like the Lady of the Lake.*

"What are you thinking about?" Undine demanded. "You make me nervous when you don't say anything."

"Grub," I said. "I was thinking about grub."

"Ha!" she shouted. "Sausages with jam! Pickled shortbread! Cold candied tongue with snail sauce!"

And so on, until we reached Buckshaw at teatime and in darkness.

Having handed Undine over to Mrs. Mullet, and begging a fierce headache ("You poor dear. You'd best go up for a nap. Bundle up warm, mind."), I made my way up the shadowed staircase, which seemed longer and steeper than usual.

Six

Alone at last in my chemical laboratory, I put my back against the door and pushed, as if hordes of barbarians with battle-axes were battering at the other side.

There had been so little time to think. I mean to *really* think.

I needed to settle my mind: to restore it to some kind of normality.

Everything was out of kilter, and it wasn't just me.

The prospect of a missed Christmas hung like a pall over Buckshaw. Memories of Christmases past danced just beyond the fringes of consciousness, taunting me with half-remembered sounds and smells: of carols, cranberries, and Christmas crackers; the fresh rustle of wrapping paper and the feel of fat, fresh snowflakes tickling our faces as we trudged through the drifts to church on Christmas Eve.

I took down a glass bell jar from a shelf

and placed it on a bench.

In spite of the imagined barbarians at the barricaded door, I unlocked it, opened it, and made my way down the stairs for a raid upon the kitchen.

One of the joys of an old house, such as Buckshaw, is its constancy. The squeaking stairs have squeaked for centuries, and the quiet ones have remained silent. Particular treads that gave out a groan under my feet had similarly misbehaved under the boots, shoes, and slippers of my ancestors. There were no surprises. We de Luces had known since time immemorial how to raid a kitchen in silence. We could do it in our sleep.

I waited until Mrs. Mullet was busy with the cooker, then slipped in and did what I had to do.

Within two minutes I was back in my laboratory, and the pantry was missing three stems of rosemary. I couldn't resist holding them to my nose and inhaling their intoxicating scent.

I tied the sprigs together with a bit of thread and set them aside.

Now, from a bottom cupboard, I brought out a round iron plate which had once been the base of a flask stand. I lit a Bunsen burner and held the heavy disk to the flame — using oven mitts, of course. Mrs. Mullet wouldn't miss them.

Within a minute or so, the room was filled with the smell of hot iron: a sharp, acrid aroma, which is what I always imagine railway tracks must smell like in the extremes of an Australian summer.

As a precaution, I opened a window sash. It wouldn't do to have someone think the house was on fire.

When the disc was nearly red-hot, I placed it on a sheet of Pyrex, sprinkled on it a layer of powdered gum bezoin, placed my bundled sprigs of rosemary on the metal, covered them with the bell jar, and sat down to watch.

The gum bezoin melted at once, causing the little world inside the glass to fill with a dense fog. As the fumes arose, the bundle of herbs took on a coat of silky white crystals: benzoic acid.

The branches of rosemary were now completely covered with artificial hoarfrost: my own private Christmas tree growing somewhere in a secret, snowy wood.

Lacking gifts and decorations, it was not, of course, as comforting as the real thing, but it would have to do.

I put my head down on my arms and fell asleep at the workbench.

■ ■ ■ ■

Hours later — I don't know the time — I was awakened by a loud clatter. My first thought, of course, was that it was Father Christmas who, in that famous American poem, makes just such a sound on the lawn.

Without even thinking — and only half awake — I dashed to the window. The snow had continued to fall, and the Visto outside was now covered with a flawless white blanket.

As I stood blinking, something hard struck the glass directly in front of my face: the same sound as before.

I opened the window and peered down into the white darkness.

"Who is it?" I called in a hoarse whisper.

"It's Carl, Flavia. Carl Pendracka. Remember me?"

Of course I remembered him!

Even though, in the long run, he was not likely to become my brother-in-law, I've always had a soft spot for Carl Pendracka, another of my sister Feely's former suitors. Carl was, after all, the one who had described to me how while swimming in St. Louis, Missouri, he had dived under an abandoned pier and found himself floating face-to-face with a bloated corpse. How could I forget him?

"Funny thing was, I *knew* the son of a gun," Carl had told me. "His name was Bobby Ryback, and we had gone to the same school. He was a year ahead of me, in the eighth grade. I knew it was him because, in spite of being blue and swollen, he still looked a lot like Bobby Ryback."

It's in the sharing of such fascinating tidbits of information that real friendships are formed.

Meanwhile, Carl must have grown tired of waiting for a response. A moment later, he came swarming hand over hand up the dead vines on the side of the house.

"Nya, what's up, Doc?" he said, wrinkling his nose and making carrot-chewing noises as he swung his legs over the sill and into the room.

Carl was an American, and he actually talked like that. I answered with the expected grin.

His wet army greatcoat and oversized boots gave him the look of a woolly cartoon caterpillar.

"How's that sister of yours . . . whatsername?"

"Ophelia," I said. "Feely. As you know perfectly well. She's engaged, thank you —

as you also know perfectly well."

"So I heard," Carl said. "I also heard she and her German pilot have gone *kaput.*"

Combined with the village gossip mill of Bishop's Lacey, the jungle telegraph of the air base at Leathcote was faster and much more accurate than even the most high-grade military intelligence — at least, according to Mrs. Mullet's husband, Alf.

"I wouldn't know," I said. "I've been away."

"Roger, wilco," Carl said. "Over and out. Canada. Land of the loon and the knotty pine."

For a supposed descendant of King Arthur, Carl could be remarkably dopey.

"What are you doing hanging round at this unholy hour? I might have called the police."

"Hoping to catch a glimpse of the dearly beloved," Carl said, and my heart almost broke for his honesty. "I saw your light — knew you were home — knew you'd let me in. Do you think she'd see me?"

"It's the middle of the night, Carl," I said. "You can't stay here. Besides, the dearly beloved is in her bed snoring away like twenty hogs. Her face is slathered with Turtle Oil, her lips are coated with Eau de Suez Vaccine Cream, and her hair is in a bag. She's hardly the Chelsea Flower Show."

"I don't care," Carl said. "If there's half a chance, it's now, while she and Hans —"

"Dieter," I interrupted. "Dieter Schrantz. He's almost criminally handsome, you know." I couldn't resist twitting him.

"I know." Carl sighed. "A Norse god."

"Tell you what," I said. "I'll make you a deal. You find out everything you can about a man called Sambridge and I'll arrange a tryst."

"A what?"

"A tryst. You know, like the ones in Georgette Heyer. A secret meeting of lovers."

I knew at once I'd chosen the right words.

A sudden fire came into Carl's eyes. He seized my right hand and gave it a couple of powerful pumps.

"Done!" he said. "And done again! Now who's this Stanfield you need to know about?"

"Sambridge," I corrected him. "He lives at Thornfield Chase, near East Finching. He's a wood-carver."

"Don't need to know that," Carl said. "I'll ask my friend Mordecai. Mordecai's in Intelligence. Say you want to find out what the King had for breakfast this morning? Ask Mordecai. Want to know how much the chancellor of the exchequer owes his banker? Ask Mordecai. Who's the smart money on for the Derby or the Grand National?"

"Ask Mordecai." I grinned. "And while you're at it, you can also ask him who won the Irish Hospitals' Sweepstake last summer."

"The horse or the lucky ticket holders?"

"Both," I told him. "If you think he can."

Carl made a rude raspberry noise with his mouth. "Leave it with me," he said. "I'll see what I can do."

He put a forefinger to his lips in a sign of secrecy, then, adjusting an imaginary gun belt on his hips, he drawled, "Well, I reckon I'll climb on my old cayuse and mosey off into the whatchamacallit."

A moment later, the dead vines outside the window were creaking with his departure.

When I was sure that Carl was gone, I lowered and locked the sash. Taking up a pencil and a scrap of paper, I scribbled a note:

Dear Dogger,
Gone up to London to see a friend.
Don't worry.

And I signed it:
        Yours faithfully, Flavia S. de Luce.

I crept through the silent house and pinned the note to the outside of Dogger's bedroom door.

He wouldn't read it, of course, until I was gone, by which time it would be too late to stop me.

Downstairs, in the library, I consulted the *ABC Railway Guide.* The first train of the day was scheduled to leave Doddingsley at 7:03. If I broke all speed records, I could just make it, and be back in time for an evening visit to the hospital.

I hadn't, of course, counted upon the snow. Fortunately, it was dry, fluffy stuff, which Gladys's front wheel cut, for the first few miles, like a saber through soft butter. The advantage of traveling so early in the day was that I had the roads to myself.

I inhaled the cold air in great gulps, willing the miles to pass, praying that we would not come to grief in a clatter of metal and ice at the end of some long incline.

Although sunrise would not be for another hour, I couldn't help wondering what I would look like to some hypothetical observer. Hypothetical farmers and their hypothetical wives were notoriously early risers, and I pictured them glancing out their hypothetical kitchen windows at the silhouette of a phantom girl in a black winter coat on a black bicycle moving steadily across a white winter landscape. An oil painting by somebody dark, like Whistler.

Flavia Cycling, it could be called — or *The Ride of the Snow Queen.*

Would they wonder who I was and where I was going? Would they care?

Halfway to Doddingsley, we came abruptly upon the tire tracks of an early morning farm tractor, and settled into them. Riding its ribbed footprints, we juddered and bumped our way towards the railway station.

From the top of the last hill, I could see the engine standing panting in the station, clouds of steam obscuring the forward carriages. The stationmaster was already making his way towards the closed crossing gates.

The engine gave out a sharp whistle. It was leaving!

Even as I watched in horror the train began to move.

"No! Wait! Stop!" I shouted, but it was too late for words.

I jerked Gladys's handlebars sharply to one side and steered her into a steep, narrow gully that ran at a right angle down to the tracks.

With a bang and a series of stomach-churning slithers, we tobogganed in a shower of snow and slush, slipping and sliding, veering from side to side, down the cutting, across the ditch at the bottom, and directly onto the tracks, where we came to an abrupt halt at the end of the platform. The train, like a panting dragon, was picking up speed. It was coming directly at us.

I couldn't help closing my eyes and waiting for the End.

It's remarkable how time slows when you're about to die, and even more remarkable the things that come to mind at such moments of peril.

It was only last summer, here at Doddingsley station, that I had witnessed the death of a stranger beneath the wheels of a train. And it was here, too, although years ago, that the Richardsons' young daughter had met her tragic end. And now, it seemed, so would I. Cynthia would soon have another death to mourn.

There came a cold, shrill sound of steel against steel and a deafening hiss of steam. My face was suddenly hot and wet.

I dared not move a muscle.

And then the sound of voices: human

voices raised in what sounded like anger. A couple of naughty words found their way into my innocent ears.

I was still alive!

I opened my eyes.

I was standing in a cloud of swirling steam, so close to the front of the locomotive that I could have reached out and touched it. But I did not.

Instinct seized me.

I picked up Gladys and marched past the driver and the fireman, both of whom had climbed down from their cab and were kicking up snow as they marched towards me with clenched fists and red, furious faces.

I dragged Gladys onto the platform, leaned her against the brick wall of the station, gave her a reassuring pat on the seat and strolled — looking straight ahead — across to the train. The guard and the stationmaster stood speechless, shoulder to shoulder, mouths open as I sailed past them in the stately way I imagined Aunt Millicent might have done.

"Carry on," I said, as I stepped into the closest carriage and took a seat.

SEVEN

A gray, grubby dawn was breaking as we arrived in London. The platform was in even more than its usual hubbub. I edged my way slowly — so as not to attract attention — into the center of a jostling mass of schoolboys. Ughhh! Somebody's sister, I would pretend to be: welcoming a grubby, jammy brother home for the holidays.

We seethed, like a mass of jellyfish, towards the station's exit.

On the street, a black cab edged forward from the rank.

"Where to?" the driver asked, squinting horribly behind his cigarette. "Buck'num Palace?"

He wheezed like a tin whistle, as if he had made a capital joke.

I climbed into the backseat in a businesslike manner. "Bedford Square," I told him.

"Any partic'lar address?"

"Number seven," I said, partly because it

was the first number that came to mind, and partly because I guessed that any square, anywhere in London, must have a number seven. A much higher number might have betrayed my relative ignorance of the city's geography.

"Right-o," he said as we jerked into motion.

I do not encourage early morning chirpiness, even in those whom I know and love. It is generally a sign of a sloppy mind, and is not to be encouraged.

Before I knew it, we had reached our destination. I paid the driver, turned away, and walked briskly to the door of number seven, where I pretended to rummage in my pocket for my keys. Judging by the nameplates at the door, the building was a nest of architects.

I waited until the taxi had driven off, then set out in search of the address I was looking for. The numbers began on the east side of the square and proceeded north, then west.

Then suddenly — unexpectedly — among the Georgian doors of solicitors, surveyors, and assorted societies, there it was: LANCE-LOT GATH, PUBLISHERS.

I tried the cold brass knob, but the door was locked. I rattled it a bit, but it was no use. There were no lights visible in the windows.

I looked up and down the square. Besides my own, there were few footprints in the fresh, unshoveled snow. The business day had not yet begun. I would simply have to wait.

I blew into my cupped hands, producing a kind of hollow owl call. I had left home without gloves or mittens, and I was beginning to regret my haste.

The temperature seemed to be dropping alarmingly. Surely it was colder now than it had been at the station.

I was weighing my options when a man in a caped overcoat turned the corner and approached along the street. In spite of the snow, he was carrying a furled umbrella and a rolled-up newspaper.

He nodded genially as he fished for his keys.

"Mr. Gath?" I guessed.

The man seemed startled at first, and then a slow smile spread across his face.

"Good lord, no. Mr. Gath, like Jacob Marley, has been dead these seven years — well, six, actually, but seven is so much more metrically pleasing, don't you think?"

I must have looked crestfallen.

"Never mind," he said. "In spite of Mr.

Gath's precipitous departure, his inconsolable successors continue to crank the sausage machine at the same old stand. Now then, what can I do for you?

"But wait — come in, come in. No point freezing ourselves to death out here on the doorstep when we could just as well be chugalugging tea in a warm study. Are you familiar with the word *chugalug*? It's an Americanism. We had it last year in a book about fly-fishing in Colorado. Far too good not to crib, don't you think?"

"Yes," I managed.

"Come in, come in," he said, putting his shoulder to the swollen door.

Inside, we stamped the snow from our feet on an ancient jute doormat, and I followed him upstairs.

Not surprisingly, his office was like a cave carved into a cliff of books. Floor to ceiling, wall to wall, teetering stacks: Every available surface had been used to create a precarious tower of printed volumes, the piles reminding me of the photos I had seen of the Leaning Tower of Pisa or the gigantic termite mounds of Ethiopia.

"Have a chair," he said, taking my coat and shifting a pile of dusty books from the seat of what looked like a Chippendale.

"Now, then," he said, when I had settled

into it, "I'm Frank Borley. What can I do for you, Miss . . . ah . . ."

"De Luce," I told him. "Flavia de Luce. Actually, I'm doing research on one of your former employees."

Because I didn't know her surname, I had to make a game of it.

I leaned forward, lowered my voice, and added in a confidential tone, "She drowned several years ago while diving in the Mediterranean."

"Good lord," he said. "Louisa Congreve?"

It was a question but not a question. I let his words hang in the air.

"She was the aunt of a friend," I said, which was more or less true. "Her family are thinking of having me write her biography."

Which was more or less not true.

"I understand she led an exciting life," I went on. "I should like to communicate with people who may have known her. I thought this would be as good a place as any to begin."

"And her family have given you permission to do this?"

"Her niece, Carla Sherrinford-Cameron. Yes. She practically begged me."

Frank Borley stuck his little finger into his ear and wiggled it about a bit, as if fine-tuning it for truth.

"Yes," he said slowly. "I remember Louisa mentioning once that she was taking a niece to the London Zoo and, yes, as I recall the niece's name *was* Carla. Yes, that sounds about right."

I gave him a smarmy look, as if to imply, *Very well then, let's get on with it.*

"Are you an author, then?" he asked.

This was an unexpected question.

"I'm considering it," I said, "— but only as an avocation."

I knew this might sound a bit starchy, but when you're caught short, starchy is sometimes the best you can come up with.

"Biographies to be your specialty?"

"I'm very fond of biographies," I said. "Especially those about the lives of the great chemists, such as Priestly and Lavoisier. I have a copy at home of Lord Brougham's *Lives of Men of Letters and Science,* of course, even though it's quite outdated in terms of recent scientific discoveries."

"And you're planning to drag it, kicking and screaming, into the twentieth century — is that it?"

I hadn't thought of this before but I saw at once the possibilities.

Lives of the Great Chemists, by Flavia de Luce.

Cavendish, Scheele, Priestly, Boyle, Hales, Hooke: The list went on and on. I would have a chapter devoted to each.

"And how does our Miss Congreve fit into all of this?"

It seemed the kind of question a publisher would ask; I had to think quickly.

"She died wearing an Aqua-Lung," I replied, improvising as I went. "A device which owes its existence to the experiments of Black and Lavoisier into the nature, chemical composition, and elasticity of air."

"Hmmm," he said. "Quite a novel idea, I must say. But hardly conducive to a bestselling, tell-all, no-holds-barred biography. Not the sort of thing we might see serialized in the tabloid newspapers."

"Except for her friendship with Oliver Inchbald," I said. "I understand they were very close."

Was it my imagination, or did Frank Borley go white?

"Good lord!" he said, gripping the edge of the table. "Is this blackmail?"

"Not at all," I said. "I'm merely making private inquiries."

"Do you realize what would happen if this got out? Oliver Inchbald's books still sell by the lorry load. The man's an *Institution*. We mustn't do anything to sully his reputation.

Think about it! We'd be letting down generations of readers."

He had now got up and was pacing the floor — what little there was of it left clear among the books.

"I should never do that, Mr. Borley," I said. "I was brought up on Crispian Crumpet myself."

"Were you indeed? And so was I! Hold on — there's something I'd like you to see. If you'll excuse me for a few minutes —"

And with that he was gone.

I didn't waste a second. Digging into my pocket, I pulled out a sheet of ship's letterhead upon which was a hurriedly scribbled series of numbers: hurriedly scribbled but exquisitely formed, each and every one of them.

I picked up Borley's telephone and dialed the digits, keeping the handset close to my mouth.

It rang twice at the other end before being picked up, but no one said anything.

"It's me," I said to the silence. "I'm in London."

"Flavia! Is it you?"

"Yes," I said. "I have to ring off right away."

"I understand," Mrs. Bannerman's voice said. "Where are you?"

Mrs. Bannerman had been my chemistry teacher at Miss Bodycote's Female Academy, in Canada, and had accompanied me on my recent voyage home. She had bid me farewell half an hour before docking, but only after pressing her London telephone number into my hand.

Having been once convicted of murder and then released after a sensational trial, she was determined to let her return to England pass unnoticed.

"I shall become the Invisible Woman," she had told me. "We shall communicate using codes and ciphers and gadgets hitherto known only to Secret Government Laboratories."

She had been joking, but I knew what she meant.

"Bedford Square," I said.

"Right. I can almost see you. There's an A.B.C. shop in New Oxford Street. Five minutes' walk south of where you are. You can't miss it. See you there in, shall we say, half an hour?"

"Perfect," I whispered, and set the receiver quietly down into its cradle just as Frank Borley came back into the room.

"I thought you might like to see this," he said, untying the worn ribbons of a flesh-colored folder. "It's the original manuscript of *Hobbyhorse House.*"

He placed it reverently on the table.

To be honest, it wasn't much to look at: a pile of dried-out musty papers — those soft, pulpy tinted sheets that look as if the cat has vomited on them. The first few pages were written in black ink in a slapdash scrawl, as if the white heat of composition had overcome penmanship.

There, before my very eyes, were those famous first words, written in Oliver Inchbald's own hand:

"I'm blowing my trumpet," says Crispian
    Crumpet
"I'm blowing my trumpet," says he.
"I shall trumpet the town till the walls
    tumble down
"And everyone knows that it's me."

The later pages were typed, and were neater than the first, except for a few surprising penciled spelling corrections. In the title poem, "Hobbyhorse," for instance, the word "equestrian" had been spelled without the *u,* but crossed out and corrected in blue pencil.

"One of our greatest treasures," Frank Borley said. "Priceless, probably. The books have sold millions. Never been out of print."

I looked suitably impressed.

"And I thought you might like to see this," he said, placing a book in front of me. "It's a first edition."

It was the same book I had seen in Mr. Sambridge's bedroom. I opened it and turned to the back flap of the dust jacket.

"Is this him?" I asked, pointing to the author's photo.

Again that mental itch that you can't quite scratch.

"Yes, that's Oliver Inchbald."

"He looks like a nice enough man," I said. "Was he, actually?"

My question caught Borley off guard.

"Well, let's say that he knew what he wanted and he knew how to get it."

"But was he *beloved*?" I asked.

You sometimes have to be persistent.

"Well, no," Borley said. "Respected . . . yes. Beloved . . . no."

"What about his son?" I asked. "What did Crispian Crumpet think of him?"

It had just occurred to me that Crispian Crumpet was probably still receiving royalty checks for his father's books.

"Hilary?" Borley said, sticking his finger in his ear again. "It's hard to say. Hilary has never been allowed the luxury of being an ordinary person."

I could well imagine he had not. I knew from my own experience that growing up famous was no bed of roses.

"Hilary Inchbald?" I asked. "Is that his name?"

Borley nodded. "He keeps pretty much out of the public eye," he said. "Actually, he's painfully — perhaps even pathologically — shy."

"I suppose he can afford to be," I said. "He mustn't have to go out to work."

"Oh, I wouldn't say that," Borley said. "He devotes his life to a charity he's set up in Gloucestershire for homeless cats."

"I'd love to meet him," I said, and I meant it.

"I'm afraid I can't be of much help," Borley said. "Confidentiality, and so forth."

I couldn't hide my disappointment.

"There is this, though," he said. "If it's of any help. I found it caught at the back of one of Louisa's desk drawers when we were cleaning out."

He rummaged through a cardboard file and removed a creased newspaper clipping.

CRISPIAN CRUMPET TOASTS CATS! the headline read.

"I'm afraid it's not in the best of taste," Borley said, "but then, what is, nowadays?"

The photograph showed a slender man

140

with prematurely white hair and alarmingly thick spectacles holding a glass of wine and a fat and contented tortoiseshell cat. He was so bent over — his shoulders so stooped — that he looked like a comic umbrella.

Crispian Crumpet Trumpets Cats Home, said the caption, and the article went on to say nothing much other than that Hilary Inchbald ("the former Crispian Crumpet") had declined to answer any questions not relating directly to his charity.

I had seen this man's face before. Was it because of his resemblance to his famous father? Perhaps it was, but somehow the rather timid-looking man in the clipping didn't look at all, as his father had, like someone who knew what he wanted and how to get it. Rather, he had the look of someone who had been ill for a very long time.

"Did Louisa Congreve know Mr. Inchbald? Hilary Inchbald, I mean."

"Oh, indeed she did. Louisa was, until her death, our in-house liaison with the Inchbald estate. As I have mentioned, Hilary is an extremely reticent man."

"And who is your in-house liaison now?" I asked boldly. Frank Borley didn't seem to mind.

"Well, *I* am." He laughed. "But as I've said

— or to be honest, as Sir John Falstaff said — 'the better part of valor is discretion,' although we now put it the other way round, don't we?"

I've always loved being with people who make you feel as if you know what they're talking about. Although it's a gift, I've been trying to cultivate it in myself.

"Right!" I said, tapping my mouth. "Stiff upper lip, and all that."

Frank Borley tapped his, too, and for a fleeting moment we were best of friends.

"It was Miss Congreve who identified Mr. Inchbald's body, wasn't it?"

The moment of friendship passed. Borley looked at me for a long time before replying.

"Yes," he said at last. "It was no secret at the time. It was in all the newspapers. I'm afraid that's all I can tell you."

"Well, I'd better be going," I said, getting to my feet. "Thank you. You've been most helpful."

I was disappointed, of course, not to have found what I came to find: how a set of Oliver Inchbald's first editions — one of them bearing the name of Carla Sherrinford-Cameron — came to be found in the bedroom of a dead wood-carver.

The clock was ticking. There were only

moments left. This was my last chance.

Then inspiration struck, as it often does when there's nothing else left.

"Did Oliver Inchbald have any interests other than writing?" I asked.

"Odd that you should ask that," Borley said. "I was reminded of that just a few minutes ago in the other room."

And without explaining what *that* was, he was gone again, but back in a jiff with a small wooden object, which he placed in my hands.

I thought at first it was a carved monkey, but upon rotating the thing and viewing it from all sides, I could see that it was a little gargoyle with a bare bottom, its fingers pulling down the corners of its mouth, its tongue protruding in what was probably meant to portray an obscene sound.

"Grotesque, isn't it? He made them for special friends."

There is a feeling that sometimes comes upon you, which I think of as *ice-water heart.* It's like a pang, but wetter. Sometimes it's no more than a trickle and yet other times a gush, but it usually comes with panic, fear, or sudden remembrance.

This time it was remembrance. There had been a similar gargoyle on the bedside table in the room where Mr. Sambridge had died.

Had Oliver Inchbald been a special friend of Mr. Sambridge's? Or a relative? Had the author carved this dark little gargoyle as a gift for him? It would certainly explain the set of Crispian Crumpet first editions I had seen in the dead man's house.

"And were *you* a special friend, Mr. Borley?"

He looked at me as if I had suddenly sprouted three heads — and then he laughed.

"Good lord, no!" he said. "I'm a mere custodian. A Johnny-come-lately. Oliver Inchbald was mostly before my time."

"And this?" I asked, indicating the ugly little gargoyle.

"He carved it for Miss Congreve," he said. "It was overlooked somehow when her family came to take away her personal belongings."

"After she died," I said.

"Yes, that's right. After she died."

"Was there anything else of interest?" I asked. "I'll need to know as much as I can before I begin writing."

He gave me the kind of skeptical look I expect to see from Saint Peter on Judgment Day.

"As a matter of fact there is. The chair you've been sitting in. He made that, too."

I looked more closely at the chair, which I had mistaken for a late Queen Anne by Chippendale. I had not noticed the carved vines.

"More gargoyles," I said. I could now see that there were several of the little monsters' faces embedded in the lattice of Gothic tracery that formed its back.

"Any particular reason he may have given this to Miss Congreve?" I asked.

"Well," Frank Borley said. "Other than that, as I have said, they were the greatest of friends . . ."

He left the thought hanging like a corpse from the gallows.

"Greatest of friends" was a phrase with which I was already familiar.

I had once, after being exposed to *Madame Bovary,* asked Dogger what the author, Flaubert, meant when he said that the lady had given herself up to Rodolphe, the gentleman in the yellow gloves and green velvet coat.

"He meant," Dogger had told me, "that they became the greatest of friends. The *very* greatest of friends."

So there it was. Further proof, if any were needed, that Carla was right: Her auntie Loo — Louisa Congreve — and Oliver Inchbald had known each other.

"You've been very helpful, Mr. Borley," I said. "I'll be sure to acknowledge your assistance in my book."

"No need to do that," he said, shaking his head. "In fact, it's much more gratifying to remain anonymous; to be one of those unsung heroes who helped keep history straight. Let's leave it at that, shall we?"

I stuck out my hand and he shook it.

"I quite like you, Flavia de Luce. I hope you'll let us have first chance to publish your manuscript."

Was he twitting me? It was hard to tell. He seemed earnest enough, judging by the expression on his face.

I turned to go.

"Flavia —" he said, and I stopped.

He seemed to be fighting his conscience, as if to keep back the words that were trying to get out.

"It's customary, you know, to put in a teaspoon of tea for each person to be served, and then to add one for the pot."

I couldn't count the number of times I had heard Mrs. Mullet repeat this ancient formula: "One for you, and one for me, and one for the pot."

Without this invocation, tea just wouldn't taste the same.

"Yes?" I said, fearful of breaking whatever

spell had gripped him.

"Louisa was a witch," he said. "Don't say that I told you, as I shall deny it vigorously."

I couldn't hide my astonishment.

"Let's just consider it one for the pot."

EIGHT

As I made my way towards New Oxford Street, my mind was in a blaze. Why had Frank Borley decided to tell me, at the very last moment, that Louisa Congreve was a witch? It had seemed almost compulsive, as if he had blurted it out against his will while under a spell.

Could it be that Carla's aunt Loo, the late witch, had him under her control from beyond the grave? Or, in telling me, was Frank Borley simply settling some ancient score?

There's an old saying, "Murder will out": a phrase which Daffy has often hurled at me as she glares balefully over her book whenever I have interrupted her reading. And it seems to be true. How many murderers have been undone by a blurt?

Murder *will* out — in the same way that one's sister's toothpaste squirts out of a tube when it's trodden underfoot — as if it has a mind of its own.

Murder, I thought, *is also like steam — although less useful.*

It was steam that had transported me to London on this snowy winter morning, and steam that would haul me home again at the end of the day. And it was a hidden head of steam, I realized, that had made Frank Borley blurt out that Louisa Congreve was a witch.

All I needed to do was to find out what fired his boiler.

Oxford Street was swarming with scores of Christmas shoppers jostling, their faces filled with a kind of happy gloom. The falling snow and the half-light of the low-hanging, leaden sky made the street seem as if it were located in some far-off mythical underground kingdom, and I wouldn't have been at all surprised to see Dante, or even old Odysseus himself, trudging along the pavement with a gift-wrapped rocking horse on his shoulder.

I had no difficulty whatever in finding the A.B.C. tearoom, and I took pleasure, as I paused in front of it, in recalling the fact that the Aerated Bread Company — which is what the large A.B.C. painted on the window stood for — had been founded not by a chemist, but the next best thing, a medical man: a Dr. Dauglish, who had invented and patented a new method of causing dough to rise, not with yeast but by an injection of carbon dioxide: good old CO_2.

I shivered with happiness at the thought.

But the very thought of bread made me realize that I was feeling distinctly peckish. It would be hours yet before I could return to Buckshaw to feed.

I tried to keep back a surge of saliva, but not with total success.

As I entered, I spotted Mrs. Bannerman at once. She was sitting in the far corner of the room watching the door.

My first thought was that she did not look like a murderess, even an acquitted one, which she was. Rather, this elfin-faced pixie might have just flown out of the pages of a fairy book by Cicely Mary Barker.

She got to her feet and flung her arms around me as if I really mattered. I'm afraid I stood there looking like a chump.

"Mrs. Bannerman —" was all I could manage.

"Let's get something straight," she said, giving my nose a mock tweak. "It's Mrs. Bannerman no more. From now on it's just plain old Mildred. Plain old Mildred and Flavia having a nice cuppa in the A.B.C., understood?"

"Yes, Mrs. Bannerman," I said. "Oh, damn. I mean . . . Mildred."

And we both laughed.

I firmly believe it is by sharing such stupid moments as these that we grow into someone other than who we used to be, and I was already feeling an inch taller.

"You're looking very posh," I said.

She was wearing a red tailored suit with a white ruffled blouse, a matching beefeater hat, and a sprig of holly berries at the throat.

"It's rayon," she said. "Nitrocellulose by another name. It makes me feel explosive." She gave me a schoolgirl grin.

"Good old pyroxylin," I said. "Hilaire de Chardonnet, and so forth."

Like any accomplished chemist, I was quite familiar with the astonishing history of the flammable fabrics.

"Top marks, Flavia. I can see you've lost none of your chemical acuity."

I'm afraid I preened a little, although in my dowdy overcoat I must have looked more like a street musician than a first-rate chemical mind.

Mildred pushed her chair back from the table and lifted a leg.

"Do you think my outfit matches my galoshes?" she asked, and she exploded with laughter.

It was not the kind of Tinkerbell laugh you might expect from such a delicate creature, but rather a full-bellied roar which caused a couple of net-hatted dowagers, dripping with pearls at a nearby table, to shoot daggers of disapproval at us from behind their menus.

"Don't look now," Mildred said, "but we're being watched."

This brought on even more laughter.

I wondered what these two old gorgons would think if they knew that Mildred earned her living by sifting through the residue that accumulates around hastily buried corpses. They would certainly be eating their tea cakes with less gusto if I told them Mildred had recommended to me Mègnin's great work, whose title could be translated as *The Wildlife of Corpses:* a fascinating pioneer study of the insects that feed on dead bodies; a book best read behind closed — or even locked — doors.

Now, here we were, Mildred and I, sitting at one of the tables of the Aerated Bread Company in Oxford Street, under the very noses of these two outraged dowagers, as if butter — or anything else for that matter — wouldn't melt in either of our mouths.

I gave them one of my supremely pleasant

smiles, which involved a very slight crossing of the eyes: just enough to make it seem as if I might be suffering a slight and unfortunate hereditary defect.

It was too much.

The old ladies got to their feet and stalked out of the shop, their noses in the air. Unfortunately, they had forgotten to pay, so that the manageress was forced to follow them out into the snowy street, where a heated argument was now taking place, with much gesticulating and pointing and the waving of arms.

"Well done," Mildred said, sipping her tea daintily.

It occurred to me that I was not the only one who was becoming a different person. This new Mildred Bannerman was not the one I had known in Canada. It almost seemed as if the two of us were changing places.

It was difficult, even for me, to realize that I was sitting across the table from a member of the Nide, that shadowy — no, not shadowy: *invisible* — branch of the secret service, of which my aunt Felicity was the so-called Gamekeeper.

As for Mildred, it was becoming evident that she was whatever she wanted to appear to be. Awkwardly put, I suppose, but what it meant was that she was a chameleon: a chameleon in black galoshes and red tailored suit, to be sure, but a chameleon nonetheless.

"How are you getting on?" she asked.

It had been only a couple of days since I had seen her last, and yet I could almost feel the force of her piercing gaze. I could tell by her eyes that she was Mrs. Bannerman again, looking out for my welfare.

"Well enough," I said, and there were a rather rough few moments during which I fought back tears. I told her about Father's illness, and she said all the right things. What else could she do?

"You mustn't blame yourself, Flavia," she said, and her words shot into me like the bolt from a crossbow. How could she possibly have known my innermost thoughts?

I did what I always do when the shot is too near the heart: I changed the subject, and I did it by blurting — yes, *blurting* — the entire story about Mr. Sambridge.

I felt better immediately. If I couldn't trust Mildred, then who — ?

"You've been busy," she observed. "The days are so short this time of year. You'll be needing to get back to Buckshaw, I expect."

I nodded.

"What can I do to help?"

"Nothing," I said politely, but wishing immediately I'd kept my mouth shut.

"Why did you ring me up, then?"

She had me there. My mind turned to mush. With most people I could talk my way blindfolded out of the Hampton Court maze, but not with Mildred.

"Well," I said, "a newspaper archive might be helpful."

"British Library, Colindale," she said, glancing at her wristwatch. "Hats, coats, boots, on! — and off we go!"

Minutes later we were hurrying down the endless steps at the Goodge Street tube station, where the Northern Line would carry us through the underworld to Colindale.

"Newspaper Room," Mildred said, handing over a card at the front desk. The bored commissionaire didn't give me so much as a glance, but pointed with a bony finger, even though it was obvious to everyone but him that Mildred knew where she was going.

Mildred filled out the necessary requests and we sat back to wait for the newspapers.

"I have a pretty good idea of when Inchbald died," she said. "But we'll begin with the latest *Who's Who* and go on from there. Louisa Congreve, I expect, won't be in such august company, so in her case, we'll need to do a bit more legwork."

"Was Oliver Inchbald a member of the Nide?" I asked, shocked at my own boldness.

Mildred threw her head back and laughed — not as loudly as she had in the tea shop, since we were, after all, in a library, which contains its own holiness.

"Whatever makes you say that?" she demanded.

"Because you said you had a pretty good idea when he died."

"Flavia! Surely you're not suggesting —"

"It was just a thought," I said.

"And a rancid one at that. Ten gold stars, though, for attention to detail. But no, nothing so romantic as that. I believe I read it in *The Telegraph*. Since I only read *The Telegraph* when I'm in the train, and since I seldom take the train, I'm reminded immediately of when it was — even *where* I was."

"Yes?" I said, fascinated with the process. "You mustn't have been very old. Oliver Inchbald has been dead for years."

"I was old enough," she said, and the tone of her voice signaled that that particular branch of the conversation had reached a dead end.

"Was Inchbald a spy?" I asked.

"Not that I know of," she answered. "But it's a good point. Being pecked to death by seabirds *does* smack a bit of Secret Agent 5, doesn't it?"

"That's what I thought," I agreed.

"No, as far as I know he was just another one of those English literary gentlemen: gardening, golfing —"

"*— and girls,*" I wanted to add, thinking of Carla's auntie Loo, but I didn't.

". . . and grenadine," she finished.

Grenadine was, I knew, a chemical concoction of pomegranate juice, often used as a camouflage for gin. One of our Buckshaw neighbors, Mrs. Foster, was an old hand in its deployment, and was seldom seen without a sample of the stuff in her hand. On one occasion, at their tennis court, I had tried to engage her in conversation about the fascinating chemical makeup of the pomegranate, such as the acids — caprylic, stearic, oleic, and linoleic — to say nothing of its rich potassium content, but she had seemed too vaporous to bother going on.

At that point, an attendant brought the papers Mildred had ordered, along with a fat bound copy of the London Post Office Directory for 1948, which she dumped in front of me.

"Congreve," Mildred said. "I expect you'll find it under 'C.' "

Saucily, I showed her the tip of my tongue and opened the book, offering a silent little prayer to Saint Jerome, the patron saint of libraries and librarians. As so often happens when you're in that Old Fellow's good books, the directory fell open at the very page I was looking for.

"Found it!" I said. "Congreve, Miss Louisa G., 47 Cranwell Gardens, Kensington, S.W.7. She's the only Congreve in the book. Western 1778. I wonder what would happen if we rang that number?"

"I should be very surprised if she picked it up," Mildred said, "in view of the fact that she's dead."

"But we might reach one of her relatives."

"You've already reached one of her relatives. Carla Sherrinford-Cameron. Or have you forgotten?"

"Yes, but we'd have an independent view of Miss Congreve's connection to Oliver Inchbald."

"True," she said. "Provided they were willing to confide in a total stranger."

"We could give it a try," I said. "We'd have nothing to lose but the cost of the call."

"Which means that you're already planning to make it from the closest kiosk. I can see right through you, Flavia de Luce."

There was silence for several minutes as she leafed through the bound newspapers, scanning each page at lightning speed before turning to the next. I noticed that she did so without licking her fingertips: a thorough professional.

"People who turn pages with licked fingers are as bad as those who wipe their noses on the table linen," Daffy had once remarked, and I had stopped doing it.

"Here we are!" Mildred said suddenly, pointing to the page. "I remembered the photograph."

In grainy black-and-white, a uniformed Boy Scout points to a pair of Wellies, which lie empty and askew, like the hands of a novelty clock pointing to four-forty.

"Nothing left of him but the bones," said Scout James Marlowe, of Wick St. Lawrence, who made the grisly discovery while doing fieldwork for a Bird Warden badge. Marlowe, 14, a young man of remarkable initiative, sailed out to the desolate island alone in the early hours of Tuesday morning.

"Human remains have occasionally been found on the island," Inspector Cavendish,

159

of the Somerset Constabulary at Weston-super-Mare told our reporter, "but they've tended to be historical and haven't been wearing Wellies."

"I think it was the gulls that got him," Scout Marlowe said. "They can go quite mad in nesting season, you know. They'll eat anything. Besides," he added, "the carrion crow, *Corvus c. corone,* also breeds on the island, and I expect they had a hand in mopping up."

The investigation is continuing.

"Hmm," I said. "I wonder how Scout Marlowe knew it was a 'him'?"

"Good point," Mildred said. "You might ask him."

This, I knew, was much more than a suggestion. It might even have been a command.

"Can't be too many Scouts named Marlowe in Wick St. Lawrence," I said, and let my eyes shift back to the rapidly turning newspaper pages.

"Yes, here we are," Mildred said. "Five days later: BONES BELIEVED TO BE THOSE OF BELOVED AUTHOR. STEEP HOLM BODY IDENTIFIED.

"Just as you'd expect. The usual chain of events. Man reported missing: the search and its shocking conclusion.

"DEATH COMES TO HOBBYHORSE HOUSE.

"You have to hand it to *The Telegraph*. When it comes to this sort of thing, they're in a class by themselves. Listen . . . it goes on:

" 'The body was identified by a Miss Louisa Congreve, of Cranwell Gardens, Kensington, who is employed at the offices of a well-known London publisher.'

"Note the 'well-known London publisher.' Everyone in the civilized world from eight to eighty knows perfectly well who that publisher is, yet someone took the trouble to keep it out of the papers."

"I wonder who," I said.

"So do I. And what I wonder even more is *how*?"

I was not following her train of thought.

"I beg your pardon?" I asked.

"You must remember that every single word in every single newspaper article is —"

"Edited!" I said. "By an editor!"

"Well done."

"But how do we find him?" I asked. "He wouldn't tell us anyway. Even if you did track him down."

" 'Elementary,' as someone once remarked. No one knows better who edited a particular newspaper article than the reporter who wrote it, and whose name, Finbar Joyce, is staring us in the face. In reporters, feelings, blood, and ink run equally deep, and nowhere more so than in Irish veins. I'll bet you a bob that Finbar Joyce would be willing to sell the soul of his editor *and* his editor's mother and grandmother — anonymously, of course — for a couple of quid and a pint of Guinness."

Ordinarily, I might have questioned such a generalization on the grounds that it was not scientific, but having met Wallace Scroop, a crime reporter in Canada who made weasels seem noble by comparison, I decided that Mildred might just be right.

Daffy had informed me that female intuition was not permissible in a sleuth, but as far as I knew, there was no rule against my making use of someone else's.

"Elementary," I agreed with a grin.

Once the date of Oliver Inchbald's death had been established, it was easy enough to order up copies of *The Times* (NOTED AUTHOR DIES), *Daily Express* (OLIVER INCHBALD DEAD IN ISLAND TRAGEDY), the *Daily Mail* (CRISPIAN CRUMPET CRE-

ATOR DEAD IN SHOCKING ISLAND MIS-
HAP), and *News of the World* (NOTHING
LEFT OF HIM BUT HIS WELLIES).

None of them shed any further light on
the story except the *London Evening Standard,* in which Scout Marlowe admitted to
making a sketch at the scene:

"It's in *Scouting for Boys,* sir. B-P" —
Marlowe here refers to Lord Baden-Powell
(1857–1941), the founder of the Boy Scout
movement, and author of the standard
handbook to which the boy alludes — "B-P
tells us that we may one day be the first to
find the body of a dead man, and if we do,
we must draw a little map. I also took a
couple of snapshots."

"None of the other papers mentioned
that," I pointed out. "I wonder why?"

Mildred looked up from the paper. "It
indicates, perhaps, that the *London Evening
Standard* is not subscribed to by Inspector
Cavendish of the Somerset Constabulary at
Weston-super-Mare."

I was instantly brimming with excitement.

"Could it be, do you think, that a clue
might be hidden like that in plain sight —
for years — without anyone spotting it?"

Even as the words tumbled out of my

mouth, I was aware that the answer was *Yes*.

Human beings were imperfect. And the police, being human at bottom, were also, therefore, imperfect. In spite of all official efforts, there was always that last stray piece of the jigsaw puzzle that lay lost and undetected beneath the drawing room sofa, and I was a dab hand at crawling in on my belly where others feared — or at least, forgot — to tread.

"Great Scott!" Mildred said, glancing at her wrist-watch and leaping to her feet. "I lost track of the time. I'd better get you to your train or we'll both be in hot water."

I hadn't the heart, or the stomach, to tell her that there was really no hot water for me to get into. With Father in hospital, no one gave a frying pan where I was, or what I was doing. Growing up is like that, I suppose: The strings fall away and you're left standing on your own.

It was sad in a way that is hard to describe.

For that reason, and others, for all I know, we were mostly silent in the taxicab, and by the time we arrived at the station, a strange awkwardness had grown up between us.

"Keep in touch," Mildred said as I climbed out and stood at the open window. "You have my number. Call if you need anything."

I gave a nod that was too abrupt, too ill-mannered; ashamed, I turned and walked away.

Why is it, I wondered, *that we can never plan a decent goodbye? Why do farewells always catch us by surprise?*

The afternoon was drawing to a close as the train moved out of the station. At the end of the platform, where the snow had not yet been cleared away, what surely must be one of London's last remaining gas lamps flickered bravely and forlorn against the growing darkness — and then it was gone.

NINE

I watched as night came creeping in across the fields and pressed itself against the window glass.

There was only one other passenger in the carriage, a gentleman who thankfully was engrossed in his newspaper. Only his hat, his trousers, and his highly polished boots were visible, giving the comic impression that he had been plastered over with printed advertising, as if he were the remains of a blitzed brick wall in Farringdon Street.

It was just as well, I thought, that the fellow kept to himself. I did not feel in the least like being questioned by a stranger, no matter how interesting or well-meaning he might be. I had been warned, of course, about falling into careless conversations with gentlemen on trains, and that was *before* I had seen Mr. Hitchcock's film on that very topic. I had already firmly resolved that, when taking the train in future, I would keep my lips zipped.

The rocking of the carriage and the *clackety-clack* of the wheels had an oddly hypnotic effect and I let myself be jostled from side to side by the movement. Railway travel always makes you think of the past, as if this beast of steam and steel, which is carrying you forward into some unknown future, causes your memories to travel backwards, at an equal speed, in the other direction. It has something to do, perhaps, with Professor Einstein's theory of relativity.

I thought of Father, and of how he used to walk across the fields with us to church, saying little but listening patiently as we prattled on about our lives: me about Chemistry, Feely about Music, and Daffy about Books. How strong he seemed — and how immortal.

Now, here he was, laid low by bacterial pneumonia, and probably because of me.

Already weakened by years of captivity in a Japanese prisoner-of-war camp, he had been shipped home at last, only to face the worry and decay of a crumbling estate and the incessant demands of His Majesty's Board of Inland Revenue, who had, apparently, never heard of gratitude. The retrieval of my mother, Harriet's, body from a Tibetan glacier had crushed him, and then to find that she had bequeathed Buckshaw to me must have been like a foot in the face, although he never said so, of course.

Outside the carriage window, an enameled sign advertising chocolate glided by in the growing darkness. *Bournville,* it said, *Home of Chocolate.*

What a cruel, grim joke it is, I thought, *that the day should come when even chocolate should have a home while my beloved father does not.*

I'm afraid I let slip an audible cackle.

The gentleman across from me put down his paper, removed his spectacles, and spoke: "Laughter makes for a good appetite, Miss Flavia — or so it is said. I expect Mrs. Mullet shall have the roast beef blackened to perfection."

"Dogger!"

I let out a whoop and clasped his hands. That Dogger should say such a thing about Mrs. Mullet's cooking was, in itself, incredible. Although her burned beef was legendary, it was one of those things that were not to be spoken of aloud, like YHWH, the four-letter name of God.

"What are you doing here?"

It was the kind of stupid question which I ordinarily hate: the kind of question one sees in the cinema or hears on the wireless. I'm sure Dogger was thinking the same thing but he smiled, nevertheless.

"The same as you are, Miss Flavia. Going home."

Whether it was the time, the place, the darkness, the snow, or the general situation regarding Father, I do not know, but I burst into tears.

Dogger unfurled a spotless white handkerchief from somewhere about his person and handed it over.

"The Christmas season is always a difficult one," he remarked. "Even at the best of times."

And with that, he turned to the window, leaving me enough privacy to mop up my face. We rode along in what I believe is called "companionable silence," Dogger lost in his own thoughts and I in mine.

Many miles slipped by before I felt I had control of my voice.

"You've been with me all day, haven't you? You followed me up to town."

"There were certain interests of Colonel de Luce which required attention . . . ," he said, his voice trailing off, and I knew that he meant "Yes."

"Then you probably know all about Mr.

Sambridge, and the fact that I found him dead."

"Indeed," Dogger said. "As does all of Bishop's Lacey and environs. I heard it from Mrs. Mullet, who had it direct from the lips of her friend Mrs. Waller, who heard it from Maximilian Brock, who heard it from the vicar's wife."

He couldn't resist a gentle smile.

"Murder," he said, "can be a particularly nasty business — or so I am given to understand."

"Max will already be scribbling something suitable for *Hair-Raising Tales,*" I said.

This was an American magazine which Daffy insisted was subscribed to by rabbit breeders but which, in reality, published articles that they claimed — with no sense of irony — were based upon "real-life murders."

Maximilian, who was both dwarf and retired concert pianist, was rumored to be one of the hired pens who published his lurid tales under various transparent pseudonyms, such as Jayne Nightwork and Sally Tell.

"I write for the little people," he had once told me, holding a forefinger to his lips, warning me to keep quiet about it. "The little people, who have no voice."

"How's Father?" I asked, abruptly switching tracks. "Has there been any improvement? Do you think Matron will allow us —"

"I hope so," Dogger interrupted. "I certainly hope so."

Clarence Mundy's taxicab awaited us at Doddingsley station. Dogger had made arrangements with Clarence to meet the train and, although I wondered vaguely, I did not ask how he knew at what time we would arrive.

Gladys was waiting patiently where I had left her, as I knew she would be, although she was now wearing, on her seat, a dunce's cap of snow, as if to welcome me home with a practical joke.

I brushed her off and, giving her a good shake, handed her to Clarence, who lashed her to the luggage rack on the roof with a strong cord.

"Place of honor," he said. "Best seat in the house. Sixpence extra."

He was teasing, of course, but I loved him for it all the same.

As we pulled away from the railway station, I remembered that Clarence had been a pilot during the war, and as I watched him now, hunched over the glowing instrument panel in the darkness, I imagined that Dogger and I were with him in the cockpit of his giant Sunderland flying boat, thundering through the night. Five thousand feet below us was the English Channel — visibility zero — nothing to be seen through the blurred windscreen but the wild, driving snow.

It was good to be in Clarence's capable hands, and I tightened my coat around my neck.

"Nasty bit of work up at Thornfield Chase," Clarence said, jolting me out of my trance. "Heard by the jungle telegraph you were the one found the body. Must have been a bit of a shock."

"Yes," I said. "It was ghastly. I'd rather not talk about it."

Dogger gave me a nearly invisible smile in the near darkness.

I was fibbing, of course. How could I tell Clarence that finding another dead body was anything but dreadful? On the contrary: It was thrilling; it was exciting; it was exhilarating, it was invigorating; to say nothing of electrifying and above all, satisfying.

How could I tell the dear man that murder made me feel so gloriously alive?

Mrs. Mullet must have been watching for

our headlights. No sooner had we come to a stop than she was out the door, not even bothering with a coat.

"Go back inside, Mrs. M," I told her, our roles reversed for the first time in recorded history. "You'll catch your death."

"You lot!" she said, planting her hands on her hips, and shifting her searchlight glare from me to Dogger and back again. "It's *you* lot'll be the death of me. Parsnips at six, I told you. Stone cold they are now. Might as well toss 'em out. Moses 'imself couldn't keep parsnips 'ot past their time. Might as well give 'em to the cat, if we 'ad one."

Her frustration, I knew, was not particularly with us, but with the fact that Father was in hospital and beyond her sphere of influence; beyond her need to advise and counsel. Pretended anger was Mrs. Mullet's way of weeping.

"It's good to be home," I told her, giving her a quick hug — but not so great a one as to draw attention to itself. "I need your advice desperately on an important matter. But first, the parsnips. We must have parsnips! Cold parsnips are my delight. Lead me to them."

Playing the clown is not an easy task. Clowns, I have come to believe, are placed upon the earth solely to fill the needs of others, while running perilously close to "Empty" themselves.

We shepherded one another into the house and order was restored.

A gloom hung over the dinner table, caused by the news that Father's condition had not improved. Feely had a spot the size of a farthing on her left cheek and she didn't seem to care. Her left hand lay limp and listless in her lap as she picked at her food with the other. Daffy was intently reading something by Pearl S. Buck, which was a bad sign.

"You'll never guess who I happened to run into," I said, trying to draw Feely out of her stupor. "Carl Pendracka."

"How utterly awe-inspiring," she said.

"He'd like to see you sometime, now that, well . . . you know."

"I do not need Flavia de Luce to organize my social life," Feely said. "I am not in need of an appointments secretary, and if ever I should be, at some point in the far, far distant future, I shall be sure to give you a pass."

"Turnip!" I said.

"Gong farmer," she shot back.

I have to hand it to my sister. As I have

remarked elsewhere, Feely can be remarkably coarse when she's cornered, and I have
to admit I admire her for it. She has a limit-
less supply of insults from the Middle Ages,
to which she is constantly adding by reading up on the lives of the great composers.
Musicians, I have discovered, can be a
surprisingly scatological (another of her
words) crew. Later, I looked up *gong farmer*
(or *gongfermour*) in the OED and found
that it meant a person who went from house
to house collecting the night soil. In other
words, a cleaner-out of privies.

I copied it into my notebook for future
reference.

"That Inspector Whatshisname called
round today to see you," Daffy said unexpectedly, looking up from her book. "He
seemed peevish to find you not at home. I
told him you were on the lam."

"Inspector Hewitt?"

"He's charging you with aggravated med-
dling," she said. "Honestly, Flavia. Why
can't you take up tatting, or pokerwork, or
paper dolls, or something civilized? Something with less blood?"

Less blood? My heart gave a *clunk.*

I could have kissed her! But not quite.

Less blood. That was just the point, wasn't
it?

In Mr. Sambridge's case, other than the clotted crust under his fingernails and the moist stains on the rope, there had been *no blood at all*. Any wound serious enough to kill would almost certainly result in blood, and yet there hadn't been a drop — as far as I could see — on either the body of the deceased or on his clothing. There was always the possibility, I suppose, that it had been extracted by some apprentice witch trying to pass her Blood & Body Fluids test, but somehow I doubted that.

Besides, Mr. Sambridge's darkened face was evidence enough that blood was present in his body: It was just that gravity had dragged it to the lowest point.

From my own studies, I knew that bloodless murder was most frequently caused by poisoning, but I knew also that poisoners do not usually follow through by hanging their victims by the heels.

On the contrary. Victims of cyanide, say, gasp their last in their own beds, or on a handy sofa, with their astonished family standing by, wringing their hands (all except one, of course) and crying out, "What is it, Cressida? What's the matter?"

But in Mr. Sambridge's case, there had been no blood, no bed, and no sofa.

Just a village wood-carver, trussed upside

down in a doorway like an inverted version of Leonardo da Vinci's *Vitruvian Man*.

It was altogether a pretty little puzzle.

How I would love to be a spider on the wall, looking over Inspector Hewitt's shoulder. What had he made of the evidence at Thornfield Chase, and who, if any, were his suspects? I knew that my name would be somewhere on his list: It only stood to reason. I had been observed leaving the house in which a dead body had been found, and the fact that the finder was me would hardly keep me out of the sights of the hawk-eyed and hawk-witted — well, you know what I mean — Inspector Hewitt.

It was too late to ring him up, which I wouldn't do, even if it weren't. The last thing on earth I'd ever do would be to disturb the dear man and his dear wife, Antigone, in their rose-covered cottage, where they would be warming themselves in front of a cozy winter fire this very minute, he with his briar pipe clutched in his mouth, she with her knitting needles clacking . . .

Knitting needles!

Oh, Flavia . . . Flavia! Where is your intelligence?

I had suspected as early as last April, when I had seen her at my mother's funeral, that

Antigone Hewitt might be pregnant. I had witnessed with my own eyes that radiant glow (in spite of the solemn occasion) and that secret squeeze of her husband's arm. But since then, I hadn't given it another thought. Swept off my feet and out to sea by the undertow of my own life, I had forgotten completely about the possibly interesting condition of the inspector's wife.

Why, even now, she and the inspector might well be sharing the heat of their comfy fire with a little stranger in a little bassinet, rocking it tenderly, cooing and calling to it and to each other like a pair of turtledoves.

It was enough to turn your stomach.

Hang the hour! I would call Antigone at once and kill two birds with one stone.

TEN

For as long as I could remember, and probably long before that, the telephone at Buckshaw had been off limits. Father had a horror of the thing, caused by certain experiences in his past of which he never spoke, and because "the instrument," as he called it, had brought him news of Harriet's disappearance and, later, the discovery of her dead body. Consequently, the telephone was to be used in only the most dire emergencies: a rule that had been — with only a few exceptions on my part — strictly observed.

The instrument was contained in a small cubicle tucked away beneath the stairs in the foyer. Once inside, you could lower your voice and whisper away unobserved with no danger of being overheard (unless, of course, you applied your ear to the tread of the seventh step from the bottom, a phenomenon which no one knew about but me).

Against all expectations, Inspector Hewitt's number was listed in the directory. *How thoughtful of him.* How many other investigators of his rank would share his private number with the riffraff? Perhaps he found that it encouraged the phoning-in of anonymous tips.

At any rate, his address was listed simply as Maybank, Hinley.

So that was the name of the rose-covered cottage! "Maybank!" I said it aloud and let the word escape from my mouth like a perfumed puff of jasmine scent as I dialed the number. "Maybank."

It was picked up at once.

"Antigone Hewitt speaking," came that soft, familiar voice, and I was nearly struck speechless.

"Uh, Mrs. Hewitt . . . Antigone . . ." (Dare I use her baptismal name?) ". . . this is Flavia de Luce. I understand Inspector Hewitt called in to see me today, but I wasn't home. I had to go up to London unexpectedly, you see, and . . ."

"Oh, yes, Flavia. Welcome home, by the way. How nice to hear your voice again."

I wanted to thank her but my mouth had gone suddenly and unaccountably dry.

"My husband *did* mention that he planned to see you, but he's unfortunately not here at the moment. Shall I take a message?"

"N . . . no," I managed. "I'll call him tomorrow — during working hours."

"I shall tell him," she assured me, and then she added, "Flavia, is everything all right?"

At least she had the good grace not to ask if anything was wrong.

"Yes," I said. And then I said, "No."

"Is there anything that I can do?"

"No, thank you. It's just that Father's in the hospital, and everything's a little muddled right now."

"I'm sorry to hear that, Flavia."

Her words should have comforted me, but they did not. Sympathy was not what I wanted. There are times when sympathy is not enough.

"How are *you*?" I asked, quickly turning the tables.

"Very well, thank you."

This was going to be more difficult than I thought. I needed to be devious.

"Have you made any interesting shopping trips lately?"

Brilliant! Just girl talk.

"Am I pregnant, do you mean? Well, yes, as a matter of fact, I am. We're expecting a blessed event; the patter of little feet; the clang of the diaper pail — however you want to put it — next month. Hello? Flavia? Are you there?"

"Son of a sea cook!" I said. It just slipped out.

Not that there was anything wrong with the words. They had been spoken by the actor Cary Grant in *Arsenic and Old Lace,* a gripping film about a family of poisoners who, in order to relieve homeless men of their suffering, spiked their elderberry wine with arsenic, strychnine, and just a pinch of cyanide.

Antigone laughed. "Indeed!" she said.

How I wanted to add, "We must go out for a glass of elderberry wine," but I restrained myself. She knew the film and I knew the film, and her single word, "Indeed," had cemented the bond. Nothing more needed to be said.

Sometimes less is more.

"Congratulations," I said. "You must be very excited."

"Yes, we are. But you knew all along, didn't you?"

"Well . . . ," I said. "Yes."

"I should have been terribly disappointed if you hadn't noticed."

Was she twitting me?

"So should I," I said, and after a second or two we both laughed.

Except for her saying that she would tell her husband I had called, that was pretty well the end of my conversation with Antigone Hewitt.

I had not really learned anything, except for the imminent arrival of a young Master — or Mistress — Hewitt, and I wasn't yet sure how I felt about the so-called blessed event.

I wasn't like Aunt Millicent, who believed that babies ought to be shellacked and framed at birth to keep them out of mischief, or like Daffy, who hated them because of the noise and fumes:

"Like smelly little motorcars," she would say, sticking her little fingers in her ears and pinching her nose shut between her thumbs whenever she spotted one.

To me, a baby was a temporary nuisance: a mere metamorphosis on its way from egg to adult. Scientists once believed — wrongly, as it turned out — that we all of us repeat the history of our species, passing in form from simple water-dwelling creatures to air-breathing mammals, and growing, in nine months, through all the various phases of human development from single-celled organism through primitive invertebrate, fish, reptile, and so forth, and ending up being your auntie Mabel, or some other mammalian horror.

As I knew from his notebooks, my late great-uncle Tar had, as a student, gently corrected Darwin on several points relating to the evolutionary process.

"Based, I presume, upon close observation of his own nearest relatives," Daffy had said when I'd told her this.

I returned the telephone receiver to its cradle, and waited for Miss Runciman, at the exchange, to work whatever wizardry was necessary with her plugs and jacks before another call could be made. She would be all agog when I requested another connection.

"Two calls from Buckshaw, and all within two minutes! Whatever is the world coming to? Tsk! Tsk!" Etc., etc., etc.

It was commonly known that Miss Runciman listened in on virtually every call made or received in Bishop's Lacey.

"Flora Runciman's got more muck in 'er 'ead than Norah's Ark," Mrs. Mullet had once told me, nodding knowingly.

Which meant that she knew where all the bodies were buried.

"Hello . . . Miss Runciman?" I said. "It's Flavia de Luce calling from Buckshaw. I'm terribly sorry to bother you again, Miss Runciman, but with Father in hospital, I'm afraid that everything is at sixes and sevens."

"Ah, yes, Flavia. I was sorry to hear about your father. How may I be of assistance?"

I'd bet a pound to a penny she had known about Father's illness even before Dr. Darby did.

"I'm trying rather urgently to get in touch with an old family friend," I said. "I'm afraid we don't have the proper directory here, but his name is James Marlowe, and he lives at Wick St. Lawrence, which I believe is near Weston-super-Mare, in Somerset. I hope you can help."

I stifled a sob.

"Poor lamb," Miss Runciman said. "Hold on a jiffy and I'll see what I can do."

Goodness knows what kind of story was forming in her mind.

I hated to drag in Father's illness in aid of a fib, but I was sure he wouldn't mind. I knew that in his lifetime, my father had been forced to use his cunning every single day, simply to stay alive. The hurts and horrors that he and Dogger had been forced to undergo during the war were never spoken of, but were written clearly in their eyes.

A series of electrical cracklings, clicks, and buzzes told me that Miss Runciman was holding serious secret talks with her counterparts in cities, towns, and villages across the kingdom. I could picture their voices speeding through the night on vast spider-webs of copper wires, linking here to there and back again, connecting all their little worlds at the press of a button.

"Hello, Flavia? Are you there?"

"Yes, Miss Runciman. I'm still here."

"I've managed to locate your Mr. Marlowe at Wick St. Lawrence. I have him on the line. Shall I put him through? There will be the usual charge, of course."

"Of course," I said. We'd count the cost later.

There was an ominous crackle of static and then Miss Runciman said, "I have your party on the line. Go ahead, please."

What do you say to a total stranger? Especially when you are being overheard by a nosy telephone operator who believes it to be a matter of life and death, and is hovering over your conversation like the spirit of God upon the Waters?

"Hello? Mr. Marlowe?"

I wasn't sure if he was a mister or not. He was certainly no longer the boy who found the remains of Oliver Inchbald.

"Hello? Yes . . . who am I speaking with?" The voice was boyish, but not completely.

186

"This is Flavia de Luce. I'm afraid my father has been taken ill and is unable to accept your kind invitation, but he's still quite interested in seeing some of the photographs of birds you took several years ago at Steep Holm. I've been told you made some remarkable snapshots of the seagulls."

I crossed my fingers, praying that birds bored Miss Runciman to distraction — and my prayer was answered — just like that! A sharp click on the line signaled her departure for greener pastures of gossip.

"What did you say your name was?" James Marlowe's voice was suddenly guarded.

"De Luce. Flavia de Luce."

"I'm afraid someone is pulling your leg, Miss de Luce. I took no particularly interesting photographs of the gulls."

"What about the crows, then?" I asked. *Corvus c. corone.* You mentioned them specifically to the reporter from the *London Evening Standard.*"

I could hear him breathing at the other end of the line, and knew instinctively that he was about to ring off. I needed to keep him talking at all costs.

"Listen . . . Mr. Marlowe. I'm going to be perfectly honest. I'm not supposed to tell you this, but I'm calling on behalf of Edgar Wallace. He's working on a new thriller

187

based upon the Oliver Inchbald murder. But please don't breathe a word. It's strictly hush-hush."

"Murder, you say?" James Marlowe asked.

"Shhh!" I told him. "It hasn't yet been made public."

"Edgar Wallace, you say?"

"Yes," I said. "But please don't repeat his name. We mustn't risk being overheard. You may refer to him as Horatio. That's his middle name. Only his closest associates are privy to that fact."

I sent up a little prayer of gratitude that Daffy had shared that tidbit of Wallace information while reading *The Four Just Men*. I was also grateful she had taught me that particular use of the word *privy*, which before that I had always thought meant something else.

I have to admit that dragging one of the most famous of all crime novelists into the discussion was a stroke of sheer genius. There wasn't a Boy Scout alive who hadn't huddled under his blankets in the wee small hours, reading wide-eyed, by the light of a shaded torch, the ingenious and bloody mystery thrillers of Richard Horatio Edgar Freeman, known to the world as Edgar Wallace, who was as much a household name as Sunlight Soap and Oxo.

"Horatio wants to keep this project under wraps," I improvised. "I'm sure you'll understand. Publishing is a cutthroat business. But if he succeeds in scooping the market, you'll be famous. I hope you don't mind."

I had him. I knew it by the change in the quality of his voice as it came filtering along the line. It was suddenly older — more self-confident. More . . . famous: the voice of someone who, in his own head, was already speaking to the newsreel cameras.

"I understand, Miss de Luce. Tell Mr. . . . uh . . . Horatio that he can count on me."

"Thank you," I said. "May I express his appreciation?"

"Of course. Tell him I'm happy to be of service."

"Now about the photographs," I went on. "I'm sure you know which ones he's interested in?"

"I believe I do," he said. "The ones of the Wellingtons, and so forth?"

"Yes," I said. "Especially the *so forth*. I think he'd be happy to pay extra for those."

"I shall drop the photos in the post first thing tomorrow," Marlowe said. "Where shall I send them?"

I gave him my address at Buckshaw.

"For safety's sake," I told him. "Horatio's

mail is not secure. It's often intercepted by certain powers — the you-know-who. Horatio is a man of *many* secrets."

"I understand," James Marlowe said. "Tell him he can count on me."

"You've already said so," I told him. "But thank you again. He will be very much in your debt."

Although somehow I doubted it. Edgar Wallace had been dead for donkey's years; he had died before either of us was born. I was counting on the fact that Scout Marlowe hadn't yet heard the news.

I rang off suddenly and without another word. It would add a touch of mystery and urgency to my call.

I couldn't resist rubbing my hands with delight. I was proud of myself.

Now for Miss Louisa G. Congreve, of 47 Cranwell Gardens, Kensington.

Or what was left of her.

"Miss Runciman? It's Flavia de Luce again. I just wanted to thank you for locating Mr. Marlowe. It was most kind of you. I'll be sure to tell Father. Yes, he'll be absolutely delighted. Now then, I was wondering if you could connect me with London . . . Western 1778 . . . ?"

It was entirely possible, I knew, that the number had been reassigned, upon Louisa

Congreve's death, to someone else. It was a chance I had to take.

I listened as the telephone rang in distant Kensington. Between rings, the lines crackled with electric excitement, as if they were as eager as I was to find out who would pick it up at the other end.

"I'm afraid there's no answer," Miss Runciman said. "Shall I try again later?"

"No, please let it ring," I told her. "I'm sure there's someone there."

I wasn't sure at all, but I had learned long ago that if you don't take command, someone else will.

"Parties are often engaged in other pursuits," Miss Runciman said briskly, half to herself and half to me. It sounded like a line from the *Telephonist's Training Manual*.

I could think of only one response.

"Exactly," I said. "I was just thinking that myself."

After what must have been at least fifty rings, the telephone was picked up and a voice said, "Well, what is it now?"

A woman's voice. A woman who was not at all happy about being disturbed while doing whatever she had been doing.

"Miss Congreve?" I asked, dropping my voice into the lowest register I could manage without making my uvula come unstuck.

There came one of those silences so awkward as to make you blush.

"Miss Congreve is dead," the voice said at last. "Who is calling?"

I had to think more quickly than I've ever had to think before. The cogs of my mind sprang into action like a grandfather clock about to strike. If Western 1778 had, in fact, been reassigned to a complete stranger, they would have no way of knowing that it had previously belonged to Louisa Congreve, or that she was dead. Nor also would they have any interest in knowing who was calling.

Something was as fishy here as the stalls at Billingsgate market.

"I'm very sorry to hear that," I said. "I had something of very great importance to communicate to her."

The silence on the other end pinkened. I could feel it.

I was banking everything on something Dogger had once told me.

"Greed," he had said, "drives everything from the stock exchange to the Engagements column in *The Times*. It's a sad fact, Miss Flavia, but true. Nobody is immune."

"Well, perhaps I can help . . . ," the voice said, trailing off but wheedling just a little.

"Are you a relative of Miss Congreve's?" I asked, my mind changing in an instant from grandfather clock to bear trap.

"A distant one, but yes . . . a relative, to be sure. I was one of the beneficiaries to her will."

I was pitting my wits against a mastermind. Within seconds she had ingeniously constructed a conduit between an anonymous telephone call and her purse.

"May I ask your name?" I said. "I'm sorry, but it's required."

"Greene," she said. "Greene with an *e*. Letitia."

I spotted the lie at once. As a fibber myself, I could easily recognize the unnecessary detail, tacked on to add authenticity. Greene with an *e*, my aunt Fanny!

I could have done better with my tongue tied to my tootsies!

And Letitia! What kind of fool did she think she was dealing with? As if the added *e* weren't a dead giveaway, the exotic Christian name was a ploy as old as the Chilterns. As I have said, I have more than once myself appended a parasitic "Sabina" to my name for one reason or another — usually as a subtle warning shot to someone who has infringed upon my dignity.

"Thank you, Mrs. Greene," I said. "I've made a note of that. I shall —"

"*Miss* Greene," she interrupted. Even

aliases have their unwritten set of rules.

"Sorry," I said. "*Miss* Greene. Could you tell me, please, Miss Greene, if the late Miss Congreve held a ticket on last June's Irish Hospitals' Sweepstake?"

It was a shot in the dark, but a bull's-eye.

I don't know what made me think of Thornfield Chase and the dead man's bedroom, but I blurted it out anyway. Anything to keep the so-called Letitia Greene from ringing off.

If the silence had been pink before, it now became red-hot. The heat of it almost singed my ear.

"Miss Greene?"

"Sorry. I was woolgathering."

Woolgathering? What flesh and blood human could possibly let their mind wander off the instant a sweepstakes ticket is mentioned?

To give her credit, the woman recovered in half a tick. "Yes, I believe she did. Buy a ticket, I mean."

But it was too late. My trap was sprung!

How could someone, dead for years, have possibly held a recent sweepstakes ticket? There was, of course, an out, but I was not going to suggest it. It was not my place in life to throw a lifeline to a liar.

"The ticket was mine," the woman said.

194

"I bought it in Louisa's name because . . . well . . ."

Because lottery tickets are illegal, I thought.

"Because single ladies like to maintain their privacy," she went on. "I'm sure you understand."

"Of course," I said, in that smarmy voice which single ladies use in talking to one another. "Of course I do."

"Could you please read me the number on your ticket?" I asked.

I was now in top gear. There could be only one outcome to this conversation.

"I'm afraid I don't have it with me. It's in a safe-deposit box at my bank."

"Oh, dear," I said. "That's too bad. Can you retrieve it? Time is at a premium."

I almost hated to do it to her: the old thumbscrew, time-is-running-out maneuver.

Time being at a premium was an idea I had picked up by eavesdropping on a conversation between Father and an insurance agent from the Prudential.

"Time, Colonel de Luce," he had said, "is like the jaws of a vise. You and me and the little man in Notting Hill Gate, we are each and every one of us being squeezed out like paste between Past and Present."

It had not seemed to me a very apt comparison, but his point was clear: The clock

195

was ticking, the fuse burning ever shorter. Time was running out, and the only salvation was to sign on the dotted line before the clock struck twelve.

It was a useful technique, and this was my first opportunity to put it to the test.

"Twenty-four hours," I said. "It's the best I can do. Our Mr. Merton would be furious, but what he doesn't know can't hurt him, can it? We single ladies must stick together, mustn't we, Letitia?"

I gave a damp little snort of defiance.

"I shall call again tomorrow at the same time," I said.

And again, like a telephonic Grim Reaper, I dropped my finger onto the cradle and cut off the call.

ELEVEN

As I stepped out of the telephone cupboard, I collided with a body in the darkness. Both of us let out muffled *oof*s.

"Who is it?" I demanded. By the roughness of his clothing I knew that it was a man, but it wasn't Dogger.

"Dieter!" His voice hissed in my ear. "Shhh! Don't give me away."

"Dieter!" I whispered back, hugging him with all my heart and strength. "What are you doing here? How did you get in? What's all this about you and Feely busting up? I don't believe it."

"Neither do I," Dieter said. "For a while we are hiring the church, then suddenly we are strangers. Women are curious creatures."

"We only do it to annoy, because we know it teases," I said, paraphrasing the Duchess in *Alice's Adventures in Wonderland*. Although I was not yet a woman, I felt confident in my opinion. Based upon my close observation of the Divine Ophelia, I knew as much about womanly behavior as the most tortured of swains.

"But why?" Dieter asked.

I could hear the pain in his voice.

"I don't know yet," I said. "But I expect that one of these days I'll find out."

"When you do," Dieter said, "let me know."

"I will," I told him. "I promise."

Much as I wanted to, I did not quiz him about his row with Feely. There are some things that are sacred between a man and a woman, and which must not be pried into by outsiders.

Besides, I could read her diary whenever I wanted to. I simply hadn't got around to it yet.

As a former prisoner of war, Dieter did not have a wide circle of social acquaintances. He had remained in England to work as a farm laborer simply because he chose to. In a way, I suppose, men, also, are curious creatures.

Besides my sister, Feely, Dieter had one other love: the English language. He had once risked his life to drop a wreath from his swastikaed aircraft onto the Brontë family's home in Yorkshire.

"How's the teaching job coming along?" I

asked as I steered him out of the narrow passageway and into the foyer. "Any news from Greyminster?"

Father had put a word in with somebody at his old school, and it was expected that Dieter would before long be putting on cap and gown to teach *Wuthering Heights* to a pack of howling schoolboys.

"There is some mix-up with the papers," Dieter said.

I nodded sympathetically.

There was always trouble with papers. Father spent his entire life plodding through reams of the stuff with the Morlocks from His Majesty's Board of Inland Revenue Department: an ongoing game of cards called "Inheritance," in which the shuffling and the dealing never ceased, and in which the only possible winner could be the stationer who sold blank paper to the players.

"And Culverhouse Farm?" I asked. "Hens laying well, and all that sort of thing?" I hated myself for making the kind of small talk that I normally despise, but what can you say to a man whose heart has been shattered, when you have no easy words?

"I heard you found another corpse," Dieter said, breaking the deadly cycle of chitchat into which we had fallen. "Congratulations!"

I grinned happily. This was more like it.

Dieter was one of those rare persons who understood priorities.

"Thornfield Chase," I said. "It's out in your neighborhood. Man called Sambridge. A wood-carver. Hung upside down on the back of his bedroom door. Cause of death unknown — at least to me."

"Roger Sambridge? They say he was a bit of a ladies' man," Dieter said.

"Really?" I said. "I hadn't heard that."

"Well, it's what you might call farm talk. I don't expect the Altar Guild would have got wind of it."

"Ho! Ho! Ho!" I said. "If you think those witches can't sniff out a ladies' man at a thousand yards, you've got another think coming."

This was sheer speculation on my part. I didn't know much about the nonecclesiastical doings of the Altar Guild, but I had it on good authority from Mrs. Mullet that at least one or two of them "weren't no better than they ought to be."

"Anything more specific?" I asked. "My mind is like a racing engine tearing itself to pieces for want of data."

"No," Dieter said. "Not for want of data but 'because it is not connected up with the work for which it was built.' Sherlock Holmes, 'The Man with the Twisted Lip.' "

I stuck out my tongue at him. "Names, please."

"Well, don't say I told you so, but the name Lillian Trench has been mentioned."

"Trench? It doesn't ring any bells with me."

I thought I was on a first-name basis with everyone in Bishop's Lacey and environs — and beyond.

"She lives near Pauper's Well," Dieter said. "Bit of a recluse; she keeps to herself — or so I've heard," he added hastily.

"Not directly across the road from Thornfield Chase?" I asked.

"I believe so, yes."

Good lord! Could it have been Lillian Trench who had twitched the curtains at me as I made my getaway from Sambridge's house?

"Anything else?" I demanded.

"Well . . . you mustn't repeat this, but I've heard it said that she's a witch."

"Dieter, you're a brick!" I shouted. I couldn't help it.

Dieter looked as pleased as punch. To him, being called a brick by an English native was probably more precious than a knighthood.

I didn't tell him that Carl Pendracka had already come calling, and I didn't think I needed to. Dieter was already miserable enough without news of a rival.

"You still haven't answered my question," I said. "How did you get in?"

"I saw myself in by way of the front door," he said. "As a former fiancé, I thought that —"

"Hold on," I said. "Who said 'former'? Was it you?"

"Well, no. It was Ophelia who put it that way."

"Feely?" I laughed in scorn, like Errol Flynn in *Captain Blood.* "Ophelia? My idiot sister? What does *she* know about love and courtship? Nothing! She pounds the piano. Period! A to G-sharp. Seven octaves and a bit. Apart from that she's about as bright as a suet pudding.

"If you don't mind my saying so," I added.

Dieter began to laugh, but not very heartily. He broke it off abruptly, looking up and over my shoulder.

I pivoted round and followed his gaze.

There on the staircase, a long strand of her hair wrapped round her fist, her face ashen, stood Feely.

I won't take the trouble to describe the scene that followed, other than to say that it was not pleasant. My sister is capable of flights of drama that would make Joan Crawford and Bette Davis crawl away whipped and whimpering into their lairs.

Without bothering to excuse myself, I trudged past the battling lovers and up the stairs to bed, leaving the two of them pleading and glaring like characters in one of the more high-pitched operas.

It had been a long day.

Next morning, I made a point of being first down for breakfast. Feely would be drained from her battle with Dieter, and Daffy had been sluggish at breakfast ever since she learned to read. Midday to her was three o'clock in the morning, tented beneath the blankets with her trusty Eveready torch and something fat by Dickens.

"Good morning, Mrs. Mullet," I said cheerily, and probably too loudly.

The poor woman had troubles enough with Father ill and the household in disruption.

"Mornin', dear," she said. "Did you 'ave a good sleep?"

"Topping," I said. "I found another body — have you heard?"

"Course I've 'eard, dear. That sort of thing gets round like 'orses on fire. Can't say as

I'm surprised. There's them what does and them what watches 'em doin' it, if you take my meanin'."

I didn't, but I nodded knowingly.

"Like Lillian Trench," I said, leaving the choice to Mrs. Mullet.

" 'Er!" she said, slamming the sausages down in front of me. " 'Er! Don't you go meddlin' with the likes of 'er!"

"No," I said. "I haven't." And that was the truth.

So far.

"There are some people best stayed clear of, an' she's one on 'em."

"Because she's a witch?" I suggested.

"Oh? And where did you 'ear that?" Mrs. Mullet asked, too casually, but by the way she suddenly made herself busy with crumbs and a little brush, I knew that she had heard it, too.

"Oh, I don't know," I said. "Daffy might have mentioned it."

Daffy was not yet down for breakfast, and could not be questioned. In any case, Mrs. Mullet had been at Buckshaw long enough to know better than to become involved in the wars of the sisters de Luce.

"Were there cats, candles, and corpses — that sort of thing?" I asked innocently, skewering a poached egg with my fork.

My knowledge of witchcraft was limited to what I had learned from a book called *The Devil Rides Out* by Dennis Wheatley, which Daffy had read aloud to me last Christmas when I was recovering from a fall. It had frightened me so badly that I had been unable to close my eyes for a week.

"Worse than that!" Mrs. Mullet said. "But I shall say no more."

"Worse than that" meant sex. I was sure of it.

Although I wasn't well up on the topic of witchcraft, I knew enough to know that it was best left to people in books and others who had nothing better to do. Dancing round a bunch of moldy stones in a wet and windy field, naked, in the dark, was not exactly my idea of ecstasy.

"He was a wood-carver," I said, steering the conversation back to Mr. Sambridge. "Churches, and so forth. Angels and gargoyles."

I did not tell her about the leering cherubs Roger Sambridge had carved on his own bedstead; the ghastly wooden imps dragging him down into the flames of Hell.

And for the first time, I found myself wondering why he had done so. Did he think himself deserving of such a fate? Could he have committed so wicked a sin as to warrant eternal punishment?

But Mrs. Mullet was not to be drawn out by angels and gargoyles.

"They ought to be ashamed of themselves," she snorted. "My friend Mrs. Waller says bonfires is all right for Guy Fawkes Night, but outside o' that there's no good comes of frightnin' the cows and wakin' the chickens. Alf says people needs to let out steam after what they seen in the war, and 'e says a good romp in the 'ills is better than a steak in the ear, but 'e was in the Army, mind, and 'as seen things 'e can't talk about on pain of death, not even with the vicar — *specially* with the vicar, Alf says. Still, I say it isn't right, and you'd better stay away from that lot, Missy, mark my words, there's never no good comes of meddlin' with the Black Carts — that's what Alf calls 'em — no good tryin' to see into next week when your feet is still all tangled up in yesterday. If all that nonsense worked, Alf says, why don't they use it at the racetrack? Why don't they use it on the stork exchange?"

"Quite right, Mrs. Mullet," I said, pushing back my chair.

I was now more determined than ever to pay a visit to Lillian Trench's cottage. It would have to wait, of course, until after our hospital visit.

I found Dogger in the pantry. He was sitting on a wooden bench, his suit protected by a green apron, polishing Father's best boots.

"Are you taking those to him in the hospital?" I asked excitedly. "Is Father coming home today?"

"I'm afraid not, Miss Flavia. I've had a word with Matron this morning. She tells me he had rather a restless night. That is often the case. Pneumonia is an exhausting disease, not only for the patients, but also for their families."

"Which means we might not see him at all today," I said. Dogger's meaning was plain enough.

"Sometimes the greatest love can only be shown by staying away," Dogger said. "It is a difficult truth, but a truth nonetheless."

"I understand," I said. "Thank you, Dogger."

Although the snow had stopped, the stuff that had fallen overnight had frozen into a crisp crust. Gladys's Dunlop tires bit into it as eagerly as if it were no more than a few stiff egg whites. The road in front of St.

Tancred's was especially hazardous where morning traffic had formed a maze of icy ruts. I was picking my way carefully across this mess when a rather disreputable American Army jeep, traveling in the other direction, went into a skid and came to a spectacular stop at right angles to the road.

"Hiya, kid!" called a familiar voice. It was, of course, Carl Pendracka.

"My name is not kid," I said, as I dragged Gladys sideways across the jagged ruts and approached the jeep. "I'd appreciate if you'd refrain from using it."

"Just *kidding*," Carl said. "Just showing off a bit for Mordecai here."

He waved to indicate the person sitting next to him. All I could see was a pair of enormous eyeglasses. Mordecai was bundled to the nose with a khaki scarf, and wore a knitted tuque or jeep-cap. His every breath was visible in the cold air, giving him the look of a teapot covered with a cozy.

"Got some gen for you," Carl said. "You got a pencil?"

"I don't need a pencil," I told him. "I have my brain."

"Spunky little gal, ain't she?" Carl said, turning to Mordecai. "Almost as bad as her sister."

I gave Gladys's handlebars a sudden twist

and moved away.

"Hey! Hold on. Don't you want to hear what I have to tell you?"

"If you can do so without condescending to me," I replied, stopping, but not looking back.

"I'm sorry," Carl said. "Sometimes I'm so full of beans I get away on myself."

I trudged slowly back to the jeep, letting the lesson sink in.

"You wanted to know last May's Derby winner," Carl said. "Tell her, Mordecai?"

Mordecai's great glasses turned towards me, but he shook his head and said nothing.

"Mordecai's shy, aren't you, Mordecai? Nervous around women."

I could have pointed out that I'm not a woman, but then I would have had to add that I am not a girl, either. It's altogether too complicated to discuss, and so I kept my mouth shut.

"Arctic Prince," Carl said. "Wasn't it, Mordecai? Two minutes, thirty-nine and two-fifths seconds. Won it by six lengths. And do you know what?"

"No. What?" I asked.

"It was the richest running in Derby history. Twenty-eight-to-one odds. Paid off twenty-two thousand pounds."

I let out an admiring whistle. I couldn't help it.

Had Mr. Sambridge been a winner? The only way to know for certain would be to turn in his ticket. Aside from that —

"Anything about Mr. Sambridge?" I asked. If the dead wood-carver had suddenly come into money, surely someone would have noticed a change in his habits in the past six months.

"Hold on," Carl said. "You promised me something, remember? A deal's a deal."

"Of course I remember," I said. "I'm not a total imbecile, you know." I crossed my arms and glared at him.

"Ah, don't be sore, Flavia," he said. "I was just reminding you. Here, have a chaw."

He held out a package of Wrigley's Spearmint chewing gum, knowing full well that there were temptations that even *I* couldn't resist.

"Take two, they're small." He grinned, and I obeyed him — except that I took three to teach him a lesson.

Carl grinned again as I shoved the gum into my pocket.

Then he turned to Mordecai. "Refresh me," he said.

Mordecai leaned over and whispered into Carl's ear, the words coming out of his mouth in a string of miniature puffs of steam, like a train emerging from a tunnel.

"Bought Thornfield Chase five years ago," Carl repeated. "Paid three thousand pounds for it. Cash on the barrelhead. No trace of him before that. No military record, as far as we can see. Mordecai reckons the wood-carving's just a front — that he's actually a racketeer, dealing with dirty money, don't you, Mordecai?"

Mordecai's spectacles steamed up as he gave a frosty nod.

"Other than that, we know that he downed an occasional pint at the Goose and Garter, in East Finching. Always got a bit morose. 'Morose' — that's Rosie the barmaid's word, not mine. But she ought to know. By the way, I suppose you know this Sam-bridge's dead?"

I nodded, trying not to communicate more than was absolutely necessary.

"Funny thing," Carl said. "Just by co-incidence, he died the same day you asked me to get the goods on him."

"Hmmm," I said, trying to sound as if I were from St. Louis, Missouri, "is that a fact?"

Carl looked at Mordecai. Mordecai looked at Carl.

"Asking questions about a dead man —

or a soon-to-be-dead man — might not look so good. We're not going to be in hot water over this, are we? With the police, I mean."

"Golly," I said. "I hope not!"

And with that I turned, gave Gladys her head, and set off across the frozen wastes in the direction of Thornfield Chase.

The rising road to Pauper's Well was treacherous. In spite of a weak sun, the temperature was plummeting and a north wind rising. More than once, to keep from sliding backwards, I had to dismount and gain a footing in the crisp, frosty dead grass at the roadside.

I should have dressed more warmly; I admit it. Mrs. Mullet was always going on about the need to bundle up. "Never get your kidneys cold," she would say. "Cold kidneys is killers, and I don't mean them as what's on a plate."

I could appreciate her concern, but what would it look like to investigate a murder wearing mittens? I would simply have to make do by blowing into my closed fists one at a time.

I leaned into the wind, puffing and panting, my lungs stinging from the cold air. The turnoff to Stowe Pontefract and Thornfield Chase could not come soon enough.

When I reached it at last, I was surprised to see fresh tire marks: so fresh, in fact that the slight watery residue caused by the vehicle's passing had not yet had time to refreeze. With icy roads, I knew, most drivers going to and from Stowe Pontefract would use the much more gentle road to the east, towards Malden Fenwick. And yet, two cars, it appeared, had passed this way: one coming and one going.

No! Hold on — it was the same car. It had either arrived from the direction of Bishop's Lacey and then returned, or had gone towards the village and then come back.

Its tire tracks — identical — sometimes ran apart and sometimes together as the car was driven in and out of the ruts.

The arrival and departure must have been at about the same time, since the watery slush was of about the same consistency in both directions.

The freezing of water, I know, depends upon air temperature. Had there been more than, say, a quarter of an hour between the car's arrival and departure, the earlier tracks would have had time to freeze harder than the later.

Such was the theory, anyway. With a sharply dropping temperature, to work out the actual effect would probably take seven Oxford mathematicians, working with seven pencils, seven years.

I noted simply that a car had come and gone in rather a short space of time.

When I reached Thornfield Chase, it all became quite clear. The car had turned in at the gates, stopped, and backed out into the road, now facing in the other direction. A passenger had emerged on the offside, and a single set of footprints led away — not towards Mr. Sambridge's house, but rather to the cottage across from it.

The house with the twitching lace curtains.

TWELVE

There is an art to staging a convincing accident. It is not as easy as you may think — particularly on short notice. First and foremost, it must look completely natural and spontaneous. Secondly, there must be nothing comical about it, since comedy saps sympathy.

I had but a fraction of a second to think before putting my plan into effect.

As I crossed the set of footprints at the cottage gate, I lurched in my seat and let one elbow come up, apparently by accident, yanking Gladys's handlebars to one side and launching her into a vicious skid which I then tried madly to correct by applying the opposite handlebar, but it was too late. Fighting for balance, I slewed and skidded this way and that, seeming sometimes almost to gain control and then to lose it again. The result was a spectacular series of vicious fishtails, slipping and sliding from side to side on the road like a drunken skater before leaving it entirely and hurtling across the ditch to land with an alarming crash and a clatter in a holly hedge with Gladys, her wheels spinning crazily, on top of me.

I lay perfectly still while I counted to twenty. Death must appear to be a very real possibility, and if not death, then at least a serious coma.

At last I opened one eye just a crack and risked a peek. One of the curtains had been lifted and a white, shocked face was staring out at me, a hand covering its mouth, aghast.

Why was Lace Curtains not rushing outside to see if I was all right?

I needed to go into Act Two of my little drama.

While raising my head slowly and painfully, using both hands to give it a series of slow chiropractic adjustments, I was able to note that the derelict Austin at Thornfield Chase had not been moved. There were, as I suspected there would be, no footprints in the snow. Nor had the police visited this morning. The only tracks on the scene were those of the car that had dropped Lace Curtains off at the gate, and the single set of prints that led from there to the door of the cottage.

Painfully, lifting Gladys out of the way, I climbed into a kneeling position, hanging on to the holly hedge to assist me. In fact, I didn't really have to act too much: I had taken more of a battering than I expected. My hands and face were scratched by the holly and my bones felt as if they had been dumped into a sack and shaken.

Authenticity comes at a cost.

I unwound my scarf and wrapped it round my head, taking care to cover one eye. A couple of holly berries, secretly seized and crushed between thumb and finger, provided an admirable substitute for additional blood, which I smeared dramatically on the far side of my face while adjusting my makeshift bandage.

That done, I hauled myself fully to my feet, staggered across the road and up the path, and banged on the door.

I listened intently but there was not a sound from inside. No footsteps, no voice calling out for me to wait. Nothing.

I banged again, harder this time.

"Help!" I shouted.

I know it wasn't the most original thing to call out, but it was short and to the point.

I put my ear to the door and was immediately overcome with the most odd feeling. It was as if someone on the other side had their ear to the door also — no more than an inch from my own. I could almost feel the warmth — almost hear their heartbeat.

I gave the spot a good raking with my fingernails — which, thankfully, I had begun to grow again since being transported to Canada and back. The wooden grating sound so close to the ear would be sickening to the listener on the other side, as if I were gnawing through the door with my teeth.

"Help!" I pleaded, more weakly this time, vibrating my lips with a forefinger to add a bubbly quality to my voice. If my calculations were correct, it would sound as if I were suffering a bronchial hemorrhage.

And by all that is holy, it worked!

A bolt clicked, the knob turned, the door came slightly open, and an eye appeared — a flustered eye, which looked me up and down.

"Yes?" asked a voice. "What is it?"

"I fell on your ice," I said, pointing painfully with my thumb. The "your" was a masterstroke. With just four letters and a single syllable it raised the twin specters of blame and a possible lawsuit.

The eye, now looking frightened, shifted

focus to the road and back again.

"You'd better come in," the voice said, and the door came open, but barely wide enough to allow me to squeeze inside.

The woman who stood facing me was no taller than I am, although her short hair was completely gray. She was dressed rather smartly and entirely in black: black jumper set with dainty black pearls and earrings, black skirt, black shoes, and I saw at once that what I had mistaken for fear in her eyes was, in fact, grief.

This, without doubt, was Lillian Trench, the witch — even though she didn't look like one.

I judged her to be about the same age as Cynthia Richardson, or perhaps a bit older, which made her about forty. There was something vaguely familiar about the woman, but I could not for the moment think what it was. Had she been at the recital at which Carla had sung? Or had I, perhaps, met her — or at least seen her, unlikely as it might seem — somewhere in Canada?

As I waited for Miss — or was it Mrs.? — Trench to speak, I had a quick look round before she found an opportunity to chuck me out. We were standing in rather a cramped and overheated hall: a bedraggled hanging fern, an ebony bench with coat rack, umbrella stand with two black umbrellas, a cast-iron frog which I guessed was a doorstop, and a coconut mat upon which were placed a pair of galoshes. A pair of *wet* galoshes. Ladies' galoshes.

Three doors opened off the little room, all of them presently closed.

I could hear the woman breathing.

"Are you all right?" she asked at last.

It was one of those questions to which a wrong answer could result in the loss of empires; the kind of question that comes up time and again in fairy tales.

"Are you all right?" she asked again, a little more impatiently this time.

"I — I'm not sure," I said. "I think I need to lie down."

It was a clever maneuver.

Had I asked to sit, she would have parked me on the seat of the hall-stand. To let me lie down, she would need to open one of the three closed doors and allow me into her inner sanctum.

She looked at me intently, making a decision. With my head still half swathed in my scarf and the backs of my hands covered with bloody scratches, I must have looked a fright.

"Very well, then," she said, raising her

voice to an unnecessary loudness. "You'd better come in."

She paused, as if to count to three, before opening the door on the right.

We passed slowly — the woman leading me — into a small drawing room, where she walked me to a Victorian horsehair sofa. I lowered myself and began to lift my feet.

"No, wait —" she said, eyeing my wet galoshes, and reached for a newspaper.

Today's *Times,* I noted.

"Put this under your feet."

I obeyed, peering meekly out at her from beneath my makeshift bandage.

"Let's have a look at you," she said, reaching out to remove it. I shrank back.

"No," I said. "I could have concussion. I'm seeing double at times."

Thanks to my Girl Guide training, I was able to bluff convincingly when required. All those wet and windy Wednesday evenings spent in cold, drafty parish halls were paying off at last.

"Could I please have a glass of water?" I asked, then quickly: "No, sorry. I think tea would be better."

I had no idea whether this was true or not, but it sounded plausible. Besides, tea took longer to make: With water, she'd be back too quickly.

"Hot, sweet tea may be beneficial in cases of shock," I added, trying to give my words that condescending and slightly snotty tone that first-aid manuals have, as if I were quoting from something I had memorized.

She started for the door, then stopped. "What's your name?" she asked.

I waited for several moments, as if racking my brains for the correct answer.

"De Luce," I said, slowly. "Flavia de Luce."

"I thought so."

And with that, she left the room.

There was no time to waste. I sprang to my feet and pressed an ear to the door panel.

Nothing but silence on the other side.

I made a quick survey of the room. Nothing unusual caught my eye — at least at first. I ran my fingers along the gap behind the upholstered seat of the sofa and came up with thruppence ha'penny and a chromium cigar clipper.

Aha! Gentlemen guests.

I peeled back the carpet: a prime hiding place for personal papers, as I knew from my own experience. Nothing under it but dust and grit. Lillian would win no prizes for housekeeping.

A small library housed on a couple of

bookshelves contained just what you would expect to find in a cottage: Dickens, Trollope, Sir Walter Scott, Thackeray, Tennyson, Ethel Mannin, Elizabeth Goudge, E. M. Delafield, Christie, Marsh, and — I must admit my heart gave a little gazelle-like leap — *Hobbyhorse House.*

I remembered something Daffy had once told me:

"One can learn from a glance at a person's library, not what they are, but what they wish to be."

Almost on instinct I plucked the book from the shelf and flipped it open to the title page:

"To Elsie," it said, *"with love and yarning."*

And it was signed, in mauve ink, by the author: Oliver Inchbald.

Elsie? Who on earth was Elsie? And what could *yarning* mean? Storytelling? Yearning? Or did Oliver Inchbald and Elsie used to knit together?

Time was running out. Lillian Trench would be back at any instant with the tea.

A quick scan of the fireplace and the hearth showed none of the witchlike implements you would expect: no cauldron hanging from an iron hook, no besom broomstick, no bundles of mandrake roots dangling at the end of a cord to dry — not so much as a trace of a black cat.

But then, I realized, a modern-day witch would work at a bank in the city. She would be a wizard at shorthand, listen to Nat King Cole on the wireless, drive a Morris Minor tourer, type up her spells on alphabetical index cards, and buy her potions — along with her Number Seven complexion milk and foundation lotion — at Boots the Chemists.

Cats, brooms, and pointed hats would be as out of fashion nowadays as whalebone corsets.

The room was disappointingly bare of clues. All that remained to search was a horrid oak sideboard: the kind of thing which would be stuffed, I knew, with Victorian sheet music, smelly Georgian chamber pots, boxes of tarnished silver cutlery, and candles and safety matches for when the lights fused.

From the kitchen came the rattle of china, signaling that tea was on the way. There was no time left for further investigation. I needed to get back to the sofa with my feet on the newspaper before Lillian Trench returned. While I was no more superstitious than the next person, I knew that snooping through the belongings of a witch might not be the healthiest of occupations.

In the seconds remaining, and in one last attempt to gather even a crumb of information, I flung open the front doors of the sideboard.

Inside, folded up like an accordion, his knees tucked up against his chin, was a person whom I took at first to be a leprechaun. A shock of white hair gave him an ageless and somehow childlike look.

His head turned slowly and he gazed out at me, his big, sad eyes made even larger by the impossibly thick glass of his spectacles.

"Ah," he said, his voice like a ghost in a bottle. "You've found me."

Then slowly, and wincing with pain, he unfolded himself into the room, as if he were an aviator emerging from his cramped cockpit after a record-breaking ocean flight.

I recognized him instantly, of course.

It was Hilary Inchbald . . . better known as Crispian Crumpet.

At one time, and perhaps still even now, the most famous boy in the world.

What do you say to someone who is as well-known as the King of England?

And then I remembered that I had actually met the King of England: his Royal Highness George the Sixth, who had turned out to be a lovely man, and not at all like his pictures. He had first thanked me for

225

returning a rare and stolen stamp to him and then gone on to chat for much of the afternoon about potassium and, rather sadly, I thought, the ways of the wasp in winter.

As I have said — an altogether lovely man.

I was still searching for words when Lillian Trench pushed open the door with her behind and entered the drawing room carrying a tea tray.

"Ah, Hilary," she said. "Had I known you were going to join us, I'd have brought an extra cup."

She seemed not at all surprised to find me off the sofa.

"You've made a remarkable recovery," she said, with an amused glance at the scarf in which half of my head and one eye was still wrapped.

Sheepishly, I unwound the thing and stuffed it into my pocket, stepping somewhat clumsily out of her way.

"Mind the Auditories," she said, placing the tray on the table. "They're difficult to see against the pattern of the carpet, but they do tend to get underfoot, the dear silly things."

I must have gaped at her.

"The Auditories," she explained, pouring milk into her tea and raising an eyebrow to ask if I wanted the same. "The Listeners."

I knew, of course, the poem by Mr. de la Mare in which a traveler knocks at the door of an abandoned house by night. Daffy had scared the blue daylights out of me by reading it aloud barely before I was out of the cradle.

"You may not believe in them," Lillian Trench continued, "but that doesn't mean you aren't stepping on them."

I stared hard at the carpet. Had something shifted against the pattern?

It was hard to say, but it made me feel uneasy.

Crispian Crumpet — or Hilary Inchbald, I should say — meanwhile stood quietly by.

If I were being asked to describe him in a word, as we often were in the rowdy and frequently violent Girl Guide game of *Name Your Poison,* I should have said *"insignificant."*

His whole being seemed to be apologizing for being there, and it was this uncanny sense of his being simultaneously present and absent that made me think I had seen him before. Had it been in the photos Frank Borley had shown me at the offices of Lancelot Gath, in London? I was too startled to think properly, and set the idea aside for another occasion.

What was Hilary Inchbald doing at Lillian Trench's cottage? Why had he been hiding in the sideboard?

One of these two people, I knew, had just come down from London, arriving no more than minutes ahead of me. I needed time to sort things out, and it seemed to me that the best way to do so was to remain in this house for as long as I could possibly manage.

Most people, I suppose, would shy away from commenting on someone who had just crawled out of a cupboard, but I am not most people.

"You must be very stiff and sore," I said. Judging by his posture and the way he was rubbing his wrists, this was obvious enough.

"Would you like me to rub your shoulders?" I asked, risking all.

Hilary Inchbald looked at me with surprise in his enormous eyes.

"Yes, thank you," he said, sitting down on a chair, trying to keep his crooked back straight.

I moved behind him and gently took hold of his shoulders. His bones were tiny, bowed and birdlike beneath my fingers, and I could have cried.

"Quite cold suddenly, isn't it?" I asked, with a glance at Lillian Trench, who was sipping her tea as calmly as if she were a duchess at a Buckingham Palace garden party.

No doubt about it: She was a cool customer.

Neither of them replied, but I could already feel Hilary Inchbald's muscles begin to relax under my probing fingers.

"They say it's to be westerly for Rockall, veering northwesterly, force six to nine, with occasional gusts to force ten," I said, desperate to keep the talk going.

I had gathered the information from the Shipping Forecast on the wireless.

Could this be Flavia de Luce speaking? Flavia de Luce — who despises small talk as the mongoose despises the snake — prattling on about the stupid weather in some godforsaken corner of the ocean simply in order to give artificial respiration to a dying conversation?

You can imagine my relief when Hilary Inchbald said, "Yes. Yes, I believe that is so."

All this civility was getting on Lillian Trench's nerves. I knew this by the way she put down her cup with a saucer-cracking clatter.

"You were seen . . . the day before yesterday . . . coming out of Thornfield Chase," she said, thrusting her chin forward into a slightly accusing position.

"I know I was," I said. "I saw your curtains move."

Two could play at this game.

Again the air went slightly frigid. I could already see that conversation with this woman was doomed to lurch along in a series of freezes and thaws, like all of the earth's Ice Ages advancing and receding and advancing again in speeded-up motion, as in a comedy from the days of the silent cinema.

A yowl and a scratching behind me made me turn round. Outside on the windowsill, a cat of many colors was standing full length on its back legs, clawing at the window frame.

"Oh, Thomas More," Lillian Trench said, moving quickly to raise the sash. "There you are. I thought you were —"

So the woman *did* have a cat after all. At least, I assumed it was hers, since cats don't cry at doors or windows other than their own.

The cat stepped in through the transom with as little regard for any of us as royalty has for the anonymous footman who holds open a door.

My scalp was already prickling with recognition as I realized that this marbled cat —

this Thomas More — was the same cat I had seen in the room where I had found Mr. Sambridge hanging dead behind the door.

I was sure of it.

"Thomas More is inclined to wander," Lillian Trench said, as if an explanation were necessary.

The cat ignored her and went straight to Hilary Inchbald, looking up at him adoringly, making little cries of pleasure as it rubbed against his legs.

The sound of its purring seemed to fill the room.

Hilary bent over and lifted the cat into his arms. They began to nuzzle each other in a way which might have been censored had they been a man and woman in a cinema film.

Still, in spite of that, I had to give him credit: He knew how to hold the animal correctly, with one hand spread under it to cradle its breastbone, the other making a firm ledge for its back feet. Altogether unlike those ignoramuses who dangle their pets as if they were a cargo of rice sacks being hoisted by a crane from dock to deck on an East China steamer.

This man knew cats.

Thomas More bumped the top of his head

against the underside of Hilary's chin.

It was obvious that the affection was mutual.

That should have told me something, but it didn't. The significance of this rather odd scene — Hilary Inchbald, Lillian Trench, and Thomas More — did not come until it was almost too late.

Perhaps it was the unreality of the day — the Mad-Hatter's-tea-party feel about the place — that threw me off the beam. I was *disorientated,* as Alf Mullet puts it: lost in a twilight world which I wasn't sure was not mostly of my own making.

I took a deep breath and forced myself to organize my thoughts.

What *was* this strange woman to Hilary Inchbald, I wondered, and he to her? What could they possibly have in common, these two odd ducks, one of them allegedly a witch and the other no more than a pale shadow in a mirror?

"Did you know Mr. Sambridge well?" I asked.

It was a bold shot out of the blue, calculated to shake up the situation; otherwise, we might have sat there all day talking of the weather, tea, and cats.

Lillian Trench glanced first at Hilary Inchbald, and then at me. And then she put down her cup.

"Get out," she said.

"I beg your pardon?" I asked.

"Get out."

I'll admit I was flabbergasted. Other than by my own sisters, I had never in my life been chucked out of a place. How awkward it felt, and how awful.

I turned to Hilary, hoping he might intervene, but my hopes were dashed immediately.

Hilary Inchbald was in tears, his frail shoulders shaking, his face pressed tightly into the tortoiseshell fur of Thomas More.

I took a step towards him, wanting nothing more than to throw my arms around him and hug him, to rub his back and say "There, there," and perhaps, even, to ask him what the matter was.

"Get out!" Lillian Trench shrieked, her eyes blazing, her voice seeming to come in blue smoke from the trenches of Hell, and in that moment, I knew that she really was a witch.

And so I did what anyone else in her right mind would do.

I got out.

THIRTEEN

I crunched my way cautiously across the icy road and, with a few words of whispered comfort, retrieved Gladys from her entanglement with the holly hedge.

Were my feelings hurt? Of course they were, and so would yours have been.

What hurt the most, though, was the fact that Lillian Trench had seen through me. She had not for a moment believed that I had fallen off Gladys and injured myself. She had known — or at least suspected — from the beginning that my "accident" was no more than an act. I was quite sure of it. In a day when everyone in England over the age of five had received some kind of Red Cross training, she had not offered so much as a sticking plaster.

Why then, had she invited me into her cottage? What had she hoped to gain by it?

Information?

If that were the case, she certainly had a

strange way of going about it.

And then I was struck with this horrible thought: *What if she had poisoned the tea?*

The usual effect of holly berries upon adults is much the same as prunes, only more so, although the berries may be fatal to children if eaten in quantity. Their poisonous element, theobromine, is contained also in cocoa, which Daffy says might explain why chocolate is so often given to children at bedtime.

There was much to think about here, but now was not the time.

It seemed unlikely that Lillian Trench, if she were a competent witch at all, would have slipped me a cup of holly berry tea. No, she would have used something far, far more subtle.

In the coming hours I would need to pay very close attention to my pulse, my vision, my taste, and my hearing — all of my senses, in fact. At the slightest sign of numbness I would ring up (a) Dr. Darby and (b) Inspector Hewitt, then race to my laboratory to concoct an antidote.

When it comes to poisoning, planning is paramount.

"Isn't it, Gladys?" I asked, giving her an affectionate pat between the handlebars to make up for having abandoned her in a freezing holly hedge.

Ahead was Pauper's Well, where I would need to make a decision.

I didn't much fancy an icy downhill run with the north wind at my back and, to be perfectly frank, I didn't really want to go home.

To the right — and not that far away — was the village of East Finching, where Rosie, the talkative barmaid at the Goose and Garter, might be willing to fill my ears with tales of the "morose" Mr. Sambridge.

I turned to the north and gave Gladys her head.

The going was grueling, pedaling against the freezing gusts. A shifting crosswind made it even more tricky, and by the time I reached the high street of East Finching, I was in need of a blazing fire.

I would walk, all rosy-cheeked, into the warmth of the saloon bar at the Goose and Garter and order a pint of hot Ovaltine, then treat myself to a dish of Christmas trifle. My salivary glands were already hanging out of my face at the thought.

Such is the stuff as dreams are made on.

The Goose and Garter turned out to be a villainous, cold, dark den with low ceilings which smelled of damaged drains and old mutton fat. A fierce draft from a broken window — crudely patched with what appeared to be the sole of an old boot — made it seem even colder than the out-of-doors.

Two old codgers in flat caps looked up from their game of checkers, then bowed their heads again in play. One of them muttered something to the other from the side of his mouth, but I could not make out the words.

A halfhearted fire guttered in the grate, as if it couldn't decide whether to stay or go out. For the moment it seemed content to spew smoke into the room, reducing the visibility to an arm's length.

A bare arm appeared out of the gloom, and then a large, red, hovering face topped with a Union Jack bandanna.

"Age?" the face demanded.

"Fourteen," I lied, without batting an eye. "Last Thursday."

"And I'm the Queen of the Royal Marines. What would you like?"

"August, please," I said, "and a plate of summer sunshine."

"Sorry, luv," the woman said, without missing a beat. "It's off the menu till next summer."

She looked me fiercely in the eye until I laughed.

"You must be Rosie," I said.

"Who sez?" she demanded, propping her arm on her hip.

This was not going to be easy.

"Mordecai," I told her.

"Ah, well, then. I must be. Mordecai is never wrong. Friend of yours, is he?"

"Not exactly," I said. "He's a friend of a friend."

She examined her fingernails. "That would be Carl Pendracka."

"A neat bit of deduction," I said with a smile, and I meant it.

"Not so much as you might think. Mordecai only has the one friend."

Like so many of us, I thought.

"You're the one was asking about Roger Sambridge."

I admitted that I was.

Rosie pulled out a chair and sat down beside me. "He's a rum bloke," she said. "Or at least he *was,* and I'm blowed if I know the reason why. Started coming in here last summer. Used to wander in of a night, sit over there in that chair with the short leg, with his back to the corner, have three half-pints of half-and-half, and never say a word. Seemed as if he was watching people. Sometimes he'd haul out a little pocket diary and pencil and write something down. 'You a reporter, then?' I asked him once, and the devil snarled at me. Snarled! 'Arggghhh!' Like one of those pirates, Long John Silver, or someone. He put his book away quick, before I could get a good look at it. I thought he might be making those lightning sketches for the newspapers, but it was writing he was doing, not drawing. I asked Bert Blaney one time — Bert used to be a churchwarden at St. Barnaby's over in Beeching Norton before his accident. Anything you ever wanted to know about the Church of England, you could ask Bert. Make your hair curl. Anyway, Bert said he — Sambridge, I mean, not Bert — was a church wood-carver. Specialized in misericords — you know the things I mean, those little devils under the seats in the choir. Wicked-looking little imps. Never could stand the sight of them myself. Give me the jimjams, kind of like invisible bats in your hair or a goose walking over your grave."

She gestured, with a nervous laugh, to a miniature above the bar of the inn's painted signpost, THE GOOSE AND GARTER, in which an enraged goose had seized hold of a frowzy — but laughing — barmaid's garter, which it was stretching to incredible lengths. One was expected, I suppose, to smile at the thought of what would happen when the goose let go.

"So you never chatted him up, then?" I asked.

"Good heavens, no! He wasn't the chatty type. Morose, is the word. That's what I told Mordecai. 'Morose, he is,' I said. 'Makes it plain he doesn't want company.' "

"Or questions," I said.

"Good point," Rosie said, biting at a blood-red thumbnail. "I never thought of that.

"Besides," she added, "he had such fierce arthritis you were always afraid of treading on one of his toes, or banging his legs, or something. Odd occupation, isn't it, for someone like him — having to hang about in those damp, drafty old churches?"

An image flashed into my mind of Mr. Sambridge hanging about on the back of his bedroom door. Did Rosie know more than she was letting on? I couldn't imagine that Inspector Hewitt had yet made public the details of the death chamber.

"Perhaps it was the pain that made him so miserable," I said.

"No, I don't think so," Rosie said. "There's pain that comes from the body and pain that comes from the heart. This was heart pain. Take my word for it. I'm older than you. I know about these things."

Ordinarily, I'd have considered her words

a slap on the wrist, but Rosie's face told me that she was speaking the truth.

I nodded — wisely, I hoped.

"How about Lillian Trench?" I asked suddenly, blurting it out on a whim.

"Her? The weekend witch? All I know is what I've heard, which isn't good. She lives in London and comes down for the full moon and the mummers."

I knew what she meant. Clarence Mundy, our taxicab driver, who had taken the part of the Hobbyhorse in the Bishop's Lacey Horn Dance — and had done so since time immemorial, except for his war service as a flying-boat pilot — was always grumbling about what he called "Horn Gawkers": those tourists who, thinking us quaint and backward villagers, came down for every winter solstice with their kit and Kodaks and littered the churchyard with their droppings.

"Like Canada geese, they are," Clarence would say. To which he would usually add a truly rude comment which I cannot reproduce here, much as I'd like to.

The Horn Dance dated back to the Middle Ages, and the Hobbyhorse, who made daring — and sometimes quite frightening — dashes at the spectators, was one of the most popular figures. It had not occurred to me until this very moment that Oliver Inchbald's book *Hobbyhorse House* was linked, at least by name, with the ancient dance at Bishop's Lacey.

Did this mean anything, or was it simply a coincidence?

And then another thought struck me: The Horn Dance was held every year on the winter solstice, which would fall, this year, on the twenty-second of December.

Which was today.

"I'm sorry," I said, leaping to my feet. "I've just remembered an appointment. I'd forgotten all about it."

"Happens to the best of us," Rosie said, getting to her feet. "Go in safety," she said. "They say the roads are deadly."

Rosie was right. The falling temperature had reduced the road to a ribbon of dark ice. In the end, I had to walk Gladys down the long hill and back to Bishop's Lacey. By the time we reached the village, it was afternoon.

In spite of the cold, a merry crowd had already gathered in the churchyard to watch the players climb into their costumes.

"No fair peeking now," Bert Archer called from the east door. "We always dress up in the vestry, and you're not allowed to look till we're ready."

Bert took the part of Hector: "A Rude Mechanical," as the character was described in the history of the play that the vicar had written to sell to the tourists for tuppence.

As Cynthia had confided, because these now cost ten pence each to print, the vicar had to make up the difference out of his own pocket.

"Prices unchanged since before the war," he used to call out to potential buyers as he went among the crowd hawking his little booklets in the churchyard.

Tully Stoker, already dressed in the Stag Man costume, crept from behind a chest tomb and into the west porch where, I knew, he would strap a great wobbling array of antlers onto his head.

After the dance he would return them to hang for the rest of the year in their traditional place in the bell tower, where visitors could view, with a shudder, for an extra penny, their impressive expanse and wickedly sharp points.

As I crossed the churchyard the music began. The tune, the traditional "Wot Sonn," which had once been played on homemade sackbuts, drums, hurdy-gurdies, and bagpipes, was now performed by members of the Bishop's Lacey Silver Band on modern cornets, tubas, and trombones made by Boosey & Hawkes in London.

It is not just cold weather that can make you shiver, I thought.

A hand seized my arm so roughly that my liver tried to escape.

"Flavia! What are you doing here?"

It was Carla Sherrinford-Cameron.

"It's my parish," I replied rather testily, shaking off her hand and sweeping my arm round in a broad circle for emphasis. "I was baptized here. My ancestors are buried here.

"And you?" I asked, not in the nicest tone of voice.

"Miss Lavinia and Miss Aurelia arranged an invitation for me to sing," she said. "Isn't it exciting? I'm doing 'Hark, the Horn.' "

"Splendid," I said, even though I thought I was going to vomit.

Why on earth would anyone invite an outsider like Carla — someone from Hinley, for heaven's sake! — to take one of the key parts in the Horn Dance: a role which had been performed exclusively by the girls and women of Bishop's Lacey since the British Lion was a kitten?

Carla was wearing a winter coat to which what appeared to be hundreds of dead oak leaves had been fastened with safety pins. In spite of the freezing air, her face glowed like a Sunday School stove.

"Miss Aurelia usually sings the part herself, but she's been stricken with a bit of tummy trouble at the last minute, and Miss Lavinia asked me to step in and fill her shoes."

I'm afraid I had rather an uncharitable thought, but I won't repeat it here.

"I've been to Bishop's Lacey so often this week that I'm beginning to feel like a native," Carla burbled. Her forehead was already covered with an oily sheen, even though the singing had not yet begun.

"Perhaps you'll be buried here, too," I said, and turned away. There is only so much that the human mind can endure.

Miss Lavinia came pushing her way through the crowd, casting horrible toothy smiles to the left and right like the sower with his seed. She was dressed in an ancient suffragette outfit which, ruffled lace and all, had gone brown with the years, and as she passed, the biting north wind brought to my nostrils the odor of naphthalene ($C_{10}H_8$) moth tablets, whose chemical makeup, I recalled with pleasure, had been described in 1826 by the great Michael Faraday.

Miss Lavinia whispered a few words to Carla, who plunged her hand into a coat pocket and pulled out an ancient throat sprayer. After an apologetic smile to the crowd, she gave a wide yawn that displayed her tonsils, stuck the silver nozzle deep into her mouth, gave the rubber bulb a couple of businesslike squeezes, arranged her adenoids, and gave the signal that she was ready. I could smell her breath even from where I stood.

Miss Lavinia fished a pitch pipe from a tiny handbag of beaded black jet and blew a frail note.

And Carla, clasping her hands, began to sing.

"Hark the horn, the sound of winter
Hark the hunter on the hill . . ."

Actually, the way she sang it was:

"Har-ar-ar-ar-ar-ark the horn, the
    sow-ow-ownd of winter
Har-ar-ar-ar-ar-ar — ark the
    hun-un-un-un-un-un-ter
    ah-hah-hah-hah-hon the
    hihhih-ill-ill-ill-ill-ill-ill . . ."

To suggest the steepness of the hill, Carla caused the intensity and pitch of her voice to rise until it was almost beyond the range of human hearing.

Distant dogs would be raising their ears in

their sleep.

Meanwhile, Miss Lavinia was conducting with both hands, glorying in the moment, and I wondered vaguely if Miss Aurelia's tummy were as upset as mine.

Carla was still at it:

"Air the speeding arrow doth splinter
Flying forth to make the kill."

To be perfectly honest, she had not too bad a voice between the gasps.

It was the custom that "Hark, the Horn" was sung unaccompanied, and as Carla's voice cracked the cold air, the members of the Bishop's Lacey Silver Band fiddled with their instruments, blew into their hands, and stamped their feet to keep warm.

I caught a quick glimpse of Feely's face among the tourists.

What is she doing here, I wondered, *with Father so gravely ill in hospital?*

But then I thought, *What am* I *doing here?* and I forgave her.

When at last Carla finished her song, there was a smattering of light applause, accompanied by more than a few heavy sighs of relief, one of them mine.

Turning to each of the cardinal points of the compass, Carla and Miss Lavinia took their bows, fetching up their skirts with thumbs and forefingers, crossing their ankles, and sinking into curtsies as overcooked as if they were a pair of rival ballerinas taking their umpteenth curtain call at the Royal Opera House.

As her audience drifted away, Carla made for me like a homing bee.

"Well done," I said, having a fried egg in mind.

"Oh, thank you!" she said, blushing. "I am so pleased to have delighted you."

Gaaaaaakkkkkk! I thought. Was someone feeding her this stuff?

"Listen," I said. "While the crowd's out here, I'm going to sneak into the church for a close look at the misericords and the gargoyles. Would you care to join me?"

Once inside, I could easily shift the topic from woodcarvings to wood-carver, and why her signed copy of *Hobbyhorse House* had been at the dead man's bedside.

"N-no," she said. "Miss Lavinia says if I am to be a truly great singer, I must look only at beautiful things."

"And do you?" I asked. I could be merciless when I felt like it.

"Mostly, yes," she said.

"Tell me about the others," I said. "What's the least beautiful thing you've ever seen?"

"I shouldn't like to say," she said, blushing.

"Have you ever been to Stowe Pontefract? Or to Thornfield Chase?"

"I — I have to go now. Miss Lavinia will be —"

"You ought to, you know," I told her. "The holly hedges there are very beautiful. They ought to improve your singing no end."

I couldn't help myself.

But I could have said more. Oh, so much more.

FOURTEEN

Perhaps I was too hard on Carla. When I realized I was treating her the way Feely and Daffy treated me, I broke off the conversation and walked away, curiously disappointed in myself.

Giving someone the benefit of the doubt is not so simple as it sounds. What it means, in fact, is being charitable — which, as the vicar is fond of pointing out, is the most difficult of the graces to master. Faith and hope are a piece of cake but charity is a Pandora's box: the monster in the cistern which, when the lid is opened, comes swarming out to seize you by the throat.

Carla could not help it that she was nauseating: the kind of person who makes your pores snap shut and your gullet lower the drawbridge.

Most irritating, however, had been the fact that I could not winkle out her connection with Thornfield Chase and Mr. Sambridge.

Until just now, that is.

It was the thought of the holly that must have done it.

I needed time to think.

With eyes fixed firmly on the ground to make myself invisible, I made my way to the west door of the church and stepped into the porch. Peering round the corner I could see that, except for Cynthia Richardson, who was arranging Christmas flowers in front of the chancel rail, the place was empty.

She nodded shyly without speaking, as one does when in a partial state of grace due to devotions. I knew enough to leave her alone until she decided to speak.

I genuflected to the altar — whether it was required or not — and walked quietly past Cynthia to the choir stalls.

Yes, here were the rows of hinged misericord seats with their carved, misshapen imps with their mocking faces, each one different in execution and detail. It was said that the wood-carvers of the Middle Ages had been allowed free rein, at the end of a long job, to mock their masters by cartooning them in wood.

This, too, I had learned from listening to the vicar show summer tourists round the church. The world can be an interesting place to a girl who keeps her ears open.

There was a monk with a goblin face, made by hauling the corners of his eyes down with his forefingers and the corners of his mouth up with his thumbs, just as we still do today behind the backs of certain members of our families. There was a mitered bishop whose eyes were popping almost to the point of explosion, like wooden grapes. There was a monk hoisting his robe to display his bare bottom as he grinned gleefully over his shoulder, and a nun with a bird on her head.

All of these had been damaged by generations of choirboys carving their initials with knives or other sharp implements, and were now, in places, almost as frail as lace. Feely had once told me that the *"W.S."* scratched onto the forehead of a wooden angel was said to have been made by a young William Shakespeare, whose family had some obscure agricultural connections to Bishop's Lacey.

It was no wonder that St. Tancred's required the services of a specialist woodcarver. How else could recent vandalism be repaired and historically important vandalism left untouched — or even restored?

I was puzzling over that when my eyes fell upon an obviously fresh bit of damage: On a clever figure, thought by experts to represent a cartoon version of the Annunciation, in which an archangel holds out, for the inspection of a surprised-looking woman, a scroll remarkably like a modern newspaper, were carved the raw initials *C.S.C.* — so fresh that they still had splinters.

I was so surprised that I broke my own ban on talking.

"Holy Moses, Cynthia!" I exclaimed. "Look at this!"

Cynthia, still pink and watery round the eyes, turned from the Christmas roses and, as a subtle reminder that we were in church, touched lightly the velvet chorister's hat which was pinned to her hair.

"Look at this," I repeated. "*C.S.C.* Carla Sherrinford-Cameron."

Cynthia said nothing, but looked at me sadly.

"How many *C.S.C.*s could have been here so recently?" I asked, shaking with excitement.

"I'm sorry you had to see that, Flavia," she said. "I told Denwyn we should have covered it with something for the holidays. We had hoped that Mr. Sambridge would be able to — oh, dear. Christmas is such a nightmare. No, I'm sorry — I take that back. It's just that with all the extra services, the parish visits, the hampers for the needy, the choir's laundry, polishing the brass, and, oh, dear — people forget that even a church needs hoovering."

"I know," I said. "And you're right, it *is* a nightmare. At least for you — and the vicar," I added. "If it isn't the deathwatch beetle, it's Carla Sherrinford-Cameron."

She nodded sadly, and her great moist brown eyes seemed as if they were about to burst, like those of the carved wooden bishop in the misericord.

"We thought we could keep it quiet," Cynthia said. "The churchwardens suggested that her parents ought to be informed; that they might be willing to make good —"

"Before they were publicly exposed." I grinned. Cynthia was the only person in the entire world to whom I could say such a thing.

"Precisely," she said. "However, Denwyn and I finally talked sense into them. We thought it a far better solution to send the girl herself to Mr. Sambridge, to confess the crime, as it were, and to beg him to make the repair."

"A little penance," I said. I could almost sympathize with Carla, having been made to do so many of them myself.

"A little penance," Cynthia repeated. "We

hated to impose upon the poor man when he suffered so horribly with rheumatism and arthritis, but our own needs so often seem more important. We forget that we can kill an old man by bringing him out in such inclement weather."

"But you *didn't* kill him," I pointed out. "He didn't come."

"No," Cynthia said. "But it might have been better if he had."

And I knew instantly what she meant.

"Listen," I said. "I have a plan," and Cynthia gave me that crazy, skeptical, but awed look she always gives me when I say such a thing.

I reached into my pocket, pulled out the chewing gum — bless you, Carl Pendracka! — shoved all of it, one stick at a time, into my mouth, and began, as they say in the instructional films, to masticate.

"Chemistry to the rescue," I said to Cynthia round the wad, although I'm afraid it came out sounding more like "Emma's three otters' red shoes."

Cynthia covered her eyes as I extracted the mess from my mouth and began rolling it into a long string between my hands. When the proper thickness had been achieved, I broke off bits and, using my thumbs, worked and smoothed them like putty into the raw gouges.

"Sit for a minute," I told Cynthia, signaling with my hands, and as she sat, I darted out the vestry door and into the churchyard, which was now almost empty. The Horn Dance had apparently moved on to other haunts, to sing at other doors round the village, where they would be rewarded with cakes and ale.

I dug out several dead oak leaves from the snow beneath the trees and returned to the choir stalls.

Cynthia's jaw fell open as I broke up bits of vegetation and began to chew them in a businesslike way.

"Flavia!"

But she said nothing else as, with no more than a bit of spit and patience, I manufactured a mouthful of oak mush: a perfect color match, if I do say so myself, for the ancient oak of the misericords. There was no risk of poisoning myself, I knew, since oak leaves had once been highly valued for their healing of all wounds.

All that was required now was to produce my handkerchief and rub the stuff into the wood.

When it came time to do my laundry next Monday, Mrs. Mullet, of course, would be furious. And I couldn't blame her.

"Job done," I said, straightening up to let Cynthia have a squint. "Flavia's Fine Furniture Repair. No task too big or too small. Satisfaction guaranteed."

"You're a genius," she said, and I couldn't have agreed more.

It was almost a miracle. My improvised stain had blended so perfectly with the ancient oak that, if you hadn't known where to look, you'd never have spotted it.

"Why would Carla do something like that?" I asked. It was a question which had not occurred to me until now.

It was unfair of me to ask Cynthia such a question. A vicar's wife hears things that would peel the paint off battleships, and yet is expected to keep them to herself.

Perhaps it was in gratitude because I had patched the pew; perhaps it was something more than that.

But Cynthia said, "The poor girl has not had an easy life. Parents off somewhere doing something noble . . ."

A pang snatched at my heart. To me, distant parents doing noble deeds was an old, familiar story.

Don't think that, something warned me. *Now is not the time.*

"She was brought up by a distant aunt, now deceased," Cynthia went on.

That would be her auntie Loo, I thought, but I said nothing.

"They've had similar problems with her destructiveness over at St. Aubyn's, in Hinley. Denwyn had a word with the vicar there and they came up with the plan to encourage her singing."

"Hence 'Hark, the Horn,' " I said.

"Hence 'Hark, the Horn.' " Cynthia smiled.

And there fell between us one of those silences which I had come to love sharing with Cynthia, and which are the sign of a true friendship: a friendship in which no words are required.

We both of us basked in it for a time, and then Cynthia said, suddenly: "I wish you'd befriend her."

Just like that. No preliminaries. *Thank you, Cynthia Richardson!*

But none were needed.

"I'll see what I can do," I said, and both of us grinned.

"The poor are always with us," she said, almost to herself. It was not entirely apt, but I knew what she meant. I myself had befriended a remarkable number of poor souls recently, including Cynthia herself and, even more recently, my own obnoxious cousin, Undine.

"Call me Undies," she had said, insisting on repeating this and shaking my hand firmly at breakfast every morning, and yet I had somehow managed to keep my cake hole shut.

True charity, I had discovered, consists in swallowing an invisible flaming sword.

"Brrrrr," Cynthia said, gathering her cardigan tightly around her. "It's too cold in here. Let's go over to the vicarage and put the teapot on."

The churchyard was now completely deserted as we made our way across the grass. Only a couple of jackdaws broke the silence, squabbling over an acorn beneath the oak where I had excavated the healing leaves.

As Cynthia opened the door, the smell of hot cloves told me that a ham was in the oven, and I suddenly felt as if I hadn't eaten for a fortnight — perhaps even longer than that. In just moments she had the teapot ready on the table.

"Electric kettle," she explained. "Gift of Bunny Spirling: *'A vicar and his vicarage ought not to be a fortress against the modern gadget,'* " she said, striking a Bunny-like stance and sticking her stomach out in an affectionate parody of Father's dear friend. "He also gave us an electric tin opener," she confided, "but Denwyn refuses pointblank to use it."

Now she was putting on the vicar's voice: *"Would our good Lord have employed an electric fish gutter or a battery-operated bread slicer, had they been handed to him at Bethsaida?"*

Cynthia was a remarkable mimic and she captured her husband's outraged remark to perfection.

We were still wiping away the tears of laughter when Cynthia suddenly shoved back her chair and leaped to her feet. Someone had entered the kitchen and was standing behind me.

"Oh! I didn't see you there," she said. "You gave me such a start!"

"I'm sorry, Cynthia," said a voice. "I didn't mean to. It was just —"

"Flavia," Cynthia interrupted, "I'd like you to meet an old and very dear friend."

"We've already met," I said, swinging round in my chair and offering my hand to Hilary Inchbald.

It is difficult indeed to describe what happened next. In the first place, it's nearly impossible to convey what it's like to sit in an overheated vicarage kitchen, with dinner in the oven, across a gingham Rexine tablecloth from a living legend, and yes, I'm not ashamed to say it, a god.

Who isn't familiar with the inky outlines of that dear curly-haired boy, striking an explorer's stance or herding the barnyard geese with a pirate cutlass? Or navigating a raft of planks in a flooded meadow with a clothesline prop for a punting pole?

Hilary Inchbald hadn't changed all that much. He was larger and older, of course, than he had been in those famous illustrations, but yet he was somehow diminished.

His confidence was gone.

I watched him as he pecked, birdlike, at his tea cake, his unruly mop of prematurely white hair giving him the look of an elderly cockatoo: surely a comedown from the little boy who had once upon a time seemed destined to conquer the world.

Is this what the world of Crispian Crumpet is really *like*? I couldn't help wondering.

It was a sad thought all round.

Did he have children of his own and were they happy?

A few words were exchanged about the weather and the flowers in the church, but all the time I was aware that, beneath the stiff superficial chat, deep currents were flowing in the conversation between Cynthia and Hilary Inchbald. Unspoken words hung in the air like the smoke of autumn bonfires — or the scent of a passing princess.

Oh, no! I thought. *Surely not!*

Love takes strange forms, I had learned — or overheard — especially in a village setting where close friendships and loneliness are one and the same thing. Hilary, to be sure, was an outsider, but probably all the more exciting to this country vicar's wife: this Rapunzel whose hair was only ever let down for market gardeners and sheep herders who wouldn't recognize a diamond if it tumbled out of heaven and bopped them on their crumpets.

To begin with, Hilary and Cynthia were far too polite to each other. For another, they were both too red in the cheek.

My heart sank deeper and deeper, like a waterlogged canoe.

The vicar would be devastated when he found them out. He would fling himself from the top of the church tower and impale himself on the sharp iron spikes of the railings which surrounded the grave of *Arabella Darling, Spinster of this Parish, who "died praising the Lord on the twenty-ninth day of November, seventeen hundred and sixty-seven. Amen. Amen. Amen."*

I was ashamed for Cynthia — more

ashamed than I had ever been for myself, and my face must have shown it.

After a while the talk ground to a halt and I realized that both Cynthia and Hilary Inchbald were staring at me.

I squirmed in my chair. I didn't know what to do. My mental hands were tied. I had been flung into a part of life that was over my head and I was in danger of drowning in ignorance.

And then Cynthia laughed.

"Flavia, dear," she said, "Hilary and I are old friends. We have known each other since we were in prams. We meet to share our sorrows."

As if she had been reading my mind.

If I had been flustered before, I was now absolutely gaga. I would need to backpedal and pretend I hadn't been thinking what she thought I had been thinking.

I looked from one of them to the other, speechless.

"Tell her, Cynthia," Hilary said. "Go ahead. I shan't mind."

No . . . no . . . no . . . , my brain was screaming. *I don't want to know. Keep your secrets to yourselves.*

I covered my ears with my hands, pleading with my eyes.

Cynthia reached across the table, offering

her wrists and forearms as if she were in a lifeboat and I a drowning swimmer.

I took hold of them and hung on for dear life.

Where did this woman get her strength? I had once — a few years ago — thought Cynthia to be pathetic. What a fool I had been! What I had mistaken for jelly was a flexible fiber of the strongest steel. No wonder my mother, Harriet, had been so fond of her.

"Hilary has been very sadly bereaved," Cynthia told me. "We thought you might have already worked that out."

Hilary? Bereaved? What was she talking about? His father had been dead for years, and his mother . . . ?

Well, that remained to be seen. If she were still alive she had been remarkably successful in keeping her name out of the newspapers.

Could I be losing my mind? Had I, without knowing it, tripped and fallen through a hole into another world in which turvy was topsy, and topsy turvy, and time ran backwards towards forever?

But for as long as I live, I shall never forget the pale, frail man who, at the same time, was also the boy, Crispian Crumpet, leaning towards me in the vicarage kitchen and saying in a voice that came to my ears like a memory of last summer's southern wind, "Roger Sambridge was Oliver Inchbald — my father."

FIFTEEN

I'd give anything to be able to say I had seen it coming — but I hadn't. I had failed miserably.

What a feather in my cap it would have been to be able to drop the bombshell at Inspector Hewitt's feet:

"Oh, by the way, Inspector, in case you haven't already worked it out, Roger Sambridge, the ecclesiastical wood-carver, was actually the world-famous author Oliver Inchbald."

"What!" he would have expostulated, and if he'd worn a monocle — which he didn't — it would have popped out of his eye like a cork.

I'd have smiled modestly and let him take all the credit, as I had so often done before.

But it was not to be. I had failed, and felt for the moment as if I had been doused with black paint.

And yet at the same time I was beginning

to burn with excitement. If Roger Sambridge *was* Oliver Inchbald, so many otherwise inexplicable things began to make sense.

I thought he might be, I wanted to say, in order to salvage what was left of my pride. But some strange new Power was telling me to keep quiet.

Except to say, "I'm awfully sorry to hear that, Mr. Inchbald. May I offer you my sympathy?"

I listened, appalled, as my words slipped out as slick and soft and insincere as black velvet at a funeral.

What was happening to me? What alien creature had seized control of my mouth? Had I been possessed by one of those slimes you see in the cinema that lurks in your lungs as it feeds on your brain?

"Thank you, Flavia," Hilary said. "You're exceedingly kind. I understand from Cynthia that you, too, have lost a parent. Your condolences mean a great deal to me."

I was thunderstruck.

Moses on horseback! I thought. Was that how things worked? Had I spent all these years barking up the wrong tree?

I lowered my eyes demurely.

"It's not easy to be deprived of a parent, is it? I first lost my father when I was eight years old. And now I've lost him again."

Those had been almost precisely my own thoughts when Harriet's body had been returned to Buckshaw — could it have been only last spring? So much had happened since that crushing day that it seemed an eternity away.

I did something that surprised me: I got to my feet, walked round the table, threw my arms around Hilary Inchbald, and hugged him.

And he hugged me back. Fiercely.

Neither of us seemed to want to be the first to let go, so that our grip on each other went on for quite some time.

Cynthia, her hand to her mouth, was unashamedly in tears.

None of us spoke, but when the long moment had passed, Hilary and I let go of each other and I returned to my chair and sat primly down, as we English do, as if some miracle hadn't happened.

Cynthia busied herself with the teapot.

"I was sent away to prep school when I was eight, you see. Far too young, but my father, being who he was, was able to pull certain strings. In order to justify my presence among the older boys, it was put about constantly that I was exceptionally intelligent — or at least clever."

Hilary spoke softly and slowly and, in spite of my acute hearing, I had to strain at times to hear him.

"At first I thought my father had sent me away because I had done something wrong: something too horrible to be put into words. No one ever took the trouble to set me straight, and so I was utterly miserable for the first few years.

"But in time, I came to equate brains with imprisonment. It was my own intelligence that had caused me to be put away. I didn't pretend to understand the reasons why, but there I was in Cheadle House, so it must be true. I had done nothing wrong, and there could be no other explanation.

"If brains were the cause of my incarceration, then the solution was evident: I would become an ignoramus. It was that simple. I don't know why I hadn't thought of it before.

"Then, perhaps, when they realized what a mistake they had made, I would be set free.

"I can still remember the exact moment this enlightenment came upon me. I was listening to Hanson, the Latin master, droning on about the future perfect tense of the verb *spero,* 'I hope.'

" '*Speravero,* my fine young gentlemen,'

he was saying. '*I shall have hoped,* if indeed you are still alive in the future, and perchance there's any of that precious substance left.'

"I chose that moment to spill my ink. And before the end of the class, I had translated *bello,* 'war,' as 'tummy' and *pudere* as something that comes forth from a cow.

"Old Hanson was livid, but my father was incandescent. I had shamed him. I had belittled him. I had brought great dishonor upon him. And he wasted no time in telling me so.

"When the holidays came round, I was packed up and sent to a house that was no longer home. My father showed me a 'talking stick' he had been sent from Borneo by someone in his club. It was a wonderful thing, made from bamboo, I believe — about the length of a common ruler and covered with carvings. It was held, generally, by the headman of the tribe who made it, and only the person holding the stick was allowed to speak. The penalty for speaking without the stick was severe: banishment, my father claimed — although I didn't believe him — or even death.

"Whenever my father wished to address me, which was seldom, and usually to take me to task for some perceived misdeed, he would bring out the talking stick from the locked drawer of his desk where he kept it, and give me a tongue-lashing.

"Once, because I wished to defend myself, I held out my hand for the stick and my father reacted by slashing me across the palm with it, drawing blood. I did not ask again. Nor did I speak.

"I could not imagine what I had done to deserve such treatment. Where was the father who had sung silly songs to me with his trousers rolled up at the seaside? Where was the father who had carried me on his shoulders to see the stone dinosaurs at the Crystal Palace? What could possibly have gone wrong?

"All I knew was that I was no longer just living in my father's shadow; I *was* my father's shadow. We could never be one. I was all that he was not, and he was all that I was not — rather like the anti-matter which the physicists are now beginning to speculate about.

"In time, of course, I came to understand that my only sin had been that of growing up."

Hilary's long fingers were spread out on the tabletop, white from pressing so tightly.

"His father beat him badly," Cynthia said softly, touching his shoulder, and Hilary glanced up at her gratefully, as if she had spared him the pain of saying this himself.

Oliver Inchbald had beaten Crispian Crumpet? That golden-haired little boy of the storybooks?

My mind almost gagged at the idea as my brain cells drew back in horror.

Until that very moment, I had never really understood the meaning of the word *obscene,* but if anything was obscene, it was this.

"He used to make me box with him," Hilary said. "He would bloody my nose, then rush out of the room and leave me to clean myself up.

"The moment I was old enough I changed my name, joined the Royal Air Force, and trained as a wireless operator air gunner. When my father found me out, he pulled strings, as he had always done, and I spent what remained of the war somewhere in Scotland, sending out coded top-secret wireless demands from the officers for tea from Harrods and hampers from Fortnum & Mason.

"I attempted at every turn to get myself posted to aircrew, where I would be in real bodily danger, but as always, my father contrived to have my every wish denied. He took away — no, *stole* from me — the single chance I ever had to commit suicide with great honor and dignity. And for that, I wanted to kill him."

"Oh, surely not!" Cynthia gasped. "You've never told me that before."

"It's true, nonetheless," Hilary said softly.

"You mustn't say that," Cynthia protested. "You simply mustn't."

"You mean in light of him lying dead in — in whatever hell he's in?"

As interesting as it was, the conversation was veering from criminal acts into theology, a subject about which I knew little and cared less.

"Did someone kill him — your father, I mean?" I asked, perhaps a little bluntly.

"I don't know," Hilary replied. "I certainly hope so."

"Hilary, dear," Cynthia said. "Take me for a little walk. I've been feeling iffish all day. A turn in the fresh air might do me good."

Hilary Inchbald, whatever else he was, was also a gentleman. He got to his feet, pulled back Cynthia's chair for her, and went to fetch her coat.

While he was out of the room I caught Cynthia's eye, and saw nothing in it but my own reflection.

I followed the two of them out of the

vicarage and watched as they walked across the churchyard towards the west.

Only when they were at a slight distance, and only when I saw him in an outdoor setting, did I remember where I had seen Hilary before he had unfolded himself from the sideboard at Lillian Trench's cottage.

I turned east towards the High Street and the Thirteen Drakes.

Howard Carter was holding up the front of the pub, his shoulders and the sole of a shoe pressed against the doorframe. Howard was something of a local character who did odd jobs around the village and kept the Thirteen Drakes afloat by spending his earnings. Since he possessed the same name as the discoverer of King Tut-ankh-Amon's tomb, Howard came in for more than his share of teasing, such as "Does your mummy know you're out, Howard?" and other village witticisms.

Howard didn't seem to mind: Fame is fame wherever you may find it.

"Could you ask Mr. Stoker to step outside, please? I'd like to have a word with him."

Tully, I knew, would not be as lenient as Rosie when it came to enforcement of the Licensing Act.

Howard examined his fingernails. This was

the sort of moment he lived for: a position of authority, even for a matter of seconds.

"Depends," he said. "What's it about?"

I glanced at an imaginary wristwatch. "It's about one o'clock," I said.

"Haw!" Howard said. "You're a rare one, aren't you, Flavia de Luce?"

"Selab Dusticafeenio," I said, pleasantly, which is a complicated tactic — a spell, actually — which I sometimes use with those who take liberties. They never know quite what to make of it. And it worked. Howard looked at me as if I had suddenly sprouted an extra head and yellow spotted fur.

He launched himself into motion and vanished inside the pub. Moments later, Tully ambled out, wiping his hands on his apron. He acknowledged me with a hint of a nod.

"Good morning — or, rather, good afternoon, Mr. Stoker. I wonder if you can help me? I'm trying to get in touch with a Professor Karl Heinz Heidecker. He's a famous chemist — Nobel Prize, if I'm not mistaken — and I've been given to understand that he may be spending a holiday in the neighborhood. I thought if he's not actually staying at the Thirteen Drakes, he might have come into the pub in the past several days."

This was unlikely, since I had invented Professor Heidecker on the spot.

Tully eyed me with suspicion, as he always did.

"I don't know Professor Heidecker by sight," I said, "but I happened to see a distinguished-looking gentleman helping you repair a broken window, and —"

"That wasn't your professor," Tully interrupted.

People are always so eager to point out to you that you're wrong that they can't wait for you to complete your sentence.

"It was Mr. Hilary and he's no chemist. I can't imagine him getting his hands dirty," Tully said, staring at my hands which, as usual, were stained and discolored by the handful of experiments I had managed to do since coming home.

Mr. Hilary! Hilary Inchbald was staying at the Thirteen Drakes under an assumed name!

Or was it simply that Tully was on a first-name basis with him?

"Mr. Hilary?" I asked, as if I hadn't heard.

"Mr. Percival Hilary," Tully said. "Of London, England."

That clinched it! Who could forget Percival the Penguin who, in *Hobbyhorse House*, escaped from the London Zoo, got lost, and — having made his way on foot past Madame Tussaud's wax museum and Sherlock Holmes's headquarters at 221b Baker Street, and having stopped to dance the Penguin Pavane on the pavement in front of each of those locations — was finally located in Hyde Park, paddling with the children in the Serpentine?

"Mr. Hilary" was obviously Hilary Inchbald. There could be no doubt of that.

But if he was staying at the Thirteen Drakes, then why on earth had I found him huddled in a cupboard in Lillian Trench's cottage, which, I couldn't help noting, was directly across the road from Thornfield Chase, where his father, Oliver Inchbald, had been living under the name Roger Sambridge?

It was enough to puzzle the sharpest saint.

"Well, thank you, Mr. Stoker," I said. "I'm sorry to bother you. Oh, by the way, please say hello to Mary for me. I haven't seen her since I've come home."

Mary was Tully's daughter, who had been of great assistance to me at the time of the Horace Bonepenny affair.

Tully's face grew dark with blood. For a moment, I thought he was going to turn away and slam the door in my face.

"Thought you might have heard," he said.

"Everyone else in the kingdom has. She's gone."

"Gone?"

"You heard me. And Cropper with her."

There are times when I've been taken by surprise, but seldom as I was at this moment.

"Gone? Mary and Ned? When? Why?"

I was gasping for words.

"Couple of days ago. Same morning your Sambridge turned up dead. The lad had words with Mr. Hilary in the Saloon Bar and a window was broke. Police were called. In the morning the lad was gone, and her with him."

It was as if he couldn't bring himself to speak his daughter's name.

"Was anyone hurt?" I couldn't resist asking.

"Yaass," Tully said, reverting to some long banished county accent of his childhood. "*I* was."

With a tragic look up and down the High Street in either direction, he turned and walked wearily back inside.

A moment later, Howard Carter appeared from the shadows of the public bar.

"You shouldn't ought to have asked him that," he said. "You've gone and broke his heart."

SIXTEEN

The remains of a roasted chicken lay near the head of the table, looking like the wreckage of the Hindenburg.

I had missed dinner.

Undine made cuckoo eyes at me as I sat down and reached for the dessert, one of Mrs. Mullet's specialties to which we referred privately as Lymph Pudding. God only knows what was in it, and He wasn't telling, although today it had an aftertaste of smoked herring.

"Ned Cropper's run off with Mary Stoker," I said to Feely. "I thought you'd want to know."

"You're mistaking me for someone who cares," Feely said.

"Alas!" I cried, throwing the back of my hand to my forehead. "Farewell flyblown chocolates . . . no more secondhand valentines."

I could be merciless when I wanted information.

But Feely wasn't taking the bait. She had already turned her attention to one of the two matching mirrors at opposite ends of the room which, reflecting each other, allowed her to see her face and the back of her head simultaneously. The temptation was too great, and she was lost at once in a series of elaborate neck contortions that put me in mind of a parrot examining its reflection in a toy mirror. *Pretty Polly!* I wanted to say.

I have always found there to be a certain sadness about mirrors, since they double the space in a house which needs to be filled with love. We don't give nearly enough credit to the people who used to drape their looking-glasses with bedsheets.

I shuddered and shook the thought from my mind like a dog shaking off water.

Undine was picking something nasty off the soles of her shoes and scraping it onto the edge of her plate. At least she was being quiet.

"Daffy," I asked, "have you ever heard of the Auditories?"

Daffy looked up from *The Catcher in the Rye,* in whose margins she was making profuse notes in pencil.

"The benches of the Roman magistrates, the stalls of the Haymarket Theatre, or that sect of the Manicheans who merely listened?"

"The fairies," I said. "The ones that live in carpets."

"Ah!" Daffy said, "those ones." Which meant she didn't know. Or was pretending not to.

Did she not remember scaring me witless with *The Listeners*?

Daffy was an incredibly complex person: not at all what she seemed to be.

If I wanted to find out what she was playing at, I needed to go along with her.

"What about de la Mare?" I asked. "Didn't he write something about them?"

Daffy shrugged. "He may have. I don't remember. Have you read his *Memoirs of a Midget*? If not, you ought to. It's about a certain Miss M, who studies death by examining the maggots in the body of a dead mole she finds in the garden. It's right up your alley."

I made a note to look up the book at once, but meanwhile, Daffy was evading my question. I needed to be more direct.

"Do you know anything about a Miss Trench — Lillian Trench? She lives out near Stowe Pontefract."

"I knew you'd get around to her sooner or later," Daffy said. "She's a witch. Stay away from her."

"Do you really believe that," I began, "or —"

"It doesn't matter what I believe," Daffy snapped. "You're in over your head. Stay away from her."

I was stunned. Had Daffy been secretly monitoring my doings? How could she possibly know where I had been and what I had been doing?

Daffy was the third person to warn me off the woman: First had been Dieter, then Mrs. Mullet, and now Daffy.

"Why?" I pouted, sounding like a petulant baby.

"Look, Flavia, believe it or not, there are things people get up to that you don't know about, don't need to know about, and don't want to know about. Take my word for it. Stick to chemistry. You're far safer piddling around at home with arsenic and cyanide than you are galloping round stirring up village gossip. Gossip has power, and some of it's black."

It was a longer speech than I'd ever heard Daffy make in my entire life. Unless she was reading aloud to us from one of her favorite books, my sister was the kind of person who is sometimes described as "monosyllabic."

(Why, incidentally, does a word meaning "a single syllable" require a five-syllable word to describe it? The world, as Mr. Partridge remarked in a recent talk on the wireless, is surely going to hell in a linguistic handbasket.)

Was Daffy trying to protect me? If she was, it would be the first time in the history of the planet Earth. There had to be more to it than that.

But before I could dig deeper, Daffy excused herself and hurriedly left the room.

"WC!" Undine said in a stage whisper. She had been following our conversation avidly.

I pretended not to hear, and picked listlessly at my pudding.

The clock ticked.

Somewhere above, a lavatory was flushed.

"See?" Undine said triumphantly.

In a remarkably few minutes, Daffy was back.

"I've just remembered," she said. "The Listeners were one of the tribes of underground fairies. Neither visible nor invisible — which means that they can be seen by some people but not by others — they exist on the threshold of vision, and have the habit of hiding underfoot where they have the least chance of being detected. Possessing small, weak, sunken eyes, but with large, powerful ears, they overhear everything, even the most secret conversations, which they use to their own dreadful advantage. They are said to endow humans with great artistic talents, but to exact a terrible price in return."

I knew at once that these were not Daffy's own words: She was quoting from a book.

I should have known! The flushing of the WC had been no more than a diversion, a decoy. Daffy had dashed, not to the lavatory, but to the library where she had consulted Professor Thorvald Fenn's great work, *An Encyclopaedic Dictionary of the Fairy Folk.* I had intended to do so myself, but she had saved me the trouble.

The fat green book was one I remembered well. I had pored over its pages in some detail after Daffy and Feely had almost convinced me that I was a changeling: a monstrous child swapped by the fairies for the real Flavia de Luce who was now, at that very moment, enslaved in some hidden cavern, a subterranean Cinderella being made to serve endless shamrock teas to the Little People.

Very much like my real life, I sometimes thought — but only when I was having a bitter day.

"Thanks, Daff," I said. "That's very helpful. I've been reading *The Golden Bough,* and it's made me think about taking up mythology and folklore."

"Jolly good choice," she said. "It will keep you away from those moonlighters."

Moonlighters? I thought. Had she let something slip?

"Those imbeciles that annoy the sheep by dancing round old stones in the rain. It's all the rage nowadays, even though it's a load of horsewallop."

But if that were entirely true, why was Daffy warning me off it?

It was no harmless specter that had killed Roger Sambridge, or, rather, Oliver Inchbald. Had the Auditories at Lillian Trench's cottage had anything to do with his death? Had they been sent marching across the road to Thornfield Chase, to do their witch mistress's bidding?

There was no doubt that the late Oliver had been granted great artistic talents, as both author and wood-carver, and it was even more certain that he had paid a terrible price for these gifts. But who — or what — had actually killed him: man or spook?

Or could it have been the alleged witch,

Lillian Trench herself? She had been a close neighbor of the dead man, so who knew what dealings she had had with him? It is common knowledge that neighborly disputes can sometimes escalate into murder, and even a lightning glance at the front page of the *Daily Mail* is enough to demonstrate this fact. A simple disagreement over a wandering cat may easily end with corpses piled up like kindling wood.

Which brought my thoughts back to the cat that had strolled so casually into the bedroom of the dead Mr. Sambridge, or, as I now knew him to be, Oliver Inchbald. It had made a second appearance at the cottage of his neighbor, Lillian Trench.

Whose cat was it, then? As I had noted earlier, cats don't generally waste their time howling at the homes of strangers.

It probably made sense when you stopped to think about it, that Lillian Trench kept a cat. Witches are widely known to keep felines as their familiars. I've never heard of a witch who didn't — except of course the Witch of Endor in the book of Samuel, but that's because there are no cats in the Bible — and it wouldn't have been mentioned even if she'd had one, just for the sake of consistency. I'd bet a fiver that she did.

By now, Daffy had given up on her conversation and returned to Mr. Salinger. I couldn't help noticing that her ears were going slightly pink.

As interesting a phenomenon as it was, I realized I was going to get nowhere with my investigation by watching someone read. There were certain questions which even my sister could not answer.

I tapped on Dogger's door with my knuckles, but there was no reply.

"Dogger," I called softly. "It's Flavia. Is everything all right?"

Was *he* all right, was what I meant, of course.

Although he had not suffered one of his terrifying episodes for quite some time, there was always the worry that I was going to find him whimpering in a corner, his head cradled in his forearms, howling like a madman as his poor brain reenacted some unspeakable torture he had endured at the hands of his wartime captors. Father and Dogger had been held in the same Japanese prison, where each of them had lost parts of his being that could never be recovered.

Although it went against my every instinct to do so, I opened the door and peeped round it. We had been taught since we were children that Dogger's room at the top of the back stairs was his Holy of Holies; that when he was in his sanctum he was not on any account to be disturbed. Although I had broken the rule from time to time — mostly with good reason, such as when he was having an attack — I had generally left him alone.

I needn't have worried. The room was empty, and Dogger's sparse bed was neatly made up with military precision.

Perhaps he was in the kitchen, I thought, as I made my way downstairs.

But he was not. Mrs. Mullet had gone for the day, and the room felt curiously empty. I vowed never to be late for dinner again as long as I lived.

And suddenly it came to me. Of course! It made perfect sense. Why hadn't I thought of it before?

I retrieved my coat and mittens from the cupboard in the foyer, retraced my steps through the kitchen, and opened the back door.

The world was a nighttime wonderland. A razor wind had stripped away most of the clouds and the trees, under a gibbous moon, were a glorious, ice-covered confection, transparent spangles glittering with a cold brightness. It was like a decorated stage set from the Russian ballet, awaiting the dancers — *The Snow Queen,* perhaps, in which human hearts are pierced and frozen by shards of ice from the trolls' shattered mirror.

In the moonlight, even the kitchen garden glowed, the red brick of the old walls illuminating the dead beds with the cold, faded glory of old silver.

The ground crunched beneath my feet as I walked towards the coach house.

I made the courtesy of knocking on the door.

"Dogger?" I called out. "Are you here? It's Flavia."

Almost as if he had been waiting inside, the door opened straightaway, and there stood Dogger.

"Miss Flavia. Is everything all right?"

"Yes, thank you, Dogger. May I come in?"

"Please do," Dogger said, and I saw as he stepped back that his sleeves were rolled up to the elbows.

In the middle of the room stood Harriet's old Rolls-Royce Phantom II, which had stood neglected for years until quite recently when Dogger had somehow managed to get it started at a time when my life was in danger. It had been brought out again at Harriet's funeral, but had since then stood alone in the coach house, thinking its own thoughts and dreaming its own dreams among the dusty beams and the long-abandoned wooden stalls.

It was like a manger scene, I thought, lit by the light of a single hanging paraffin lantern, in order to conserve electricity.

Dogger had placed a milking stool in front of the towering nickel-plated radiator, which he now resumed polishing with a surgeon's touch.

"You're cleaning her up to go fetch Father, aren't you?" I asked.

I had known it all along.

Dogger picked at a reluctant bit of road grit with his fingernail.

"Bert Archer has offered to iron out some of her wrinkles," he said. "He can't resist an old Rolls — especially one that has suffered indignities."

He was referring, of course, to the damage the car had suffered in rescuing me from the Pit Shed behind the library, an incident which I preferred to forget — except for the happiness of my father's face on that occasion.

"Bert tells me that if we run her over to his garage this evening, he'll get to work straightaway."

"But the cost —" I said, thinking of the piles of papers and unpaid bills that littered

Father's desk like the crumbling towers of Angkor Wat. In spite of my having inherited Buckshaw, the affairs of the estate were still in shocking disarray after years of siege by those gray men, His Majesty's Revenue Rats, as Father called them when he thought I wasn't listening.

"Bert has offered to carry out the necessary repairs gratis," Dogger said.

"He says it's the least he can do," he added somewhat mysteriously. "Would you care to assist?"

Would I!

"I think I should like that," I said, stuffing my happiness down my throat. If I were to become the lady of the manor I'd better start playing the part.

Dogger put on his jacket and held the door open for me. I stepped up into the front passenger's seat.

"I hope you'll teach me to drive her one day, Dogger," I said.

"I hope I shall, too, miss," he said.

The Rolls started without a hitch. On almost the first turn she was trembling with silent life in the lamplight.

"Tally ho," Dogger remarked.

"Tally ho," I replied.

Even at walking pace, the journey into the village was a relatively short one. There was no time to waste.

"It turns out that the late Mr. Sambridge was actually Oliver Inchbald, the author," I remarked.

Dogger nodded. "Interesting, but hardly surprising," he said.

What did he know that I didn't?

"Meaning?" I asked.

"Meaning that it is interesting but hardly surprising," he said, and I knew I was going to get no more out of him. If there was one thing Dogger was not, it was a gossip.

It was time to change the subject.

"What's a black thing that can be hung up as a wall decoration?" I asked. "Rather like a cross section of a brain — a silhouette — a fan with a distinct stem and various branches. It's hard to describe."

"It sounds much like a gorgonian sea fan," Dogger said. "And your description is a very good one. *Rhipidigorgia,* if I'm not mistaken. Polyps of the family Gorgonaceae, which are easily distinguished from their neighbors, you will recall, by their axes not being effervescent in muriatic acid. They are wrenched, sadly, from the sea-floor of the northwest Mediterranean and are lugged home to be pasted up until they return to dust on our parlor walls."

A shiver ran through me. Hadn't Carla's

auntie Loo met her fate while diving in the Mediterranean? Could it have been she who had brought a sea fan home as a gift to Oliver Inchbald?

They had, after all, been great pals. Or so I was led to believe.

Was Oliver's death somehow connected to hers — even though the two events were separated by several years? I needed to think this through, and to do so properly.

"You seem to know a great deal about natural history," I said, and Dogger smiled.

"As a boy," he said, "I was very keen — as we used to say. I suppose I had rather a crush on Mother Nature. I did a bit of botanizing."

"Botanizing?"

"Plants and grasses and so forth. Thought it might come in handy someday."

"And did it?" I was only partly serious.

"It did," Dogger said, and left it at that.

And in that moment, a sudden dark image welled up in my mind, of Dogger and Father flushed from hiding at the edge of a steaming field somewhere in southeast Asia, leaping from cover in a ditch to twist garrotes of steel-sharp grasses around the necks of their ambushed hunters.

"And the sea fans?" I asked, wanting to change the subject as quickly as possible.

"A sideline," Dogger said. "I gave my specimens eventually to the Museum of Natural History in Oxford."

"Why?" I asked.

"So that they would be viewed by those who could enjoy them more than I did."

"Ah," I said, because I couldn't think of anything else.

By now we were pulling up outside Bert Archer's garage. In spite of the cold, Bert came out to greet us. He guided the Rolls in through the open doors with a series of elaborate hand signals.

"Magnificent piece of machinery," he said as we came to a stop. "Had Lady Denniston's Silver Ghost in last month for a noisy clock."

He grinned horribly, as if he had made a capital joke. "Now, then," he said, rubbing his knuckles together in anticipation. "Let's get the old girl up onto the hoist and find out what's under her skirts."

Dogger frowned, but ever so slightly.

"If you please, Mr. Archer," I said. "Little pitchers have big ears."

Bert took it lightly, but I had the distinct feeling that he had learned his lesson.

"Found another body, so I hear?" he said. It sounded almost as if he took personal pride in my accomplishments. "That Sambridge fellow, out at Thornfield Chase?"

"That's right," I said quietly. I was trying to teach myself not to burble.

"I shall miss his custom. Regular filler-upper he was."

How odd, I thought. Roger Sambridge's old Austin had looked to me as if it had been parked since dinosaurs roamed the earth. I couldn't resist.

"Did he have a second car, then?" I asked.

"Ha!" Bert said. "Didn't need one, did he? Not with a neighbor like Lillian. Man who has a neighbor like Lillian, therefore shall he want for nothing, as the vicar likes to say."

I hadn't seen a car at Lillian Trench's cottage, but that didn't mean she didn't own one. Even witches have to get around when brooms would be too obvious.

"Thank you, Mr. Archer," Dogger said. "We shall leave you to your work."

And so, with the Rolls in dry dock, as it were, Dogger and I were left to walk home across the moonlit fields to Buckshaw.

Halfway across a field that has been known, since the Middle Ages, as Breakplough, we stopped for a breather, and to look back at our own footprints, which receded in the direction of the village, our trail growing smaller and smaller in the distance.

"Rather like 'Good King Wenceslas,' isn't it?" I said, ticking off the points on my mittened fingers (which isn't as easy as it sounds). "Snow lying round about, deep and crisp and even? Check. Brightly shining moon? Affirmative. Cruel frost? Check. It's just perfect, isn't it, Dogger?"

"Perfect," Dogger said.

"Except, perhaps, for a poor man gathering winter fu-oo-*el*."

At that very moment, a single headlight swept the field as a farm tractor came bumping out of a nearby lane, pulling a trailer full of firewood.

We both laughed.

No one would have believed it, and I knew that Dogger and I would keep this moment to ourselves. There is a kind of magic that cannot be shared. Even talking about it robs it of its power.

Oliver Inchbald had known that, hadn't he?

We saunter the shore, holding hands,
Sharing the silence of the sands . . .

He had written that in one of his books, about walking by the sea with his son. I could still remember the illustration: no living persons in sight — simply two pairs of footprints, one large, one small, vanishing in the distance.

How like they were to our own footprints in the snow, Dogger's and mine. A different season, to be sure, and a different setting, but still much the same: an adult and a younger person walking side by side in a sort of wilderness with no more than their footprints to tell us where they've been.

How could a man capable of writing those lines possibly be cruel enough to beat a child? Had Hilary Inchbald been telling the truth?

And if he hadn't, what else might he be lying about?

Overhead, the stars twinkled vividly. They don't care about humans, the stars, except in picture books.

"Have you ever wondered, Dogger," I asked, "if wickedness is a chemical state?"

"Indeed I have, Miss Flavia," he said. "I have sometimes thought of little else."

We began walking again, silent for a while, save for the crunching of the brittle snow.

Although I was aching to talk to Dogger about Father, I found myself unable to do so. Dogger was burdened with enough grief of his own without my adding to it.

"Do you have any brothers or sisters, Dogger?" I asked. It was a thought that had never occurred to me before.

"Yes, I do, Miss Flavia," he said at last, after a very long pause. "Do you wish me to tell you about them?"

"No," I said.

"Thank you," he replied.

Again we walked on in silence for a while: silent because there was far too much to say.

"Dogger, do you think it's right that some of us should live for ages while others are doomed to die?"

Dogger laughed. He actually laughed!

I had never heard him laugh before, and it was a strange and pleasant sound.

"It makes no difference what I think," he said. "We had an old saying in our regiment: *'It matters not if we march with the March-morts or the Mortmarches; our final destination is the same.'*"

I nodded sadly, because I knew that this was true.

"On account of the chemistry," I said.

"On account of the chemistry," Dogger agreed.

SEVENTEEN

I couldn't sleep. Outside my bedroom window, the winter stars were blazing even brighter — if that were possible — than they had while Dogger and I were walking home.

Beyond the Visto, Castor and Pollux, the Heavenly Twins, had risen well above the eastern horizon.

Oliver Inchbald had written something about the stars, hadn't he?

What was it? Of course! It wasn't from *Hobbyhorse House,* but its companion volume, *Bedtime Ballads:*

Old Castor says to Pollux,
"A little lad I see,
A-strolling on the distant Earth.
Could he be watching me?"

Old Pollux says to Castor,
"How vain you are, my twin,
'Tis me! 'tis me! the little lad

Has seized an interest in."

It was all a matter of viewpoint, wasn't it?

The motives for killing a village wood-carver would appear to be entirely different than those for murdering a much-beloved author. As would the suspects.

Who in their right mind would even dream of doing away with Oliver Inchbald — a man who had brought so much pleasure into the world?

The Death of a Household Name, I should call it, if I were writing up the case disguised as fiction, as Miss Christie has done.

It was far, far easier to think that a morose wood-carver and part-time tippler might have made a mortal enemy.

Which meant that my prime suspects should be the dead man's present-day friends — mostly his acquaintances from church and village: those who knew him only as Roger Sambridge. As opposed, say, to those who had been acquainted with the blessèd Oliver Inchbald, who had been supposedly pecked to death by seagulls.

How had he managed to pull it off?

A death so sensational — so dramatic — could not have been enacted successfully without an enormous amount of planning. And — the hair at the back of my neck bristled at the thought — a great deal of assistance. One does not stage such a spectacle without planning the actual event with military precision.

Why hadn't I thought of this before?

Why hadn't I thought to question Lillian Trench about her neighbor? Had I been too intimidated by coming face-to-face with a would-be witch? Or had the sudden jack-in-the-box appearance of Hilary Inchbald from the sideboard thrown me off the track?

It wasn't until that very moment that the penny dropped, but when it fell, it fell like a load of lead bricks.

Of course! How could I have been so feebleminded? Shame on you, Flavia de Luce!

What a colossal fool I had been! Like everyone else, I had been taken in totally by what was probably the most magnificent piece of stagecraft in recent memory.

Hang your head, John Gielgud! Sir Laurence Olivier, go stand in the corner in shame! Oliver Inchbald — alias Roger Sambridge — has bested us all.

At least he did until he was overtaken by Fate, who apparently has no sense of humor.

What were his last thoughts? I wondered. *Had he, at the end, and alone with his killer, had even a moment to regret his life? Had there been time for a final "Dash it all!" before his eyes were closed forever?*

His final years could not have been easy ones. I knew that he had suffered with arthritis, and that many of his hours had been spent alone in a pub — not spinning tales and making men laugh as you would expect, but sitting by himself. "Morose," Rosie had called it, which meant, if I understand the word correctly, that he was a sour old crab apple.

What a comedown that must have been for the creator of Crispian Crumpet.

As my mind shifted into a higher gear, a new landscape of questions revealed itself. It was like riding Gladys to the top of the Jack O'Lantern and seeing, suddenly, a vast, fresh perspective of Bishop's Lacey and vicinity laid out like a carpet at one's feet.

A matter of viewpoint.

Castor and Pollux.

There was, for instance, the question of the wooden frame upon which I had found the dead man hanging. Who, among his acquaintances, could have constructed such an instrument of torture, and how had they brought it to Thornfield Chase and set it up? Who had the necessary woodworking skills?

Well, Boy Scout James Marlowe, of Wick

St. Lawrence, I thought with a smile, was the first that came to mind. Boy Scouts were famous from pole to pole as being able to whittle up, upon demand, anything from a toothpick to a cantilever bridge. It had been he who made the grisly discovery of Oliver Inchbald's first death, while I, Flavia de Luce, had been left to discover the second.

Had Oliver Inchbald stood idly by and watched as the fiendish device was hauled into his cottage and set up? Or was he already dead by then?

The latter seemed more likely. In spite of my own mental powers I could scarcely imagine anyone assisting at his own crucifixion.

Fiction. The word rang in my brain. Oliver's first "death" *had* been a fiction, cleverly contrived and staged by himself, with the assistance of others yet to be discovered. The second, alas, had been all too real.

Had it been an accident?

Had some unspeakable ritual gone suddenly and horribly wrong?

With these unpleasant thoughts in mind, I rolled over in bed, wrapped the quilt around my shoulders, and fell into the deepest and most restful sleep I've had since the day before I was born.

■ ■ ■ ■

When I awoke, a winter sun was already slanting in through my window, its low angle illuminating the peaks and valleys of the baggy Georgian wallpaper with which my room was covered.

I remembered that for simply ages I had intended to take further scrapings, for examination under the microscope, of the various mold colonies that flourished on its ancient paste, but now was not the time. Molds, when you stop to think about it, are really no more than large, happy families. If you could make yourself small enough — like Alice — you would probably be able to hear them laughing and singing their moldy songs, teasing one another, playing harmless moldy practical jokes, and swapping moldy ghost stories.

In rather an odd way, I envied them.

I have a confession to make: In spite of being as tolerant as the next person, I found myself unable to face my own family at breakfast. The very thought of spending even part of an hour under the eyes of Feely, Daffy, and Undine made my brain begin to dissolve. I could already feel it.

I leaped out of bed and scrambled into

my clothes, my breath making absurd little puffs as if I were a character in the comics, saying nothing. Although the unheated east wing of Buckshaw was a trial in the winter, it was the price I was willing to pay for solitude. The only thing missing was dog-sleds.

By a somewhat devious route, I made my way downstairs to the pantry. Mrs. Mullet was so busily fussing with the Aga, she did not notice as I tiptoed in behind her and made off with a liberal supply of uncooked bacon and eggs and several slices of bread.

As I lit the Bunsen burner, back upstairs in my laboratory, I sent up a brief prayer of thanks for not having been spotted.

Holding the bread to the flame with a pair of test-tube clamps, I toasted it to perfection. Eggs scrambled in a glass beaker and bacon sizzling on a stainless steel dissecting tray soon filled the room with the most delicious odors. Claridge's and the Ritz — even the Savoy, I was willing to wager — had never smelled half so deliciously tantalizing on a cold winter morning.

I ate, as Daffy once remarked, with gusto. It was a word I hadn't heard before, and I at once imagined her sitting at a linen-topped table on a terrace by the sea with an elderly, white-haired foreign gentleman —

Greek, perhaps — with a red carnation in his buttonhole, passing her the kippers.

This was Gus Toe, and he lived on in my imagination long after I had been set straight about the word.

I was mopping up the last morsel of egg with the last bite of toast when there was a knock at the door.

"Come in, Dogger," I said, knowing it would be no one else.

The door opened and Undine stuck her head into the room.

"Surprise!" she screeched.

"Go away," I said.

I still hadn't been able to work out why the child annoyed me so much. The fact that I could not had caused me to retreat behind a curtain of insults.

I had tried referring to her at every opportunity as Pestilence, but it had done no good. I had told her that when she dies, I would pray not *to* the Virgin Mary, but *for* the Virgin Mary.

All of which had bounced off Undine's back like H_2O off an Aylesbury duck.

"Go away!" I repeated, in case she hadn't understood.

Undine raised her curled fingers to her lips, sticking a thumb between her teeth to form the mouthpiece of a makeshift trumpet:

"Ta-rah! Ta-rah! Ta-rah-ta-ta-rah-ta-rah!" she trumpeted. "A visitor is announced! Miss Flavia de Luce is desired at the door!"

I laughed in spite of myself.

"If the visitor has a butterfly net, it's you they want, not me," I said.

"The visitor has no net for the lepidoptera," she said, dropping her voice into a lower register that was not only wonderfully done, but also spine-chilling.

"His name is James Marlowe," she added. "And he has a knife."

EIGHTEEN

Undine was right. He *did* have a knife. Or what seemed at first to be a knife.

"Go to your room, Undine," I told her and, incredibly, she obeyed me.

Which left me alone with an armed man.

James Marlowe stood in the foyer, head thrown back, gaping at the ceiling as if he were studying the dome at St. Paul's Cathedral. He was short and stocky, with a barrel chest, and by the way his arms hung out from his sides, I knew that he had developed the kind of biceps that are required for swarming up ropes and so forth.

He had unbuttoned his winter coat, and I could see that he was wearing a hand-me-down blue suit and a striped tie from one of the lesser schools. When he had finished with the foyer, he peered at me owlishly through a pair of round, black-rimmed spectacles.

More for show, I thought, than anything,

since the lenses were of little, if any, magnifying power. I had to admire his brass, though, since I had used the same trick myself when I wanted to gain sympathy or suggest a certain nonexistent weakness.

I judged him to be about eighteen or nineteen, which would be about right.

"Miss de Luce?" he asked, sticking out a square hand.

I took it and I shook it, not trying to hide my glance at the object in his other hand, which was not at all what I had imagined. I'd been expecting the standard Boy Scout knife, with black checkered horn handle, and a blade for every occasion, such as a screwdriver, a corkscrew, a tin-opener, a button hook, and a prong for removing stones from horse's hooves.

Far from it: This tool, which he held out to me on an open handkerchief, was a slender steel blade with a wooden handle: a blade that went from square in the center to round to a doubly sharpened wedge at the tip. It was more of a chisel than a knife, and I have to admit I'd never seen anything like it.

"It's a wood-carving tool, called a firmer," he said. "I found it beside what was left of Mr. Inchbald."

I wanted to shout "Yarooo!" but somehow

I managed to swallow the word.

"Put it in your pocket and follow me upstairs," I said.

I was nervous, of course, about inviting anyone into my sanctum sanctorum, especially a stranger with a sharp-edged weapon, but I needed a place to talk to him without fear of interruption or of being overheard. It was too cold outside, which left the laboratory. I would simply have to risk it.

"Take a pew," I told him, gesturing towards a wicker chair. It was something, I thought, that would be the sort of thing an associate of Edgar Wallace might say: hard-boiled but friendly. I didn't want to appear too intimidating.

I sat myself down in Uncle Tarquin's old oak office chair behind the desk.

Like the beam of a lighthouse, James Marlowe's eyes scanned the room, widening as they went at the sight of the scientific equipment and the rows upon rows of chemical bottles. He was barely able to keep his mouth from falling open.

"I thought I'd deliver the photos personally," he said, passing them across the desk. "Rather than sending them by mail. I thought Mr. Wallace might appreciate —"

"I'm sure he will," I interrupted. "But first, I'd like you to set the scene for me. I like to form my own first impressions."

Like Inspector Hewitt, I couldn't help thinking.

"We can look at the photographs later."

He looked at me rather dubiously. "You seem awfully young to be an assistant to Mr. Wallace," he said.

I gave him a stern glare. "Scout Marlowe," I said. "If Mr. Wallace had not placed his complete trust in me, I should hardly have been placed in this position."

This made no logical sense, but it served its purpose.

"I'm sorry," he said. "You may call me James."

"And you may call me Flavia," I said, softening just enough to encourage him. "Tell it to me in your own words — from the beginning, if you please."

I pulled an unused notebook from a drawer and picked up a pencil.

James opened and closed his mouth several times, his tongue clicking nervously as he licked his lips. But he said nothing. Had I been too forceful?

I raised an encouraging eyebrow. "Whenever you're ready," I said, doling out a little smile.

"The island of Steep Holm," James said, "lies in the Bristol Channel, approximately five miles west of the town of Weston-super-Mare. About a mile and a half in circumference, it rises two hundred feet above the channel . . ."

He sounded like the narrator of one of those dreadful travelogues in the cinema that you have to sit through before you get to Boris Karloff, and I guessed that he had told this story more than once.

"Hold on," I said. "It's human interest Mr. Wallace wants. We'll get to the geography later. Start with the corpse and work outwards."

"It was horrible!" he said, and by his sudden pallor I knew that his mind had instantly flown back to the scene of his grisly discovery. "At first I didn't know what it was, you see. A cluster of old rags — a discarded beef bone — I almost stepped on it."

He stopped to swallow heavily. "I had gone there alone in a small sailboat to map the Victorian fortifications, and to observe the gray plover and the dotterel for my Bird Warden Badge. I had always been interested in the migratory —"

"The corpse," I reminded him.

"It was horrible," he repeated. "Gulls, you see — when they attack — the skull — the eyes were gone. Bits of gristle — connective tissue, I suppose — glittering in the sunlight. It was sickening."

Connective tissue? This was more like it. Edgar Wallace would have been proud of me.

No wonder they hadn't wanted the Inchbald family to view the corpse!

I wrote down James's words in the notebook, taking great care to record them accurately.

"To be honest," he added, "I vomited. They didn't put that in the newspapers, though."

I nodded sympathetically. And yet I remembered that at the time James had been interviewed by *The Telegraph,* he had been quite matter-of-fact about it all. Indeed he had positively rhapsodized about the habits of the carrion crow, and the madness of the birds in nesting season.

And to the *London Evening Standard* he had babbled on about Lord Baden Powell's advice on mapping a corpse.

Hardly the words of a lad who has just tossed his cookies.

Or was I being too hard on the boy?

It was odd, the way in which I kept thinking of him as a boy. Although the James Marlowe who was at this very moment sitting in my laboratory was now nearly a man, he had been only fourteen at the time of his allegedly grim discovery.

Was there more to this man/boy than met the eye?

"Go on," I told him, and he did:

"I tried to convince myself that the . . . remains . . . weren't human. But the firmer, the pipe, the wallet, the . . . the wedding ring . . ."

Again he seemed on the verge of breaking down.

"Wedding ring?" I said. "I don't remember a wedding ring being mentioned."

"No," James said. "They didn't put that in the papers, either. The police thought it might be murder."

"Did they say so?" I asked.

"Well, no. But I'm no fool. I was a bright boy. Inspector Cavendish told me to button my lip about it or he'd have my guts for garters."

Inspector Cavendish was a man after my own heart. Even though the news of Oliver Inchbald's death had gone round the world by wireless, they wanted to keep quiet about the evidence by which his identity was established.

Which was interesting in itself.

Had Inspector Cavendish himself been in on the plot? It was uncharitable of me to think such a thing, but that's how my mind works.

Heaven only knows the author of *Hobbyhorse House* had more than money enough to pay off a couple of trusted confederates. But where had he managed to find a dead body to substitute for his own? If, in fact, that is what had happened.

It may sound far-fetched, but in the annals of crime, far stranger things have happened.

"Tell me about the island," I said. "Mr. Wallace will want to know about the geography. Setting is important in stories, you know."

"Well, it's desolate," James said. "Yes, desolate, I should say. It's only half a mile long and a quarter mile wide, and has just two accessible landing places. There's not much on it, really, except for a few military remains, some old, others more recent. And the birds, of course. Birds by the thousands."

His eyes lit up.

"You're very fond of birds, aren't you, James?" I asked.

"To be honest, I like birds better than people. I suppose Mr. Inchbald did, too, or he wouldn't have gone there."

This was an interesting thought. No one

had mentioned — at least in my hearing — that Oliver was keen on birds. Or had he gone to Steep Holm for some other reason — a walking tour, perhaps — and recognized it as a perfect setting in which to fake his death?

Suppose he had planned it all from a cozy armchair in London?

Authors are known to have fiendishly clever minds, and the authors of children's books are more fiendishly clever than most.

What if Oliver Inchbald *had,* in fact, staged his own death without ever leaving home? What if — like some shadowy puppeteer, or chess master moving his pieces on the board — he had planned and executed his devious plan without ever taking off his slippers?

The important question, though, was *why?*

Why would a man who has the world at his feet — a man who was read aloud from drawing room to nursery, a man beloved by old and young — wish to throw it all away, to vanish from the earth like a music hall magician, in a puff of smoke?

Or a cloud of seagulls.

That, as Hamlet is supposed to have said, is the question.

I was proud of myself. I had finally managed to distill the entire case into a single word:

Why?

"Sorry," I said, tapping my pencil on the notepad. "I was speculating. Getting back to the gulls —"

Slowly, almost reluctantly, I thought, he pulled from an inner pocket a white envelope, which he held out to me.

"These are quite gruesome," he said. "You might not want to —"

"Gruesome is my game, James," I said. "Mr. Wallace demands nothing less."

I took the envelope, opened it, and removed an inner glassine envelope, in which were a number of photos and negatives.

As I thumbed through the prints I couldn't help letting out a whistle. "Crikey," I said. "These don't half take the cake!"

The photos were, as James had warned me, gruesome. In fact, they were more than gruesome: they were ghastly.

There was the bundle of rags, badly mauled, with bits of bone visible through rips and tears; there was the toothless skull with its empty eye sockets.

"They go for the eyes," James said. "They have a fondness for eyes."

I nodded wisely, but wondered if the gulls had taken the teeth as well.

"Did the police see these?" I asked. "You mentioned the photos to the reporter from the *London Evening Standard.* You also mentioned making a sketch."

"I gave them the sketch," he said.

"And the photos?"

He looked away.

"And the photos, James?" I insisted.

"He seemed like a nice chap," he said. "The reporter, I mean. Offered me a cigarette. I didn't accept it, of course. I told him about the photos but I mentioned them to no one else."

"Did he ask to see them?"

"No. He was in a rush to get back up to London for some kind of newspaper beanfest. Besides, I hadn't developed them yet. The film was still in my camera. I have a folding pocket Brownie. It belonged to my father. He carried it all through the war — in spite of personal photos being forbidden."

Like father, like son, I thought.

I leafed through the photographs, examining each one carefully.

"These are very nicely done," I said. "You printed them yourself?"

"Developed *and* printed. I had already earned my Photography Badge, you see, so I was quite good at it."

I returned the prints to the envelope and removed the negatives. At first glance, it seemed that each of them corresponded with one of the prints.

"Hold on," I said. "There are eight negatives, but only seven prints."

"Yes," James said. "I spoiled one of them. I was fiddling with the aperture and overexposed a shot. I could have kicked myself. I had only one roll of film, and it was the last shot left."

I took up the photos again and placed each on top of its corresponding negative.

There was one negative left over. I held it up to the light of the window: a dark and nearly opaque rectangle of about two and a quarter inches by three and a quarter.

"Not much to see, is there?" I asked. "What was it a photo of?"

"I don't remember," James said quickly. "At any rate, it didn't turn out, as you can see."

He didn't remember? A Boy Scout drilled in the arts of observation?

What did he take me for?

I decided to say nothing. Instead, I beckoned him, with a wiggled forefinger, to follow me.

I took down two bottles from a shelf of photographic chemicals. "You are familiar with Farmer's Reducer, I expect?"

The look on his face told me he was not. So much for his Photography Badge.

"Nothing to do with fat farmers," I said, "but named for Ernest Howard Farmer, who published the formula in 1883. It's a solution of potassium ferricyanide. . . ."

I picked up the bottle of bright red salt crystals.

James was now crowding closely behind me, peering over my shoulder — a little too close for comfort, considering that he might still turn out to be a killer.

"We mustn't ever mix this with an acid," I said, "because it produces hydrogen cyanide gas. We'd be dead before we could say 'coconuts.' "

This had the desired effect. James took a hasty step backwards.

I picked up the other bottle, which was half full of clear crystals resembling crushed ice.

"Sodium thiosulfate," I told him. "Hypo. Ordinary fixer."

"It's not acid, is it?" he asked, taking another step backwards.

"No," I said. "Actually, it happens to be the antidote to cyanide poisoning.

"God moves in mysterious ways," I added,

"His wonders to perform. Hand me that bottle."

I stirred three quarters of a cup of the sodium thiosulfate into a quart of water.

"There's our Solution A," I said.

To a second half-cup of water, I added just over half an ounce of potassium ferricyanide. As the red crystals dissolved, the liquid became yellow.

"Solution B," James guessed.

"You're a fast learner," I told him, and he glowed with pride as I prepared my trays and bottles.

"Now then — four parts Solution A . . ." I poured it into a tray. "And one part Solution B . . ."

As the solution turned to an even deeper yellow, I wondered vaguely if Lillian Trench was ever so happy gloating over her witchly brews?

"This is powerful stuff," I said. "We'll dilute it with a bit of water — to slow down the chemical action."

I picked up the negative with a pair of photo tongs, immersed it in the liquid, and began swirling it gently but steadily beneath the surface.

"Nothing's happening," James remarked, after a few seconds.

I pulled the negative from the tray and

plunged it into a tray of water.

I held it up to the light.

"Look again," I told him. "There's been a change in the transparency."

Something had begun to appear.

Back into the reducer, now . . . swirling . . . swirling . . .

An image was swimming into being.

"This is the exciting part," I said, but James was strangely silent.

"Now we stop it," I said, plunging the negative into the hypo.

After a fix and a decent rinse, I cleaned up my chemicals, for the Lord abominateth a sloppy chemist.

"Hello!" I exclaimed, holding the negative up to the light. "What's this?"

"I don't know," James said, far too quickly.

I thought I recognized the object, but I didn't want to jump to conclusions. The image was a negative, of course: Whites were blacks and blacks were whites.

"Let's make a print and find out," I suggested.

"No, wait — it's nothing. I remember now. It's a photo of my Scout knife."

Really, James? I thought. *A photo of your Scout knife? You've just stumbled upon a mutilated corpse on a desolate island, and you choose that particular moment to take a photo of your beloved Scout knife? Come off it. I may be a girl but I'm not a mooncalf.*

I was now, as Feely would have said, "on the horns of a dilemma." Although I wanted desperately to make a print from the negative, I wasn't so keen on locking myself into a darkroom with a possible killer.

The darkroom was at the back corner of the laboratory and was, as all darkrooms are, light-tight. I would not be able to keep an eye on him for the ten or fifteen minutes it would take to produce a positive image. Could I trust James enough to be left alone in the lab while I carried out the process?

"Come with me," I said.

In the darkroom, I prepared the developer and fixer. Nothing new here: I had done it a hundred times.

I switched on the safelight and turned off the room light.

We were plunged immediately into a blood-red gloom. I glanced over my shoulder at James, who was breathing down my neck.

How had the corpse at Steep Holm died? I wondered. Had he been strangled? From behind?

I slipped the negative into the enlarger and made the exposure.

I knew that I was rushing it somewhat but

all I needed was a useable image, not a work of art to be hung by the Royal Photographic Society.

James was strangely quiet as I went about my work. The sound of his breathing now seemed to fill the room. Why was he so reluctant to have me make a print? Why had he lied about the photo? Why had he claimed it was no more than a snapshot of his knife?

I immersed the exposed paper in the developer and waited for the chemicals to work their magic. It didn't take long.

"Look," I said after just a few seconds. "It's coming."

Again, as with the negative, a faint image appeared on the photo paper, then gained rapidly in intensity.

I gasped.

James gasped.

It was a photograph of a knife — and a good one, at that.

"You see?" James said, breathing a hot cloud of relief onto the back of my neck. "I told you so."

"So you did," I said, plunging the print into the rinse water, then into the tray of fixer.

I switched on the overhead light with relief.

"Phew!" I said. "It's hot in here."

I led the way out into the blessed daylight of the laboratory.

"You didn't believe me, did you?" James said. "I could tell."

"Of course I believed you," I told him. "But I have a scientific mind. My eyes need their own proof."

I could tell that he was becoming sulky, as boys and men do when they're caught bluffing. And I ignored him, as girls and women do when they catch them out.

I would wait only for a few minutes before removing the developed print from the fixing bath.

I have to admit that something else was on my mind: Sooner or later, Inspector Hewitt would see my handiwork. It would be entered as evidence. I wanted him to praise my photographic skills.

Silly, perhaps — but sometimes *silly* is all there is to grasp at.

"Someday, my prints will come," I said, making a little joke to relieve the tension. It was not a brilliant one, but it did the trick.

"Haw! Haw! Haw!" James exclaimed. He had caught on to it, and his vanity was restored.

Thank heavens he had seen *Snow White and the Seven Dwarfs*.

"Now then," I said. "Let's see what we've got."

I brought the tray from the darkroom out into the lab.

We both of us leaned over it, our heads together.

"You see," James said. "I told you — it's just a knife."

"Yes," I said. "A knife. A knife with initials engraved on the handle."

I pointed, and read them aloud. *"O.I."*

Oliver Inchbald.

NINETEEN

I let my eyes rise slowly up from the submerged print to meet the gaze of James Marlowe.

There was no need to say a word.

Each of us could see in the eyes of the other that the jig was up.

"You disappoint me, James," I said. "Have you already forgotten the first law of Scouting? *A Scout's honor is to be trusted.* Mr. Wallace will be extremely disappointed in you, as well."

This was laying it on a bit thick, but it did the trick. I had learned the ten Scout Laws by eavesdropping on the troop meetings in St. Tancred's parish hall, never dreaming that they would come in so handy.

Tears welled up in his eyes. In an instant he was a boy again, taking — and breaking — his pledges.

"I didn't mean —" he said. "It was just that —"

I held out my hand, but not in sympathy. "Let's have it," I said.

With a sly look, James reached hurriedly into his pocket and dropped something into my palm.

It was the wood-carving tool he had shown me downstairs.

I gave him my most reproachful look and handed it back. "Come off it, James. You know perfectly well what I mean."

Unable to meet my stony stare, he dug into another pocket and extracted the object I wanted.

The knife was the one in the photo. The engraved initials *O.I.* proved there could be no doubt about it.

I walked slowly across the room, opening out the two blades, which glinted wickedly in the light from the window.

Was this the weapon that had killed the man on Steep Holm? No point worrying about fingerprints now. If this *was* the murder weapon, James had already been soiling it with his dabs for years.

I pulled a magnifying glass from the desk drawer, and examined the thing closely.

"Phew!" I said. "Cartier, London. You have exquisite taste, James."

I could tell at a glance that the case was fourteen-carat gold, the owner's initials elaborately engraved. I held the knife to my nose and sniffed, then tapped it on my hand.

A couple of dark strands fell out and into my open palm. I sniffed again. "Pipe tobacco," I said. "And if I recall correctly, you don't smoke. Right, James?"

James nodded.

"Let me guess . . . ," I said. Guessing was not permitted in the art of detection, but I was enjoying myself, so hang the rules.

"Correct me if I'm wrong. You came ambling along on your bird hunt, stumbled upon a corpse — or what was left of it — spotted the knife in the grass, picked the thing up, had a squint, saw the maker's name, and pocketed it."

James said nothing.

Law number eleven, I thought: *A Scout is stubborn.*

"Come on, James, I'd have done the same myself. It's a Cartier, for heaven's sake!"

I wasn't sure if I would have done, to be honest, but let's face it: Gold is gold.

Slowly and grudgingly, James nodded, unable to meet my eye. "I thought no one would know," he said. "I'm sorry."

But I was barely listening. My thoughts had sprung ahead and left James Marlowe in the dust.

If this was Oliver Inchbald's pocket knife

— and there could be little doubt about it — how had it come to be found in the grass near the body of some as-yet-unknown victim?

One thing was perfectly clear: It was far too convenient.

I remembered what Carla had told me. I could hear her voice in my head: *"Auntie Loo said there wasn't much left of him but a few ribbons, his wallet, and his pipe."*

No mention of a knife.

Of course. There wouldn't be, would there? James had already pinched it.

And Auntie Loo. Carla's aunt Louisa. I had almost forgotten about her.

What role had she played in this deadly little drama? In due course, she would be called upon to identify the corpse — or what was left of it.

And so she had.

Wrongly.

Whether it was intentional or a simple mistake on her part — the stress must have been terrible — she had viewed the tattered remains and pronounced them to be those of Oliver Inchbald.

And not long afterwards, she herself would perish in the Mediterranean, in an Aqua-Lung diving tragedy.

"That day on Steep Holm, James . . . did

you see anyone else? Anyone at all?"

It was a shot in the dark, and I knew it.

James shook his head. "I swear I was the only living soul."

Of course he was. I knew in my heart that he was right. The body had obviously been there for some time before he stumbled upon it.

Long enough for the seagulls of Steep Holm to reduce the corpse to wreckage.

"By the way, James," I asked. "You told the reporter, 'I think it was the gulls got him.' How did you know it was a man?"

James curled his lip as if he were puzzling over a mathematical calculation.

"By the pipe," he said suddenly.

"And the penknife," I added.

"Yes, of course — by the penknife."

"Well, thank you," I said. "You've been very helpful. I'll pass this information to Mr. Wallace, and I'm sure he'll be in touch if there are any further questions."

"Shall I leave the knife with you?" he asked.

"No, thank you," I said. "I've seen quite enough."

When he was gone, my thoughts flew like a bird back to Louisa Congreve.

"Hello, Mrs. Bannerman? It's Flavia de

Luce again."

"Flavia! How lovely to hear from you. But it's Mildred, remember? Compliments of the season, by the way. How's your latest hobby coming along?"

Mildred was as sharp as a cutthroat razor, and twice as fast.

"Spool knitting? I think I'm getting the hang of it." I fell into her game without batting an eyelash. "I've picked apart one of Father's old cardigans, and I'm using the yarn to make Christmas wool dollies for Feely and Daffy."

A somewhat exasperated *click!* on the line announced that Miss Runciman had thrown in her hand.

In spite of that, I did not let down my guard. "I'm coming up to London today. I'd like to make another visit to your friend, the canary breeder. What was her name . . . Congreve? I'm thinking of surprising Aunt Felicity with a young bird for Christmas. It was such a pity about her Orpheus, wasn't it? She adores the Belgian birds, but I might surprise her with one of the German singers from the Hartz Mountains or the Tyrol."

All that I knew about canaries had been learned from several forced viewings of a stale instructional film that was dragged out regularly for our church fêtes. It was called

"Wonderful. She'll be so happy. I shall look forward to seeing you later, then."

"Oh, and Mildred —" I added, "I'd like to visit that other gentleman — the one in Fleet Street — about a cage."

"Finbar Joyce, you mean?"

"Roger. Roger. Over and out," I said.

I couldn't resist.

"Dogger," I said, "I'm going up to London again. I shall be leaving straightaway. Mrs. Bannerman is meeting me, so you mustn't worry. I shall be back at the usual time."

"Of course, miss," Dogger said. "Shall I ring for the taxi?"

As the train rolled through the winter landscape, I reflected upon what a true stick Dogger was. As an old soldier, nothing surprised him. He had quite willingly taught me how to palm the queen of spades when playing Black Lady with Feely and Daffy, and he had not begged off when I had asked him to help me extract, for a practical joke involving Feely's Eau de Violet scent, certain of the volatile terpines from the caudal gland of a dead badger I had found in the woods.

Truly a gentleman of the old school.

As we approached London, the winter landscape shifted subtly, mile by mile, from the white of angels' wings to a relentless gray muck. It was hard to believe that Christmas was now only days away.

True to her word, Mildred was waiting for me on the platform.

"I have a taxicab waiting," she said. "Cranwell Gardens awaits us."

The street was indistinguishable from any other in Kensington: Tall white Georgian houses gazed down haughtily with closed faces upon a narrow street.

"If we're not out in ten minutes, come back in an hour," Mildred told the cabbie.

"Right you are," he said, tipping his cap. We climbed out of the taxi and stood on the pavement.

Ionic capitals stared like a parliament of owls from the pillared face of number 47. A few steps up from the street found us on the porch. Mildred already had a key in her hand.

"I believe it's flats," she said. "But if it isn't, we'll pretend we blundered into the wrong house. They do all look alike, don't they?"

She tried the door and found it unlocked;

I followed her into a narrow hall with three doors, a staircase, and an aspidistra that seemed in need of artificial respiration.

The place had a stuffy smell, in which I could distinguish woodworm, old sofas, and tinned soup.

Mildred was right: The house was divided into five flats, and number 47 was right here at the bottom of the stair.

Mildred knocked. We waited. She knocked again. Nothing.

"Would you like to do the honors, or shall I?" she whispered.

I signaled her to be my guest.

She selected a hooklike wire on her keychain and applied it to the lock, and before you could say "housebreakers" we were inside.

If I had thought my own lock-picking skills to be excellent, Mildred's were divine. *Saint Peter,* I thought, *had better keep his eye on the Pearly Gates.*

The room in which we found ourselves was unremarkable. Table, chairs, sofa, dresser, and desk seemed all to have been stamped from the same mold.

Mildred eased open a door that opened towards the back of the flat and peeked inside.

"Ditto," she said. "Ugh."

335

"It's as if no one lives here," I whispered. "As if it's waiting for a boarder to turn up."

"Spot on," she said. "This is not the flat of a woman who taught Albert Einstein to tap-dance, or whatever it was."

"She smoked his pipe," I said, remembering Carla's words. "Maybe they redecorated since she died."

"I think not," Mildred said. "This furniture looks to have been bought as a job lot in Tottenham Court Road. Late 1930s, I should say at a guess — all cheap veneer and scrollwork. Might as well have been knocked together by Cousin Claude in the cellar."

I could see what she meant.

"Could we have the wrong flat?"

"Check the phone," Mildred said. "Is that the number you called?"

I walked to the desk and glanced at the telephone. Its number, Western 1778, was printed on the dial.

"Yes," I said.

"Are you sure?"

"Quite sure," I said.

How could I forget 1778? It was the year that the great Antoine Lavoisier discovered oxygen and gave it its name.

There could be no doubt that this was the flat I had telephoned. Someone had cer-

336

tainly been here within the past few days: Miss Letitia Greene, who had picked up the handset and talked to me about the sweepstakes ticket held by her distant relative, the late Louisa Congreve.

Miss Letitia Greene, who had been a beneficiary to Louisa Congreve's will.

"There must be papers somewhere," I said. "People can't live without papers."

But a thorough search of the flat failed to turn up a single scrap. The place had the look of a film set, where all the furnishings were simply for show: the sad belongings of make-believe people.

Perhaps that was the point.

"Do you suppose this could be a front?" I asked.

Mildred laughed. "A bolt-hole? You might have a point there. It's traditional, isn't it, for those who have something to hide — such as Sherlock Holmes — to maintain a place for grabbing forty winks, or for putting on or taking off their various disguises?"

"Do you suppose Miss Greene might be a private detective?"

Mildred stroked her chin with a long forefinger. "A private detective," she said, ". . . *or* a public criminal."

I shivered. Something about the place was giving me the heebie-jeebies.

Snooping through someone else's belongings is generally quite invigorating, but a place with an empty clothespress, empty dresser drawers, and empty cupboards left me feeling somehow on edge.

"There's not much to go on," I said, looking round uneasily.

"No," Mildred said. "But not much is much better than nothing."

She saw the puzzled look on my face.

"That maidenhair fern, for instance," she said, pointing. "One can see at a glance that it's been well cared for. Note the lush growth. The maidenhairs, as you know, require coddling. Otherwise they have a tendency to sulk."

She reached up and, having poked a finger into the pot, held it out for my examination. "Dry," she said. "Not watered for several days. Conclusion? Householder left in a hurry. The fact that she cleared out her clothing lock, stock, and barrel might mean that she had no intention of returning. I'm assuming it's a she, since men on their own don't generally grow ferns."

"The bird has flown," I said.

"Precisely. The question is not *Whence?* but *Whither?* Let us gird up our loins, Flavia, and do likewise."

The taxi was waiting at the curb, the

driver craning his neck in all directions.

"These 'ere traffic wardens come at yer like carrion crows," he said as we pulled away. "Oughtn't to be allowed. Where to?"

"Fleet Street," Mildred told him. *The Telegraph.*"

"Thought as much," the driver said.

TWENTY

Not far from St. Paul's Cathedral, the office of *The Daily Telegraph* was in a part of the city flattened by the Blitz. Even after ten years, blackened bombsites still remained scattered round the church like rotting teeth in the mouth of some ancient duchess.

We stared out at the passing narrow streets, silenced at the sight.

With a sudden swerve to the curb, our driver pulled up with a jerk and stared at Mildred in his mirror, waiting for her to pay the fare.

"Thank you, Bert," she said, handing him a couple of notes. "You are truly a pearl among cabbies."

Bert fought to hold back radiance, then tipped his cap.

We paused for a moment on the pavement, looking up at *The Telegraph*'s towering pillars.

"Designed by the same person who did

the pylons for Sydney Harbor Bridge," Mildred said with a sniff, and I nodded knowingly.

Inside, we asked directions and fought our way through hordes of people in a maze of brightly lighted corridors. The racket from regiments of typewriters and armies of shoes shuffling on marble was overwhelming.

"Here we are," Mildred said, and tapped lightly with her knuckles on a glass-windowed door.

There was no answer.

She tapped again and then opened the door.

"Finbar Joyce?" she asked.

I had somehow imagined Finbar Joyce as an elderly, rumpled reporter in a reeking, wrinkled mackintosh with a cigarette in his mouth and a notebook and pencil clutched in his nicotine-stained fingers.

Instead, he turned out to be a large, youngish man in flannels, with an orange and blue silk cravat tucked into a creamy Fair Isle pullover. He looked more like a wealthy fisherman on holiday than a Fleet Street reporter. The only signs of dissipation were the faint red rims of his eyes and the curve of his belly, which reminded me of a sail full of wind.

341

"Mildred Bannerman," Mildred said. "We spoke on the telephone."

"Ah, beloved Miss Bannerman," Finbar said, without getting up from behind his desk — without even looking, in fact. "The Inchbald affair."

He waved us to a couple of criminally hard-looking wooden chairs.

"You knew him, I believe," Mildred said.

"I reported on his death," Finbar said. "I should hardly say I knew him, no. Rubbed elbows with the Great Man once or twice, perhaps, in the clubs. Raised a glass or two on small occasions. The world of books and newspapers is not a large one — quite the contrary to what you may think."

Although he was speaking to Mildred, he was looking closely at me.

"This is my friend Flavia de Luce," Mildred said.

"Ah! Sylvia Silence, the girl detective." Finbar grinned. "I know you by reputation of course. Your fabled name has crossed this desk on more than one occasion. The Case of the Purloined Penny Black, for instance. If I recall correctly, His Majesty the King was thinking of making you a Knight of the Garter."

I blushed. I did not much care for such personal talk coming from the mouths of strangers.

"About Oliver Inchbald," I said.

"Just so," Finbar said. "I expect you were fattened in the nursery on *Hobbyhorse House.*"

It was an insult, and I recognized it as one instantly. I was not going to let this self-important scribbler get away.

"I was, Mr. Joyce," I said. "And I suspect you were, also."

"By the river Liffey, I sat down and wept!" Finbar exclaimed. "Touché! Hallelujah! You've smuggled in an unexploded bomb, Miss Bannerman. A veritable UXB in pigtails. More than I had bargained for."

What *had* he bargained for? I wondered. Hadn't Mildred said that the man would sell the souls of everyone in sight for a couple of quid and a pint of Guinness? What had she offered him in exchange for dishing up the lowdown on Oliver Inchbald?

"*Mrs.* Bannerman," Mildred corrected him.

I beamed at her. We were on the same team.

"You were sent to the scene of his death?" I asked.

"Assigned," Finbar corrected, "by old Bartleby, my editor. Dispatched, as it were. Thence wafted on the swift wheels of the

Great Western Railway to Weston-super-Mare, where I proceeded to —"

"Tell us about the corpse," I interrupted, at the risk of seeming obnoxious. I was growing tired of listening to this windbag.

"Ah, the corpse," he said, and his face grew suddenly solemn as he drew in a deep breath.

"Bones, flesh, and feathers — as if an angel had crashed."

Now, this was reporting! I couldn't recall if angels actually had flesh, but otherwise this was journalism with real juice. I allowed my mouth to fall open in appreciation.

"But you didn't say so in your article," I said.

"No. One is not allowed a soul when the Proprietor is paying for the ink."

I felt suddenly sorry for Finbar Joyce.

"The Proprietor?" I asked.

"Lord Ruffley. He who holds all of us in the palm of his hand, there to be fed like feasting flies — or flicked off into oblivion."

"You are being very honest, Mr. Joyce," Mildred said quietly.

Finbar's eyes swept slowly round to her, like a lighthouse in the night. "There are occasions, Mrs. Bannerman," he said, "when honesty is the only option left."

"Are you telling us that Lord Ruffley

intervened in your reporting of Inchbald's death?"

"I am telling you that Fleet Street is a harsh mistress. No more, no less."

"As I well remember," Mildred said.

As in a blinding flash I recalled that Mildred had been subjected, as few humans before her, to the full glare of the newspapers' headlights. As a convicted murderess, she had been shot and shamed by a hundred thousand cameras, all of her newspaper photos chosen to make her look cruel, haunted, gaunt, and guilty.

But why was she telling him this? It made no sense. I looked from her face to his, as if to find the answer.

"You know each other!" I exclaimed as the light dawned. "You're old pals!"

That whole business of "*Miss* Bannerman" and "*Mr.* Joyce" had been a sham — a show put on for my benefit.

Why, then, had they suddenly dropped it?

"There was a time," Mildred said, "when Finbar was . . . was . . ."

"A lifeline in a stormy sea," Finbar said, grinning. "A rock . . . a rocket in the night . . . a comforter . . . a warm blanket . . ."

"Stow it, Finbar," Mildred said, and we all laughed.

Now that their secret was out, the room became a warmer place: so much so that I removed my coat and hung it with Finbar's on the nearby stand.

"What was he really like?" I asked. "Oliver Inchbald, I mean."

"Glossy. Slick. 'Brittle' is the word that's sometimes used. A walking mirror: a piece of cold glass that reflects all that it sees without ever giving of itself."

"A bully?" I asked.

"Ah! You've heard that, too."

"Who loved him?"

Finbar laughed — a short, barking noise like a fox. "What a question! Not the usual 'Who hated him?' asked by the men in wrinkled suits with a whiff of handcuffs and the river about them. Look after this girl, Mildred. She's a menace to murderers."

A menace to murderers? I quite liked that. If I ever have a business card I shall have that motto printed on it with an image of a never-sleeping eye.

"Was Mr. Inchbald murdered?" I asked.

"Who knows?" Finbar said. "The autopsy was inconclusive. The body had been too long on the island before it was discovered."

"And the seagulls?" I asked.

"There was nothing to contradict such a theory," Finbar said, "except that it had never happened before, which doesn't make it an impossibility. The idea was actually floated by the Proprietor."

"Lord Ruffley? Why?"

"It's the way of the world," Finbar said. "A famous man suffering a heart attack on an island sells thousands of papers, perhaps. The same man pecked to death by maddened seagulls sells millions."

"That's disgusting," I said.

"Welcome to our wicked world, Flavia de Luce," Finbar said. "Enjoy your stay."

"Who loved him?" I asked, repeating my question.

"Well . . . nobody," Finbar said. "Except perhaps that woman at his publishers. What was her name — ?"

"Congreve," I said. "Louisa Congreve."

"Congreve! Yes, that's the one. She was his amanuensis, his dogsbody, and his whipping boy, all rolled into one. Or so it seemed to me."

How odd, I thought. Louisa Congreve hadn't sounded like the type to be anybody's dogsbody. And whipping boys were not noted for teaching the tango — or whatever it was — to Winston Churchill.

Or were they?

Could there be shadier sides of life of which I was not yet aware?

I didn't like to think that there were —
but at the same time I didn't like to think
that there weren't.

By now I was feeling quite benevolent
towards Finbar Joyce. Perhaps I had mis-
judged him. I found myself on the verge of
blurting out that the body he had viewed
on Steep Holm was not that of Oliver Inchbald. But I managed somehow to hold my
tongue.

Detection is a game of cards, I had already
decided. It is not necessary to show your
hand to the other players — such as Inspector Hewitt, for instance. Not even to Mildred. For some reason which I could not
yet explain, I hadn't confided in her all that
I had found out at Thornfield Chase.

I was thinking this when Finbar got up
from his desk, looked out the window, then
drifted to the door, which he opened and,
after a glance outside, quietly closed again.

"Listen," he told us. "I oughtn't to be doing this, but since we're all hail-fellows-well-
met — and as long as you keep quiet about
it, at least until the papers are on the street
—"

"You have our solemn word," Mildred
promised, without consulting me.

"It's just come through this morning. The
body found on Steep Holm was not that of

Oliver Inchbald."

He looked from one of us to the other to judge the impact.

I've learned in my short life that surprise is the most difficult of all the emotions to fake. By contrast, happiness, fear, anger, disgust, and sadness are a piece of cake.

But surprise takes some real acting skill. One must avoid shooting the eyebrows up in inverted Vs, like a circus clown, or throwing up the hands, palms outward, or widening the eyes until they are, like the dog's in the fairy tale, as big as saucers.

Letting the mouth fall open is the mark of an amateur — even though I've occasionally done it myself for variety.

Instead, one must begin with a barely perceptible blink, followed, after a count of three, by another, this one more noticeable. Each of these must be accompanied by an inhalation of air, the first through the nose and the second through the mouth.

Only then is the hand allowed to make a slight movement towards the throat, but it must be stopped forcefully before it has gone half a foot.

"I beg your pardon?" I said.

Making a person repeat their surprising statement robs it of some of its power; gives you a little more time to go through your rigmarole.

"The body found on Steep Holm was not that of Oliver Inchbald," Finbar repeated.

"No!" I said.

"It's true." Finbar nodded, and he seemed gratified by my response. "Someone in the pathologist's office had an early pint with one of our lads and — well, by this evening it will have circled the world."

I shook my head, as if in disbelief, and stared at him expectantly, like a dog waiting for the third biscuit.

"Turns out to be the remains of a tramp named Walter Glover. Spent his life driving wooden stakes into remote places to mark the spots to which the Holy Ghost and little men from Mars had both descended.

"At any rate, they didn't find his marker on Steep Holm until a couple of days ago, so that there was no reason to connect him with the place. His family didn't really bother keeping track of him, which explains why he was never reported missing."

"Men from Mars," Mildred said. "It is very sad, isn't it?"

Finbar nodded. "Mr. Wells has much to answer for," he said.

As we put on our coats and made ready for the cold outdoors, Finbar stood up behind his desk.

"Farewell, fair Flavia," he said. "I shall mark this day with the traditional white pebble, so that in my latter years —"

"What about the pipe?" I interrupted.

"Pipe?" Finbar said, surprised.

"Yes," I said. "The pipe with *O.I.,* or something similar, engraved on the stem."

Carla and James Marlowe had both mentioned the pipe that had been found beside the ravaged body. I'll admit I was speculating about the monogram, but a man with money who monograms one thing will likely monogram everything in sight.

"How could you possibly know that?" Finbar said, whitening noticeably. "Inspector Cavendish removed it from the scene with his own hands. Its very existence has been a most closely guarded secret. I was in on it myself only because I happened to be there.

"How could you *possibly* know?" he asked again.

"A lucky guess," I told him.

"You really oughtn't to do it," Mildred said outside as she hailed a taxicab. "But I suppose you can't help it, can you? I was much the same at your age."

I bit my lip visibly as a signal of remorse, but said nothing. We drove to the railway

351

station in silence.

As I stepped out of the taxi, Mildred reached across and took my hand.

"Good luck," she said, and I gave her fingers a squeeze.

This time, there was no Dogger on the train, and I was left to sit alone, staring out at the ever-darkening countryside.

At the last stop before Doddingsley a man and his young daughter came into the carriage, arms loaded to overflowing with prettily wrapped gifts. When they had settled, he began to explain to her in great detail how the surface tension of water kept certain insects from sinking.

And I felt suddenly as if I had been plunged into a vat of sadness.

I thought of Father, of course. Without meaning to, I had been keeping him at arm's length in my mind for far too many days.

Why? I wondered. Was it for his sake or for mine?

Why didn't I take a taxi to Hinley and to the hospital? Why didn't I barge in and demand to see my father? It wasn't as if I hadn't done such things before.

It was a failure on my part.

A failure of what?

Of love?

Of trust?

Of understanding?

When it came to thoughts such as these, my mind became a tiny boat tossed on a vast, dark sea. With no compass to guide me — no stars, no oars, no sail, not even a bailing bucket — I was at the mercy of God . . . or Fate . . . or Chance . . . or Mrs. McCoo in the Sky, or whoever it was in cosmic charge of things.

At such times I could only retreat for safety into the Castle of Chemistry: the only hiding place in the universe where relationships would never — could never — change.

TWENTY-ONE

I shoved a note under Dogger's door, telling him I was safely home, then went to my room and shot the bolt. I fished out a stack of gramophone records from under the bed and sorted through them, blowing off the dust. The one I wanted was, of course, as always, at the bottom of the pile.

Pavane pour une infante défunte, or *Pavane for a Dead Princess,* is a piano piece by Maurice Ravel, and I wished to hear it because it suited my soggy mood.

Years ago, when I was younger, Feely had forced me to lie on a sofa in the drawing room with my eyes closed and a lily in my folded hands as she played the *Pavane* at a glacial pace from beginning to end.

"If you move so much as an eyelash," she had told me, "we shall have to start over from the beginning."

I wound up the machine, dropped the needle onto the record, and, as the sad music began to ooze from the horn, stood on my head on the bed with my heels against the wall and began to organize my thoughts.

I had less than five minutes before the music ended.

I would first gather the known facts, and they were these:

I had discovered the dead body of Oliver Inchbald, who was living under the name of Roger Sambridge, in his cottage at Thornfield Chase. The author had apparently staged his own death on the remote isle of Steep Holm in the Bristol Channel. How he had done so, and with whose assistance — even the reason why — remained to be discovered, but it seemed reasonable to assume that he had happened upon a dead and badly bird-mauled body while on a hiking trip, and seen at once the opportunity to vanish without a trace.

He was, after all, an imaginative inventor of tales, wasn't he? The idea could have occurred to him in a flash. All he needed to do was rummage through the tattered clothing to make sure that no means of personal identification remained, and then dump his own belongings beside the body. It was all too easy.

It was the woodworking tool — the firmer

— that gave the game away. The firmer was the straw that broke the camel's back: the unnecessary detail.

Oliver had been so eager to have the body identified as his own that he had gone too far. How clever he must have thought himself! Who else would think to leave a token of some obscure hobby, such as wood-carving?

How lucky he had been to have had it with him!

He hadn't counted, of course, on the acquisitive James Marlowe happening upon the scene and pocketing two key pieces of evidence.

The skull, as I had observed from James Marlowe's photographs, had been toothless. The tramp, Walter Glover, had evidently worn false teeth, which Oliver Inchbald must have removed from the remains, in order to foil identification.

I couldn't help wondering idly what he had done with them. It seemed more than likely he had ditched the dentures some-where in a rubbish bin, and that they were now in some unknown tip for eternity, or until unearthed by some future archaeolo-gist.

As I had learned from my own inspection of his body, Oliver himself had possessed a full set of perfect — and quite likely very expensive — teeth.

Had Inspector Cavendish of the Somerset Constabulary not wondered why or how the seagulls had managed to extract a perfectly serviceable set of teeth from the famous author's mouth? Perhaps he had, but was still keeping that curious fact as the ace up his sleeve — even though several years had passed.

The possibility still existed, of course, that James Marlowe had pocketed the teeth as a grisly trophy, as he had done with the pocketknife. For all I knew, there was a Boy Scout badge called Relic Collector.

Stranger things have happened, as I know from personal experience.

Who else had been at the scene of the discovery?

Had Carla's aunt Louisa been summoned to the barren rocks to have a squint, or had her identification of the corpse taken place in a proper morgue, with sliding slabs of stainless steel and dramatically pulled-back sheets and so forth?

How, when it came to that, had she managed to identify the body — other than by its possessions — when there was so little left of it?

Perhaps the police had decided that she

was the only one of Inchbald's family and acquaintances with a strong enough stomach to view the remains.

It was too late to know. Auntie Loo had since joined Walter Glover and Oliver Inchbald somewhere in the Great Beyond, where they were probably looking down at this very moment, nudging one another in the ribs and cackling at my puzzlement.

And then, of course, there was Finbar Joyce. Finbar had gone at once by train to Weston-super-Mare and then by boat to Steep Holm. By the time he arrived, the remains would have been under police guard, making souvenir hunting impossible.

Had other reporters been on the scene? They must have been, but Finbar, having received an early tip-off from his master, Lord Ruffley, must surely have been the first.

What similarities had there been between the body on Steep Holm and that of Oliver Inchbald, alias Roger Sambridge?

Very few, at first sight: One was not much more than a bundle of bones on a rock and the other a fully fleshed man hung up on a door: a healthy-enough-looking person except — of course — that he was dead.

I allowed my mind to return to Hilary Inchbald, the dead man's son. He had certainly been in the neighborhood — at the Thirteen Drakes, in fact — at the time of his father's death.

Or had he been even closer? It was obvious that he was more than just a casual guest at the home of Lillian Trench, less than a stone's throw from the death scene.

If anyone had a motive for killing Oliver Inchbald, it had to be his son who, as a boy, had been so horribly abused by his father. It would, in a complicated way, be tit for tat, or a case of turnabout's fair play.

And what about Carla?

Other than the fact that the vicar and his wife had suggested she go apologize for mutilating the misericords, I could still not explain how her personal copy of *Hobbyhorse House* came to be in the bedroom of its dead author.

The only reason that even remotely made sense was unthinkable.

Even by me.

And then, of course — inevitably — there was Lillian Trench herself, whose name kept bobbing to the surface like a rotten egg in ice water.

And at that very moment, the *Dead Princess* ended. The phonograph needle went *skrork-skrork-skrork*ing at the end of its groove, and I allowed my legs to fall with a thump down onto the bed.

It is a well-known fact that standing on one's head stimulates not only the brain, but also the digestive system, and — to put it delicately — I heard the sudden "Tally-ho!" of nature.

I clattered down the stairs to the small closet on the landing and seized the knob.

The door was locked.

" 'Oo is it?" called a startled voice from inside.

It was Mrs. Mullet.

"Flavia," I said.

"You mustn't come in, dear," she said. "I'm 'avin' a vowel movement."

"All right," I said. "Sorry."

One never knows quite what to say in such situations, but some of us have discovered a strategy that works as well as any.

"I need to know about Lillian Trench," I called out in much too loud a voice, as if she were in Africa rather than on the other side of a thinly paneled door. "How do you know she's a witch?"

There was a slight pause, and then Mrs. Mullet said, " 'Cause I 'eard it from my friend Mrs. Waller, that's 'ow."

"And how does Mrs. Waller know?" I persisted.

" 'Cause she 'eard it from the woman's

own lips, that's 'ow."

"Lillian Trench told Mrs. Waller she was a witch? I mean that Lillian herself — not Mrs. Waller — was a witch?"

"That's right, dear," Mrs. Mullet said. "Now walk away, please. I'm comin' out."

It is from small encounters such as these that great feats of detection are born.

Having made my ablutions — as Feely says to Dieter when she's trying to throw him off the scent — I made my way downstairs.

Although it was now well after dark, there were things still to be done. I simply could not allow Inspector Hewitt to get there before me and take all the credit.

But first, as they say in the cinema, I needed to make a clean getaway. The last thing I needed was to have that twerp Undine dogging my footsteps.

I needn't have worried. The house lay in perfect silence.

To tell the truth, I was enjoying this new freedom to come and go as I pleased, and the slight sense of danger produced by prowling round the village alone in the dark simply added spice to the occasion, like curry powder to dumplings.

"Come on, Gladys," I whispered, easing open the greenhouse door. "There's skulduggery at the crossroads. The plot is thickening and our services are craved."

The wind was still well up, polishing the icy road to the glossy sheen of black crystal. The white, bright winter moon shone down, transforming the familiar countryside into a fantastic kingdom of cold glass.

Freezing air is conducive to clear thinking, and as I rode, I reviewed in my mind the implications of Mrs. Mullet's remark.

Why would Lillian Trench put it about that she was a witch? According to Mrs. M, she had told Mrs. Waller that in so many words. Volunteered it, so to speak.

A woman living alone in a country cottage would hardly risk the glare of village gossip without a powerful reason for doing so.

There could be only one explanation: She wanted to frighten people off.

And why, I asked myself, *would she want to do that?*

To keep them away, of course. There was no other logical answer.

And why would she want to keep them away?

I thought I knew.

But the only way to be certain was to confront the woman herself. A single question would do the trick. I would know in an instant from her reaction if I were right or wrong.

In spite of the ice, I took my hands from Gladys's handlebars for a moment and gave myself a good hug.

I was proud of myself.

Father would be proud of me, too.

As I was passing St. Tancred's, I dismounted and walked Gladys across the road. The surface was especially slick at this point and I didn't want to risk a tumble. The de Luce family fortunes were at a low enough ebb already. A broken arm or a broken leg — or even worse — would be the last straw.

As I picked my way across the icy surface, a pair of headlights swept the road to my right, towards the village high street. A car was approaching from the east.

I don't know what made me do it, but I picked up Gladys bodily and carried her quickly through the gate and behind the stone wall of the churchyard, where I crouched, scarcely daring to breathe.

To be spotted and questioned would be to fail. I simply couldn't risk it.

As it approached, the car slowed as it shifted down through its gears, and my heart began to sink. Peering out between the loose stones on top of the wall, I could see that it was Inspector Hewitt's familiar blue Vauxhall.

Had he spotted me? Had his headlights picked me out? I couldn't be sure.

I huddled down in the darkness, trying to make myself as small as possible.

The Vauxhall hadn't come to a complete stop, but was still crunching slowly, carefully, inch by inch across the slick ice.

Surely they could not see me in the darkness of the churchyard.

I risked a peek.

Although the car had gone too far past for me to identify the driver, the drawn, white faces of the two passengers in its backseat were clearly illuminated by the moonlight.

Hilary Inchbald and Lillian Trench.

Both of them looked like death warmed over.

After what seemed like an eternity, the Vauxhall, having waddled its way slowly across the treacherous patch of ice, accelerated towards Hinley.

"Blast it all!" I said. My opportunity was lost.

There could be no questioning now of the would-be witch. Inspector Hewitt had beaten me to the punch.

It was clear that he had come to his own

conclusions about the death of Oliver Inch-bald — alias Roger Sambridge — and had made his arrests.

In spite of myself, I couldn't resist a little smile.

There was nothing left for me to do now but to return to Buckshaw and read about it in the morning papers.

Did the inspector know the half of it? I wondered.

I would have to wait upon the *Hinley Chronicle* to find out.

As I rounded the gate, a faint sound came to my ears, blown on the wind.

Something was groaning behind me in the churchyard, and it wasn't the wind. Whether it came from a human throat I could not tell.

I am not normally nervous in country churchyards; in fact some of my most pleasant hours have been spent among the dead, who are, after all, harmless.

Why, then, was my hair suddenly standing on end? Why was every nerve in my body shrieking at me to run?

Was it the dark, tattered cloud which went suddenly scudding across the face of the moon? Was it my childhood memory of tales of terror told to me by Daffy before I could even walk? Edgar Allan Poe can have a powerful effect on the mind of a child.

The wind moaned among the tombstones — hummed horribly among the bells in the tower overhead.

The very air was electric. A storm was rapidly approaching. The moon vanished and reappeared — vanished again.

The noise came again — closer this time — different than before.

The sound of singing.

Singing is not out of place at a church, especially two days before Christmas, but the church and the vicarage were both in darkness. This was no last-minute choir practice.

Could it be Christmas carolers, I wondered, *making their way from door to door in the village, in hopes of a bowl of hot cider or something stronger?*

But no, this was the sound of a single human voice, and it was coming clearly now to my ears, carried crisply upon the cold air by the north wind.

"Hark the horn, the sound of winter
Hark the hunter on the hill . . ."

The song was the Horn Dance. And I recognized the voice.

"Carla?" I called. "Is that you?"

There was no reply. Only the weeping of the wind in the winter churchyard.

"Carla?" I called again, louder this time. I didn't want to risk arousing Cynthia and the vicar, although the chance seemed slight. They would be too exhausted from their pre-Christmas labors to hear anything less than the arrival of the Apocalypse.

Besides, the wind was whipping Carla's voice away to the south and away from the vicarage. She was unlikely to be heard by anyone but me.

"It's all right, Carla," I called. "Don't be frightened. It's me, Flavia."

Did I imagine it, or did a chilling giggle reach my ears? A giggle so cold as to make the bones of the buried dead seem warm by comparison?

"Carla?" I called again.

I needed to establish communication.

"Carla?"

Another giggle from somewhere among the tombstones.

It is not the dead who are to be feared, I thought, *but rather the living. Only the living can cast you down among the dead.*

Echoing among the ancient monuments, Carla's stony voice seemed suddenly to be coming from everywhere.

"Air the speeding arrow doth splinter
Flying forth to make the kill."

With those words, she came rushing at
me out of the darkness, her eyes blazing like
lanterns and her face hideous to behold.

On her head were strapped the antlers of
the Horn Dance.

A fierce heat seemed to radiate from her
features, as if she had been possessed by
some ancient sun god.

She's mad, I realized. Quite mad.

She came to a sudden stop, grasping at a
leaning tombstone, breathing heavily, her
feet pawing at the ground and steam issuing
from her nostrils like a stag at bay.

"Well done!" I said, because I could think
of nothing else. "Sing it again, please,
Carla."

If she obeyed my veiled command, I
would have a few more moments to think,
and heaven knows, I needed them.

Oh, if only Dogger were here, I thought.
He would know what to do. When it came to
dealing with disturbances of the mind, Dogger had a great deal more experience than
I.

I don't mean that to sound condescending. It's the truth, and Dogger himself
would be the first to admit it.

If he were here.

But he wasn't.

It was too much to expect — I knew it already — that fond Fate might have caused him to follow me to the churchyard in the same way that he had followed me on the train to London.

Although Fate loves coincidence, it does not chew its cabbage twice.

I was on my own.

Carla was still glaring at me, mad-eyed in the moonlight.

"Please, Carla," I said again, quietly. "Sing it again. Please."

She clasped her hands at her waist in the familiar crustacean pose.

"Hark the horn, the sound of winter
Hark the hunter on the hill
Air the speeding arrow doth splinter
Flying forth to make —"

"The kill," I said. "That's what you think you've done, isn't it, Carla? You think you killed Roger Sambridge. Or should I say Oliver Inchbald? But you already knew perfectly well who he was, didn't you?"

Carla looked dazed, the ancient antlers rocking crazily from side to side on her head; the gleam of old, polished bone in the

369

moonlight.

"I know you were there, Carla. I smelled your throat spray."

It was true: the sulfurous dioxide solution had been a dead giveaway.

I had only just realized this — perhaps prompted by the smell of lightning. A whiff of brimstone had definitely been present in the death chamber and my overactive mind had allowed itself to substitute Satan for science. It's a well-known fact that sulfurous acid (H_2SO_3) is the main ingredient in throat sprays used by opera singers from Caruso right down to the current American heart-throb Mario Lanza.

It is an even better known fact that a solution of sulfurous acid has a more clinging and long-lasting odor than its more famous relative, sulfuric acid. Which is why it lingered in the room.

"He was probably already dead," I said. "You just happened along and blamed yourself."

"He wasn't dead!" Carla shrieked. "He *laughed* at me!"

Laughed at her?

My mind was turning mental gymnastics as the remaining facts fell into place as smoothly as oiled tumblers in a lock.

"You went there to apologize for damaging the misericords, didn't you? And to butter him up by begging him to sign your copy of *Hobbyhorse House.*"

"He insisted I sing for him first," Carla blurted, her face an agony.

"And did you?" I asked, already knowing the answer.

"He laughed at me!"

I had no trouble imagining the scene: the pain-racked old man hanging suspended head downwards in his homemade surgical frame . . .

She must have taken him by surprise.

He had probably meant to put her at ease — to reassure her — but Carla had taken it the wrong way.

"Your aunt had forbidden you to go there, hadn't she? But then the vicar ordered you —"

"I have no aunt," Carla said in a surprisingly calm voice. "My aunt is dead."

"Come off it, Carla," I scoffed. "What do you take me for? Your auntie Loo has been living here for years — right across the road from her old swain, Oliver Inchbald — and putting it about that she's a witch to keep the neighbors off. Isn't that true?"

"Swain" is a nice touch, I thought. The word was used in "The Lass with the Delicate Air," and even Carla could hardly miss

371

its meaning.

That stirred her! Carla shook herself like a bear coming out of an Alaskan river.

"Auntie Loo is dead," she said in a dull, resigned voice.

"Perhaps she is," I told her, "but Lillian Trench lives on. Isn't that the truth?"

With a gulp, Carla let loose a tattered scrap of laughter. I thought for a moment she was going to vomit.

But she did nothing of the sort. Instead, she lowered her head and charged directly at me.

She was trying to impale me on her deadly antlers.

It is at moments such as these — moments of great distress — that time becomes treacle and things go into a peculiar, oozing sort of slow motion: the kind of thing we see in documentary films where bullets burst water-filled balloons.

This was precisely what was happening now as Carla came hurtling towards me, floating like lazy thistledown upon the air, her hair lifting and falling in slow, sweeping waves like owl's wings and her mouth opening and closing in a slow, rubbery grin.

Because she was considerably larger than me, Carla had the advantage of both weight and speed.

The crusty snow between the graves had been polished by the wind, and footing was treacherous. I tried to sidestep — slipped — and fell.

Carla went rocketing past and, with an almighty crash of ringing antlers, collided with a crooked tombstone. In an instant, she was on her feet again, shaking her head groggily.

I managed to claw my way round behind a tall marble monument upon which the finger of a sculpted hand pointed to heaven. I rolled over, hauled myself to my knees, and sucked in several deep breaths.

I hadn't realized how shaken I was.

A low moan and a moist slobbering sound told me that Carla was on her feet again. I could see her shadow on the snow, the antlers motionless, her head cocked — listening.

I held my breath.

But here she came again. She had spotted my trail in the snow and was lumbering heavily towards me.

Although I could not yet see her, I could hear clearly each clotted gasp of her breathing.

I stood up and peered round the monument. Since she already knew where I was, there was no point in hiding. *Better to have her in plain view,* I thought.

"Listen, Carla," I said. "Inchbald or Sambridge or whatever you want to call him died because he couldn't release himself from the rack he built. The gear was jammed. The stupid thing was broken. I saw it with my own eyes. You're not responsible for his death. Do you understand?"

There was a long pause, during which I could almost hear her thinking.

And then there came one of the most spine-chilling sounds I have ever heard: a soft, sucking laugh that was hardly human.

"Ss-omething ss-lipped." She giggled, her words coming in machine-gun gasps. "He ss-creamed. Couldn't — get loose. He begged me. I could — have cut — him down. I could — have gone — for help."

"But he had laughed at you," I said, trying to sound as if I understood.

Carla nodded, looking almost relieved. I saw that tears were running down her face.

"I left — him there . . . to die."

And with an ear-splitting wail she came running at me again, passing so close this time that I could feel the heat radiating from her body. I could even smell the distinctly rank and goatish odor of her sweat.

She was the hunter and I was the quarry. How easy it would be, I remember thinking, to lose an eye to that vast expanse of pointed antlers.

"Carla!" I shouted, as firmly as I could. "Sing to me! Sing to me, Carla!"

I had heard of disturbed people being calmed by someone taking sudden command. I could think of nothing else, and it was worth a try.

And it almost worked.

Having stopped, she stood motionless for a moment, her mouth writhing, her lips twisting in a horrible tortured grimace, as if something unspeakable was trying to escape her body.

Had she heard me?

Her voice came on the bitter air.

"Hark the horn, the sound of winter . . ."

But this was no longer Carla's voice. It was the voice of some poor tortured soul crying out to be released from whatever hellish prison it had fallen into.

"Hark the hunter on the hill . . ."

The voice of a madwoman.

"Air the speeding arrow doth splinter
"Flying forth to make —

"THE KILL!" she shrieked, lunging at me again.

I spun away, my frozen fingers clawing at the buttons of my coat. I dodged behind a tombstone just long enough to extract my arms frantically from the sleeves.

With a shrug, the coat was off — clutched in my hands.

Carla's head oscillated from side to side as if she were an adder zeroing in on the position of her prey. From her mouth was oozing the most unspeakable slime.

Without another word she launched herself at me, head down, and as she did so, I sidestepped, spun round, and flung my coat over her head, entangling the antlers, putting every last ounce of my remaining strength into giving it a powerful twist.

With a sickening thump, she went down into the snow.

I threw myself on top of her, holding on in spite of her thrashing.

I was surprised to find myself sobbing.

Only then did I notice that the vicarage lights had come on and that dark figures in windblown dressing gowns, carrying torches, were approaching cautiously through the snow.

TWENTY-TWO

An hour and a quarter had come and gone. Dr. Darby had been summoned and had arrived quickly on the scene to calm Carla with a sedative.

By the time Inspector Hewitt returned — called back by the magic of automotive wireless, and still in the company of Lillian Trench and Hilary Inchbald, who had reported Carla missing — the scene in the vicarage drawing room was one of near normality.

Wrapped in ancient eiderdowns, Carla and I huddled in front of the fireplace. Carla, in a glassy-eyed trance, stared fixedly at the flames as if she had never seen fire before, while I sipped distractedly at the cup of hot Oxo Cynthia had somehow managed to rustle up.

Lillian Trench rather furtively eased herself onto a stool beside me.

"Meddler!" she hissed in a whisper. "You

had no business —"

"You were all in on it, weren't you?" I interrupted. Inspector Hewitt was busy with Hilary Inchbald, and this was my chance.

"Frank Borley was in love with you, wasn't he? He'd do anything to help you."

"Is this blackmail?" Borley had asked me in his office. *"Do you realize what would happen if this got out?"*

Proof positive that something was going on, if only I'd been paying attention.

I had wondered at the time what fired his boiler, and know I knew.

It was Lillian Trench.

"He helped cover up, didn't he?" I said, keeping my voice as low as possible. "With that business of your death in the Mediterranean, I mean."

Shooting me a look that would have killed spiders, Lillian got up and crossed to the other side of the room, where she stood hugging herself.

Well, it made no difference. Inspector Hewitt would be left to find out all of this in his own sweet time. There was no need for me to steal his thunder.

I glanced across at him and could tell that the inspector was mildly peeved — although he didn't show it — to find that Carla was in no fit state for questioning.

"I'd hoped to have a word or two," he said, not looking directly at the doctor.

"She's still a young woman," Dr. Darby said. "Plenty of time for that. Besides," he added, unwrapping a mint and popping it into his mouth, "they're expecting her at the hospital. Mustn't keep Matron waiting. Matron doesn't fancy being kept waiting, if memory serves."

And with that, Carla, Lillian, and Hilary were gone, given over to the care and keeping of Detective Sergeant Woolmer, who shepherded them to his car as if they were three lost lambs.

"Now, then," Inspector Hewitt said, as soon as they were gone. "Out with it."

He opened his notebook and stared at me expectantly.

"Well," I said, "Cynthia — Mrs. Richardson, I mean — asked me to take a message to Mr. Sambridge."

Cynthia nodded confirmation. "It's true," she said, as she had done before.

"Thank you, Mrs. Richardson," Inspector Hewitt said. "We needn't trouble you further. You've been most helpful."

With an almost audible sigh of relief, Cynthia got to her feet and left the room, muttering something about silver to polish and surplices to iron.

I was alone with the inspector at last.

"Carry on," he said.

"I found him dead. Hanging from the door. Trapped in a surgical frame of his own invention. Broken release catch."

I thought the inspector would appreciate professional brevity.

"Yes," he said, glancing at his watch, "We know all that. Get to the point."

I thought I had, but I began again. "As I came away from Thornfield Chase I saw the curtains twitch across the road. I know now that it was Carla, who was visiting her aunt Louisa, alias Lillian Trench."

I couldn't resist the "alias."

Inspector Hewitt said nothing, but scribbled something in his notebook.

I told him about my trip to London and my visit to the offices of Lancelot Gath; I told him about my visit to the newspaper archive at Colindale; I told him — somewhat fearfully — about my snoop round Louisa's flat in Cranwell Gardens (where, I claimed, I had found the door conveniently open). In the interests of truthfulness, I even told him about my interview with the former Scout James Marlowe.

I did not, of course, tell him about Mildred Bannerman.

Some things, after all, are sacred.

During all of this, his Biro scarcely left the paper.

"You'll want to share these with Inspector Cavendish of the Somerset Constabulary," I said, laying out in front of him the negatives and prints that James had made that dreadful day on Steep Holm, when he had stumbled upon the ravaged body of the deceased Walter Glover.

Ratting on poor James caused me a momentary pang of regret, but hadn't the police had years to question him? It was hardly my fault if they'd bungled it.

A ghastly silence fell as Inspector Hewitt thumbed slowly through the photographic prints. I had brought them along to shock Louisa, should she decide to deny the truth of my deductions.

"I expect I shall," he said at last, setting them aside.

And then he sprang the trap. "Incidentally," he asked, "how did you connect Louisa Congreve with Lillian Trench?"

It was the question I had been dreading.

"It came in bits and pieces," I said. "But it began with Thomas More."

Inspector Hewitt looked at me blankly.

"The cat," I said. "The cat at Lillian Trench's cottage was the same cat I'd seen in Roger Sambridge's bedroom."

"I see," Inspector Hewitt said, his Biro going like fury. "Please explain."

"It was her cat, not his."

"I see," the inspector said again. "And how did you deduce that?"

Was he twitting me? I wasn't sure.

"Cats don't meow at the doors of strangers," I said. "And yet it meowed at hers."

"Please go on."

"Well, it seemed evident that someone from Miss Trench's cottage had been inside Thornfield Chase on the day that Roger Sambridge died — at least, that was one possibility. The cat had come in with them and had been locked in when they left."

"That seems hardly conclusive," Inspector Hewitt said.

"No," I agreed, "but as I've said, it was only the beginning."

"Pray continue," he said. Was he twitting me? I couldn't tell.

"Well, when I met Hilary Inchbald at Lillian Trench's — sorry, I mean Louisa Congreve's — cottage, I knew at once by the way Thomas More snuggled that the cat was his."

"Are you saying that Hilary and his cat were living with Miss Congreve?"

"Yes. At least for a time. I suspect he was keeping a room at the Thirteen Drakes for the sake of appearance."

"Hmmm," the inspector said, but it was an agreeable "Hmmm," and not at all the kind with a sniff of condescension in it.

"Louisa was like a mother to him," I said. "She took his side against his father's bullying. When I first began to suspect that Lillian Trench was actually Louisa Congreve —"

"Hold on," Inspector Hewitt said, writing furiously. Could all of this be news to him? There was no way of knowing.

Having caught up, the inspector nodded, and I continued.

"Well, if Oliver Inchbald could vanish, so could she. She did him the favor of identifying his 'body,' and now it was her turn. Compared with helping a world-famous author to disappear, a convenient diving accident in the Mediterranean must have been a piece of cake."

"So that the two of them could live happily ever after at Stowe Pontefract," Inspector Hewitt said.

"Exactly! He grew a beard and became an ecclesiastical wood-carver, and she —"

"Became a witch," Inspector Hewitt finished for me.

I hugged myself. I couldn't help it.

For a moment we were partners, the

inspector and I, and what a warm feeling it was! And for a moment, I wanted to share everything. I didn't care if he took the credit.

"Things went along well enough at first," I said. "But they went sour quite suddenly. Last summer, I should say."

"Why last summer, particularly?" Inspector Hewitt asked. He couldn't hide the hint of a smile.

"Because that's when he suddenly began paying visits to the Goose and Garter, in East Finching. The barmaid, Rosie, described him as 'morose.' "

"Any ideas why?"

"Well," I said, "I suspect it was because Hilary had turned up. As I've said, Louisa was like a mother to him — very protective. She and Oliver must have had words."

"Must have?" the inspector asked, with a sharp look.

"*Might* have," I corrected myself. "Sorry."

Blast! I had been too cocky for my own good. I needed to draw attention — discreetly, of course — to the excellence of my deductive skills.

"As I see it," I said, "Louisa had gone up to London the day of Oliver Inchbald's death — perhaps to bring back some papers, since her flat was stripped bare. Did she know he was dead before she left? I don't know. She told me I had been seen leaving Thornfield Chase, but perhaps it was Carla who saw me. I believe she left Carla alone in the cottage, and that Carla decided to go across to Thornfield Chase — both to apologize for her vandalism at the church and to ask Oliver to sign her copy of *Hobbyhorse House.* She found him suspended in that arthritis frame of his. He asked her to sing for him — possibly to reassure her; to keep her from being alarmed.

"But when she did, he laughed at her. Laughed so hard that something slipped. He became trapped in his frame. He couldn't reach the release. He begged her to free him. But he had laughed at her. She walked out and left him there, not caring if he died."

"Steady on," the inspector said.

I had not realized that my fingernails were slicing into my palms, and that my knuckles were bone white.

"Was it murder?" I asked. "Will Carla be charged with murder?"

"I can't say," Inspector Hewitt said.

"Can't say, or won't say?" I asked.

I couldn't hide my look of scorn.

"Listen, Flavia," he said. "We are both of us bound by the same great restrictions. The Law demands that you tell me everything you know, and yet at the same time, the same Law demands of me that I tell you nothing."

"It isn't fair," I said, trying not to pout.

"Of course it isn't fair," Inspector Hewitt agreed. "But it isn't meant to be. It's worth remembering that some of the greatest things in life are completely *un*fair."

He waited for a moment, fiddling with his notebook, giving me time to unruffle my feathers.

Which reminded me of Esmeralda. That hadn't been fair, had it? And yet her death had probably saved Father's life.

"I see what you mean," I said. "And you're quite right."

"Getting back to Louisa Congreve," Inspector Hewitt said. "You telephoned her at her flat in London . . ."

"Yes," I said. "She pretended to be a Letitia Greene. I pretended to be a representative of the Irish Hospitals' Sweepstake. I'm sorry — I shouldn't have. But I knew that thinking the ticket a winner — whether it was hers or Oliver Inchbald's — would lure her back to Thornfield Chase. And it did. When I went there next morning she had just been dropped off. I saw the tracks of the turning car. I was quite certain, by then, that Louisa and Lillian Trench were one and the same person."

Privately, I was thinking that I should simply have followed the cat across the road. It would have been so much simpler; would have saved so much trouble.

The inspector, meanwhile, made another note, but said nothing.

It was all about identities, wasn't it? Oliver Inchbald was living under the name of Roger Sambridge; Louisa Congreve under the name of Lillian Trench. Even Hilary Inchbald had registered at the Thirteen Drakes as Mr. Hilary.

Had any of it changed anything?

When you come right down to it, we are each of us our own creations.

Who, really, am I? Is Flavia de Luce the person everyone thinks she is? Is she who *I* think she is?

We never know, I suppose, until we become someone else.

It's sad, I think, that Oliver Inchbald and Louisa Congreve had been so unhappy as to kill themselves — in a manner of speaking — and to invent new lives which turned out to be every bit as miserable as the old ones they had taken such pains to obliterate.

"That which we call a rose by any other name would smell as sweet," as Daffy was so

fond of saying.

But would it?

Did names matter? Would I have been a better or a happier person if Harriet and Father had baptized me Brünnhilde? Or called me Cordelia?

"What's in a name?" Inspector Hewitt said suddenly.

I'd almost forgotten he was there.

"I beg your pardon," I said, borrowing the words of the fictitious Letitia Greene. "I'm sorry. I was woolgathering."

"I was thinking of the inscription you said you found in Lillian Trench's copy of *Hobbyhorse House. To Elsie,* I believe it said."

"Yes: *To Elsie, with love and yarning.* It's so obvious, isn't it?"

"Not to me it isn't," Inspector Hewitt said. "Would you care to enlighten me? Who the devil is Elsie?"

"Elsie is *L.C.* Louisa Congreve. Elsie must have been his pet name for her. To throw people off the scent, you see."

"Good lord!" the inspector said.

"They were very good at camouflage," I said. "I suppose they needed to be. That whole witchcraft business, for instance. She even tried to scare me off. 'Mind the Auditories,' she told me, as if there were trolls in her carpets. And I almost fell for it."

The inspector smiled an absentminded smile.

"And with Louisa Congreve on the scene," I said, "I knew that Carla couldn't be far away. I had already caught a whiff of her throat spray in the bedroom at Thornfield Chase, but of course I wasn't able to make the connection until I saw her use the same atomizer when she sang at the Horn Dance."

"Well done," Inspector Hewitt said.

"Sulfurous acid," I explained, not wanting to let this moment of glory pass. "H_2SO_3."

"Yes, I seem to remember that from my college days," the inspector said, and there was for a moment an unbreakable bond between us: the eternal bond of chemistry.

I glowed with all the fire of a newborn galaxy.

The inspector closed his notebook, put away his Biro, and got to his feet.

"Come along," he said. "It's late and the wind is bitter. I'll give you a lift home."

We said our goodbyes and offered our thanks to Cynthia, who seemed to be all hands and apron.

"Merry Christmas," she said. I had forgotten all about it.

The snow was beginning to drift among the tombstones as we made our way to the car, the wind pushing at our backs.

"How are you bearing up?" Inspector Hewitt asked suddenly. "It's been quite a day."

I knew he was referring to my encounter with Carla.

It was suddenly more important than anything on earth to show him I could cope, even if it called for a little deceit.

"I'm all right," I said.

Would he notice if I changed the subject? A light bit of banter would show him what I was made of.

"You told me once that His Majesty King George did not permit anyone but policemen and criminals to ride in official vehicles. Has he changed his mind?"

Inspector Hewitt laughed — he actually laughed! — as he stowed Gladys in the boot and held open the door for me.

He did not reply until we were in the car and he had started the motor. And then he said: "His Majesty King George allows us to make an exception in the case of persons who have been extraordinarily helpful to his officers."

I think I fainted.

I'm not quite sure, but for some indefinite

amount of time I was definitely in a swoon.

I became aware of the sound of the car heater — of the official tires crunching through the ice and snow.

Suddenly the inspector said, "I was very sorry to hear about your father. How is he?"

I was jerked back to reality. What was I to tell him? How could I say that I didn't know?

"He's not been allowed visitors," I said, which was only partially true. Everyone in Bishop's Lacey — even the wretched Undine — seemed to have seen Father. I was the only exception.

"I'm planning to visit him in the morning," I said. "I shall tell him you were asking."

"Please do," Inspector Hewitt said.

And then, unaccountably, we were stopped at the door of Buckshaw. Time had jumped like a bad splice in a film at the cinema.

The inspector and I were sitting there looking at each other in the way you do at the end of a journey, not knowing quite what to say when there's only one thing left.

"I hope you'll go easy on Carla," I said, taking advantage of the moment. "She's not had the same advantages as some of us."

"Justice does not distinguish," Inspector

Hewitt said. "She wears a blindfold, remember."

"I'm sorry," I said, leaving him to decide what I meant by it.

"Nevertheless," he added. "I shall whisper in her ear."

Tears welled up in my eyes. I couldn't help myself.

"Antigone Hewitt has a very fine husband," I said.

"Hasn't she, though?" Inspector Hewitt said, and we both laughed.

The moment had passed.

I had pulled it off.

Twenty-Three

Some sleeps are washed with gold, and some with silver. Mine was molten lead.

I awoke feeling hot and feverish, my throat feeling stuffed with razor blades. I could tell from the shambles of my bed that I had tossed and turned all night, although I could not remember dreaming.

Dreamless nights, I knew, can be the most troubling, since you come back not knowing where you've been or what you've done.

As I swung my legs out of bed, I was shattered by a sneeze — and one of the worst kind.

I mopped up and was reaching for my clothing when the door opened and Mrs. Mullet backed into the room carrying a breakfast tray.

"Not so quick, miss," she said. "Back into bed with you. I've brought you some nice toast and jam and ginger tea."

"But I've got to get up," I said. "We're going to the hospital to see Father."

"They've already left," Mrs. Mullet said. "You need your sleep. You ought to 'ave 'eard yourself, 'awkin' and 'ackin' somethin' wicked. You've got a stripped throat, you 'ave.

"Worse 'an that," she added, fixing me with a fierce glare, "you was whimperin' in your sleep. What you been gettin' up to, miss — and don't tell me it's nothin'. I may be a fool, but I'm not a new fool."

"Already left?" I echoed in my nutmeg-grater voice. It might have been funny if I hadn't been so close to tears. "What do you mean, already left?"

"Left. Gone, is what I mean," Mrs. Mullet said, punching up my pillows with far more force than was strictly necessary.

"Who's gone?" I demanded.

"All on 'em. Miss Ophelia and Dieter, Miss Daphne, Miss Undine. Dogger's drove 'em."

What treachery! How could they do this to me?

How could someone like Undine be allowed in to see my father — not once, but twice — while I was kept at bay as if I were some kind of pariah?

"Dieter?" I said. "I thought Feely had tossed him over?"

"Fmmmphh!" Mrs. Mullet said. "A temper in a teapot. Girls go all silly when they've got themselves a beau. You will, too, when your time comes."

I was too upset to pull even my standard gargoyle face.

"Thank you, Mrs. M," I croaked. "You're right. I think I need my sleep."

And without another word, I rolled over, burrowed into the pillows, and pulled the eiderdown up to cover my head completely.

I gave a few convincing twitches as I settled.

After a moment, I heard the rattle of dishes and the sound of the door closing.

She had taken away my breakfast.

I counted slowly to four hundred, because you never know, and I'd been tricked before.

I dressed quickly, pausing from time to time to suppress a cough with both hands. Although there was now no one else in the house but Mrs. Mullet, it wouldn't do to be caught.

Bundled to the eyes in coat, jumpers, mitts, and scarves and weighted down by heavy rubber galoshes, I looked to myself in the mirror like a World War I aviator about to take off on a high altitude reconnaissance flight.

Which gave me an idea: I still had the

goggled flying helmet I had worn when Aunt Felicity took me for a flight in *Blithe Spirit,* Harriet's De Havilland Gypsy Moth. I hauled the thing on over my hair, strapped it under my chin, and was ready to go.

I slipped quietly — or as quietly as one can when one is dressed like Sir Ernest Shackleton — out into the hall and into my laboratory.

I raised the sash of one of the east windows overlooking the Visto — the same window, in fact, by which Carl Pendracka had made his entrance and his exit.

Settling on the sill, I swung one leg out, and then the other. If the dead vines on the brick wall would support Carl, they would certainly support me.

I worked the window closed and began my descent. The vines creaked and groaned dreadfully, as if I were climbing down a ladder of old bones. It didn't much matter, though: The east wall of the house was far enough away from the kitchen that there was no danger of Mrs. Mullet hearing my clatter.

After only a few slips and plunges, I reached the ground and made my way round the back of the house. The wall of the kitchen garden would hide me most of my way to the greenhouse, and as for the rest of it — well, I would simply have to be stealthy.

It helped to know that Mrs. Mullet wasn't much of a one for gazing idly out the window.

"I keeps my nose to the Aga and my eyes on the pots," she had once told me when I'd caught her peering out at the sky. *"But it pays to know what kind o' weather you're goin' to 'ave to walk 'ome in when your 'usband's gone and lost your only umbrella."*

Luck was on my side. I managed to reach the green-house without raising a siren voice from the kitchen door.

"Come on, Gladys," I urged. "No more lollygagging."

Not that she was. She'd know I was only teasing.

We shoved off — literally — towards the west, with me pushing her like a battering ram through the dunes of snow, which varied from patches of drifts to little seas of glaring ice, with Gladys groaning all the while like an ancient dowager being dragged against her will across the fields.

It was a private joke. Gladys loved to pretend she was being abducted. She was being amusing, I knew, and because it helped pass the time until we reached the road, I did not discourage her.

Now, finally, after a mile or so, I was able to drag her across the last ditch and set her wheels upon what should have been the tarmac, but was in fact no more than a dark and hardened trail of snow and ice leading towards Hinley.

Fortunately, there was very little traffic as we wobbled westwards. The occasional car coming from behind us to the east would give a little honk to indicate that they were overtaking, but aside from that, there was only the howling of the crosswind and the crunching of the icy mulch beneath Gladys's Dunlop treads.

What a week it had been!

To keep from thinking about Father, I had allowed my mind to be consumed by the nasty business of Oliver Inchbald, alias Roger Sambridge. Although I was certain I had solved a crime, I still wasn't quite certain what that crime had been.

Would Carla Sherrinford-Cameron be found to be a murderess? If so, had her aunt, Louisa Congreve, been an accessory? Had Louisa known that morning, before she set out for London, that her neighbor — to be charitable — was dead?

Why had Oliver Inchbald, showered with literary glory and years of success, decided to fake his own death and vanish from the world? Had he been threatened with some kind of exposure? Had it been, as I suspected, that his wife — Hilary's mother — was still alive? That he had faked his death to avoid the shame of exposure? That he had tired of his own fame?

My mind boggled. I could think of a score of reasons but I didn't want to.

In the same way, I suppose, that the perfect crime is extremely rare, so is the perfect solution. In real life, we are never able to dot every *i,* cross every *t,* or tease out every last strand of what we think of as the evidence.

Real life is messy, and it's probably best to keep that in mind. We must learn never to expect too much.

It was a relief, in a way, to hand things over to Inspector Hewitt, and to have my own life back again — such as it is. Perhaps one day he and Antigone would invite me to tea at Maybank, and he would fill in the blanks about Oliver Inchbald.

But even if he didn't, I was satisfied. I had done my best.

The temperature was plunging and the goggles of my helmet were frosting up. Could it be that warm air was leaking from my eyes? I scrubbed at the lenses with my coat sleeve, but it didn't much help.

My vision was so restricted that I was finally forced to raise the goggles and expose my frost-rimed eyes to the blowing snow.

My every cough was visible on the freezing air: little explosions of white, like smoke from the rifle shots in a cinema western.

And then, mercifully, Hinley came into view, the stony spine of its skyline like the bones of a dinosaur still half embedded in the earth, barely visible through the snow.

I wobbled at last into the high street, Gladys's wheels sliding sideways into the icy ruts. I wanted nothing more than to dismount, tear into the nearest tea shop, and gorge myself on hot toast and steaming tea. How I regretted leaving Buckshaw without breakfast.

But nothing, now, could keep me from Father. He was only minutes away and I had a plan.

What a scolding I was going to give him! I would show him that I was no longer the girl who had gone away to school in Canada; that I had grown up and come home a different person.

I would begin by giving him the very dickens for catching pneumonia; for not looking after himself. I would tear a strip off him that he would never forget.

I would tell him that I was only doing it

for his own good, because I loved him so much. Yes, that's what I would do.

But that was nothing compared with what I would do next.

The idea had popped into my head as if by magic, and I suddenly understood how Saint Paul must have felt on the road to Damascus.

At the first opportunity, I would make an appointment with Father's solicitors. I would instruct them to draw up whatever papers were necessary for me to sign in order to return the estate to Father.

I would make him a gift of Buckshaw!

It was brilliant! Why hadn't I thought of it before?

My mother, Harriet, of course, had left Buckshaw to me: a loving and thoughtful act, I suppose, but one which had imposed an enormous and crushing burden on my mind.

Giving it to Father as an outright gift would solve all of our problems. I didn't know the ins and outs of inheritance tax, but surely we could sort it out together.

I chuckled, coughed, and laughed. Yes, that was it. We would sort it out together.

From the market square, the street to the hospital rose up so steeply that I was obliged to dismount and walk. The snow on the stone cobbles was treacherous, and only by clinging to Gladys's handlebars could I keep from falling on my face.

At the top of the hill, I stopped and stood staring up at the hospital's dark, stony face.

On the porter's lodge, as I knew it would be, was the sign ALL VISITORS PLEASE RE-PORT. I had been here before, and knew my way around.

I couldn't run the risk of being stopped for any reason. My barking cough alone would be reason enough to be tossed out on my ear.

To one side was a grim stone archway, which led, I remembered, by way of a pinched and gloomy passage, to a small courtyard which was used mostly by under-takers and others whose secret work was carried out away from the public view.

Here was the loading dock, which would give unquestioned entry to the hospital.

I hoisted Gladys up onto the dock, leaned her against the stone wall, and promised her that we'd be going home with Dogger. No more struggling through the snow.

The wind tore the heavy door from my hands and slammed it shut.

But I was inside.

I flattened myself against the wall and waited to be caught. But the only sound was the growl of distant machinery.

The air was heavy with the smell of super-heated laundry and somewhat less super-heated institutional soup, both equally un-appetizing.

I set off down the long corridor at a military pace, as if I were carrying important dispatches. A chin-up, shoulders-back pos-ture and a brisk pace is generally enough to discourage any but the most officious door-keepers.

Just let them try! I was gaining confidence with every yard I walked.

Father would be proud when I confessed. We would have a good laugh about it later.

I made it past the kitchen with no alarm, and then the X-ray department. Beyond lay the wards, and I glanced quickly into each as I passed.

No sign of Dogger, or of Feely or Daffy.

And then I remembered there were also wards upstairs on the second floor.

Of course! It made perfect sense that Father would be up there on the top deck — not down here in steerage, so to speak, with the kitchens and the laundry boilers.

I couldn't risk going into the foyer and inquiring at the desk, I thought, as I smoth-ered a cough with both hands. When I got to Father's room I would wrap my scarf across my mouth to avoid contagion.

To my left was a door marked STAIRS and I took it, slipping through as silently as a ferret on the hunt.

At the top, I peered cautiously out into the corridor, but I needn't have bothered: There was no one in sight.

The hospital seemed to be in a dreamy daze, the hum of voices somewhere in the distance. At the end of the hall someone had even put up a Christmas tree, its colored lights and tinsel managing to make even the ghastly brown and green walls look cheery.

The wards were to my right. I stepped into the hall and walked confidently forward, yet fully expecting Matron to come bearing down upon me at any moment, like a pirate ship under full sail.

I must say, though, that I was not afraid. I would deal with her.

The new, stony Flavia de Luce would turn her away: send her scurrying with her tail between her legs.

The very idea delighted me.

As I glanced in at the third door, my heart lifted.

Dogger was sitting on a chair beside the bed in which Father was lying peacefully, his eyes closed.

How surprised they would be to see me!

There was no one else in the room — just the two of them. The others must have stepped out for a break.

As I entered the room and drew closer, I could see that Dogger's shoulders were shaking. Was he having one of his episodes? If so, I needed to get him out of here. It wouldn't do for Father to be disturbed by such a sight.

Hoping not to startle him, I reached out and touched Dogger, giving his arm a reassuring squeeze.

"Dogger," I said quietly, "it's me, Flavia."

His head came slowly round and he looked up at me, and I saw that his eyes were brimming with tears.

"What is it, Dogger?" I asked.

"I'm afraid, Miss Flavia . . . ," he said. "I'm afraid —"

"No need to be afraid, Dogger. Everything is all right."

And then as I saw the reason for his weeping, a howl escaped my throat and went echoing round the room.

I was shaken as if by a fierce but invisible wind. I could barely breathe.

"Oh, Dogger," I gasped, clutching at his shoulder. "Whatever shall I do without him?"

"You must cry, Miss Flavia," Dogger said, looking up at me from his haunted, tearstained face. "You must cry as long and as hard as ever you can."

ACKNOWLEDGEMENTS

Special thanks (and congratulations) to Dana Cameron and Carla Coupe, of the Femmes Fatales, those ferociously creative and talented women dedicated to the fine art of crime fiction. Dana and Carla were the successful bidders in an auction at the 2015 Baker Street and Friends weekend in New York City, for the right to name a character in the next Flavia de Luce novel in support of the very worthy Watson Fund.

Oh, yes . . . their character? Carla Sherrinford-Cameron. I hope I haven't treated her too cruelly.

Thanks also to legendary Sherlockian Peter Blau for helping make all of this possible. It was inspiring — and awe-inspiring — to meet Peter at last, after having heard of him everywhere for so many years.

Thanks, too, to Les Klinger, Mike Whelan, and Mary Ann Bradley, and to Steven Rothman, all esteemed members of the Baker

Street Irregulars, for extending so cordial a welcome to an ailing Sherlockian.

To Peter Calamai, C.M., and Mary Calamai for so warmly welcoming a wandering alien. As they (almost) said in *My Fair Lady:* We could have talked all night.

Again, with thanks to Roger K. Bunting, Professor Emeritus, Inorganic Chemistry, Illinois State University, for sharing his vast knowledge of historical photographic chemical arcana.

To Nick and Lynne Ingham, and to Steve and Lesley Ingham, who, far beyond the call of duty, rolled up their sleeves and pitched in when it mattered the most. Without them, there would have been no —

Well, let's not even think about that!

To cousins Garth and Helga Taylor for their hospitality and for providing, not just a warm oasis in the bitter cold, but also a forgotten piece of family incantatory lore.

To Jim Sherman, of Perfect Books, in Ottawa, who was the perfect host. And to Barbara Fradkin, compère without compare. Thank you, Barbara!

To Elvira Toewes for arranging an unforgettable homecoming in Toronto, and to Bill and Barb Bryson, cousins also, on the Bradley side, for re-creating the family circle of vanished years.

To Ben McNally, of Ben McNally Books in Toronto, for making a dream come true.

One of the great — and unforeseen — joys of writing the Flavia books has been in hearing from friends I had thought long lost. One of the chiefest of these has been Jim Richards, now of Colorado. Although Jim and I labored together in the vineyards of radio long ago, at a time when the vines were still young, we lost touch for more than half a century. Jim went on to even greater great glory in the television racket, becoming one of the most internationally award-winning writer/producer/directors ever. His many suggestions — based on his own growing up in England during the years in question — have added immeasurably to the world of Flavia de Luce. As Webster said in *The Duchess of Malfi:* "Old friends, like old swords, still are trusted best."

Thank you, Jim!

ABOUT THE AUTHOR

Alan Bradley is the internationally best-selling author of many short stories, children's stories, newspaper columns, and the memoir *The Shoebox Bible.* His first Flavia de Luce novel, *The Sweetness at the Bottom of the Pie,* received the Crime Writers' Association Debut Dagger Award, the Dilys Award, the Arthur Ellis Award, the Agatha Award, the Macavity Award, and the Barry Award, and was nominated for the Anthony Award. His Flavia de Luce novels are *The Weed That Strings the Hangman's Bag, A Red Herring Without Mustard, I Am Half-Sick of Shadows, Speaking from Among the Bones, The Dead in Their Vaulted Arches, As Chimney Sweepers Come to Dust, and Thrice the Brinded Cat Hath Mew'd.*

alanbradleyauthor.com

Look for Alan Bradley on Facebook

The employees of Thorndike Press hope you have enjoyed this Large Print book. All our Thorndike, Wheeler, and Kennebec Large Print titles are designed for easy reading, and all our books are made to last. Other Thorndike Press Large Print books are available at your library, through selected bookstores, or directly from us.

For information about titles, please call:
   (800) 223-1244

or visit our Web site at:
   http://gale.cengage.com/thorndike

To share your comments, please write:
Publisher
Thorndike Press
10 Water St., Suite 310
Waterville, ME 04901